WISHFUL
SEEING

Praise for Janet Kellough and the Thaddeus Lewis series

On the Head of a Pin captivated us from the beginning. Janet did a great job of weaving her characters into a mystery that keeps you turning the pages.... This is a four-star selection that will be loved by all mystery fans.
— *Suspense Magazine*

On the Head of a Pin works on several levels; the murder mystery is woven into the larger story of Canada's wild, pre-Confederation era.
— *Quill & Quire*

Kellough does a fine job of bringing life to the times and to her ministerial hero on horseback.
— *National Post*

[*Sowing Poison*] is a thoroughly well-done historical mystery.
— *Globe and Mail*

Kellough manages to work all these ingredients to conjure another rich tale of murder and intrigue in the County.
— *The Wellington Times*, review of *Sowing Poison*

[In *The Burying Ground*] Kellough weaves a tale that is almost as much a history lesson as it is a thrill ride.
— *Publishers Weekly*

Love the *Murdoch Mysteries?* Then you need to discover Janet Kellough's terrific series set in 1851 and featuring preacher/detective Thaddeus Lewis.
— *Globe and Mail*

[*The Burying Ground*] is an engaging historical mystery.... Fans of Chesterton's Father Brown or of Anne Perry and others who set their mysteries in Victorian England will find this Canadian variation much to their liking.
— *Booklist*

WISHFUL SEEING

A Thaddeus Lewis Mystery

Janet Kellough

DUNDURN
TORONTO

Editor: Allison Hirst
Design: Laura Boyle
Cover Design: Courtney Horner
Printer: Webcom

Library and Archives Canada Cataloguing in Publication

Kellough, Janet
    Wishful seeing / Janet Kellough.

Issued in print and electronic formats.
ISBN 978-1-4597-3537-8 (paperback).--ISBN 978-1-4597-3538-5 (pdf).--
ISBN 978-1-4597-3539-2 (epub)

    I. Title.

PS8621.E558W57 2016   C813'.6   C2015-908174-2-
                                              C2015-908175-0

1   2   3   4   5   20   19   18   17   16

 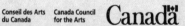 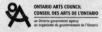

We acknowledge the support of the Canada Council for the Arts and the Ontario Arts Council for our publishing program. We also acknowledge the financial support of the Government of Canada through the Canada Book Fund and Livres Canada Books, and the Government of Ontario through the Ontario Book Publishing Tax Credit and the Ontario Media Development Corporation.

Care has been taken to trace the ownership of copyright material used in this book. The author and the publisher welcome any information enabling them to rectify any references or credits in subsequent editions.

— *J. Kirk Howard, President*

Printed and bound in Canada.

Visit us at
Dundurn.com | @dundurnpress | Facebook.com/dundurnpress | Pinterest.com/dundurnpress

Dundurn
3 Church Street, Suite 500
Toronto, Ontario, Canada
M5E 1M2

For Sam and Alex

Committal Proceedings, Cobourg Courthouse, September 21, 1853

Thaddeus Lewis was not in the least surprised that the court-room was packed with spectators. The newspapers had been full of lurid details about the Paul Sherman murder, and the fact that the accused was a woman made the case even more sensational. As he elbowed his way to the front of the room, he couldn't help but overhear snatches of speculation and opinion. The circumstances surrounding the arrest of Ellen Howell had been thrashed over many times in the days leading up to the committal, but now everyone seemed to expect that the prosecution would present new evidence, something they hadn't heard yet, facts that were not yet common knowledge.

In Thaddeus's opinion, most of the people he pushed out of the way were gawkers and idlers, there out of nothing more than curiosity. They would repeat the details of the proceedings later in the streets and taverns. Others would crowd around to hear news of the latest developments. Some of them would even pay for drinks in exchange for eyewitness accounts.

Thaddeus managed to find a seat in the second row of benches on the right hand side, near the prisoner's box. Mrs. Howell had asked him to attend. "So I know for certain there's a friendly face in the crowd," she'd said; but his presence would be no comfort if she couldn't see him. A beefy man and an elderly woman with a cane had glared as he shoved past them and slid into a vacant seat. Under any other circumstances, Thaddeus would have stood back and let the woman take the space. Today, he firmly claimed possession of a few inches of bench.

The hubbub in the room grew louder as the prisoner was led in from a door at the side of the courtroom. She walked with her head down, looking neither left nor right, but just as she reached the box she stumbled slightly and reached out to steady herself, grabbing the rail in front of her. At that moment she happened to glance up. Thaddeus caught her eye and nodded. She smiled slightly.

The crowd quieted and everyone rose as three grim-faced justices of the peace entered and took their places at the front of the room. Thaddeus rose only far enough to show the requisite respect. He wasn't taking a chance on losing his seat.

When they had all settled themselves again, the clerk read out the charges, alleging that "Mrs. Ellen Howell did feloniously, willfully, and with malice aforethought, on the night of September fourteenth in the Year of Our Lord, eighteen fifty-three, in the Township of Hamilton, kill and murder Mr. Paul Sherman."

Mrs. Howell's head sank lower as the accusation was read, and the audience in the courtroom was strangely silent as the gravity of the charge struck home. Newspaper reporters scribbled furiously, recording every detail so they could later describe it all for their readers.

One by one the prosecution witnesses were called and swore to tell the truth. The first to testify was the coroner, who had determined that the death was suspect and had called together a jury who agreed. He described the scene he encountered when he'd arrived on Spook Island, and read the autopsy report stating that Paul Sherman had died from a gunshot wound to the chest.

The prosecutor thanked the coroner and then walked the other witnesses through their testimonies.

Donald Dafoe, the man who had found the body, repeated his account that he had been fishing, and had put ashore on Spook Island to cook a pickerel, whereupon he discovered the dead man.

Two people testified that they had seen Ellen Howell on the shore with her husband earlier on the day in question. Two more swore that they had later seen her walking along the road from Sully in the direction of the Howell farm, although "she was ahead of us," one said, "and turned down the lane before we reached her." Both claimed that she was alone and that she was wearing a blue dress. And one witness testified that Ellen Howell had previously attended a Methodist meeting wearing that same blue dress. He said he remembered it because his wife had remarked upon it and had been badgering him for one just like it ever since.

The crowd became restless as the testimony proceeded. This was all old news. These details had been discussed and debated long since. They were hungry for something new to talk about.

The next witness was a man from Close Point who had rented his skiff to "an Englishman." He was a newcomer to the area, and did not know the man's name.

"And was this man alone?" the prosecutor asked.

"No," the witness replied. "There was a woman with him, a woman in a blue dress. She stood a little way away, so I didn't see her face."

"Nevertheless," the prosecutor continued, "can you say with any certainty that this same woman is in the courtroom today?"

"No, I can't be certain at all. She was about the same height and build as the woman in the prisoner's box, but she wore her bonnet low and I wasn't close enough to see her clearly."

Thaddeus thought the lack of positive identification was a point in Mrs. Howell's favour, but then he realized that all the testimony did was confirm that both the Howells were present when the skiff was hired.

It was Chief Constable Spencer who finally gave the spectators what they had come for.

"I personally interviewed a number of the witnesses called today," he reported, "and there was ample evidence to warrant a visit to the Howell farm, just south of Sully. My intention was to interview both Mr. and Mrs. Howell."

"And what did they have to say for themselves, Mr. Spencer?"

"Mr. Howell said nothing. He was not present, being away, according to his wife, on business. Mrs. Howell claimed not to know Paul Sherman, and denied ever having set foot on Spook Island. We commenced a search of the premises and discovered a blue dress soaking in a washtub in the summer kitchen."

The prosecutor was on sure ground now. "And did this dress match the description of the blue dress as reported by the witnesses you interviewed?"

"It did. And on further examination, it was evident that its laundering had not been sufficient to remove a large stain on the skirt."

"In your opinion, what was the cause of the stain?"

Thaddeus felt, rather than heard, the crowd's sudden intake of breath.

"It looked to me for all the world like blood."

A gasp, and then an eruption of comment from the crowd, as though this was proof of guilt indeed. The bailiff called for order and gradually the chatter died away.

The prosecutor thanked the witnesses, signalling that the presentation of his evidence was at an end.

One of the justices turned to Mrs. Howell, asking if she cared to cross-examine any of the witnesses. She didn't look up, only declined with a quick shake of her head.

The deliberation took little time. The clamour of the crowd was deafening when one of the justices announced that evidence in the case was sufficient to proceed.

Ellen Howell would be tried for murder.

Thaddeus remained in his seat, deep in thought, while the courtroom emptied. He would have to find some way to help her.

PART ONE
The Hope Circuit,
Summer 1853

I

Thaddeus shifted his weight into a more comfortable position as he waited impatiently for his assistant, James Small, to find a way around the knot of construction that blocked the road ahead. Upper Canadian summers could certainly be steamy at times, but August had ushered in an unusually long stretch of very high temperatures, making travel uncomfortable and enclosed spaces unbearable, and there was no sign of any relief to come.

The aggravation and discomfort of heat and travel were made worse by the delays he encountered whenever his route took him near the rail line construction. It was tempting to believe that the surveyor had deliberately laid the route out in such a way as to cross Cobourg Creek as many times as it possibly could, solely for the purpose of annoying travellers, but Thaddeus knew that the route had been designed to skirt along the bottoms of hills and run as levelly as possible for as far as possible before it had to tackle the steep climb to Rice Lake. The local newspaper had been full of breathless articles detailing the route, the method of construction, and the extraordinary benefits the Cobourg to Peterborough Railway would bring to the entire community.

For the umpteenth time that day Thaddeus pulled out his handkerchief and mopped away the sweat on his face. He was beginning to wonder if he had made the right decision when he'd accepted this appointment. He had been of two minds about taking any posting at all when Bishop Smith offered Hope as a reward for having been so obliging about the Yonge Street Circuit.

"The meetings are already well established on Hope," the Bishop had said in his usual persuasive manner. "There's strong support in the whole district. It's not nearly the challenge that Yonge was."

Thaddeus knew it was a plum, but he was also familiar with the geography of the district. The villages along the shore of Lake Ontario were easily reached, but a rolling landscape climbed steeply from the swampy ground around Cobourg to the oak plains at Rice Lake. There would be an endless progression of steep rises and deep valleys, sudden descents into little dales followed by precipitous climbs up a series of never-ending hills. If he took the posting, he would have to cover it on horseback rather than in the buggy he had grown so used to on Yonge Street.

He protested that he couldn't stand up to that kind of punishment anymore. He was old and had grown soft after two years of riding in a cart and dining a little too well at his son's table in Yorkville. Bishop Smith listened to him politely, and then offered the enticement of an assistant, a man named James Small, a young probationer not experienced enough for his own circuit yet, but certainly qualified enough to lead prayer meetings.

"You can limit your appointments, if you like," Smith said. "Take as many rest days as you need and let your assistant do the bulk of the work."

And then he threw out the clincher. The circuit came with a comfortable manse, a four-bedroom house with a garden and a good barn for his horse.

In the end, Thaddeus agreed, but only for a year. He had no other prospects in sight anyway, and he wasn't entirely sure what he would do instead if he turned the appointment down.

Now, as heavy lumber carts clogged the roads and churned up the dust, he was becoming exasperated and wondered if he had made a mistake. He was in a hurry. He and Small had agreed that it would be best to make an inaugural tour of the circuit together, and circumstances played nicely into this plan when a farmer in Haldimand Township offered the use of an enclosed field for a camp meeting. Given the continuing fairness of the weather, it was likely to draw a large crowd. All of the Methodist Episcopal ministers within riding distance had been invited to speak, and as an old hand at camp meetings, Thaddeus was offered four stints on the platform. It was a splendid opportunity for an initial introduction. But only if he could get there.

He shifted in the saddle again and fanned his face with his hat. He wondered how the men on the railway crews could bear such hard physical labour in such high temperatures. They were well paid, he knew. There had been an advertisement in the *Cobourg Star* offering a dollar a day in wages. Even so, most of the workmen were immigrant German or Irish, and Thaddeus could hear guttural tones clashing with Celtic lilts as the workers called to one another. Few local men were willing to put in the ten or twelve hours a day of back-breaking effort required to build the railway. They could make better coin from supplying the enormous quantity of timber and gravel that was needed, or from selling food to the store that fed the crews. But the one thing they all agreed on was that, once built, the railway would bring them enormous riches, whether it was from working on it, supplying it, or investing in it.

As annoyed as he was by the delay, Thaddeus had to admit that he was fascinated by the construction. While he waited for Small, he watched a work crew scrape away at the roadbed, levelling the soil in preparation for a second crew who would lay down wooden ties to cushion the iron rails. It was not unlike the way a plank road was built, he realized. One of these ran from Cobourg to Gores Landing to connect with the steamers that crossed Rice Lake to Peterborough, but there was constant complaint about the condition it was in. The planks that had been laid across the boggy lowland parts of the road refused to stay put. Every winter the frost heaved and twisted them and every spring the road was found to be nearly unusable. No one seemed able to say for certain that the same thing wouldn't happen to the rail line, but if the amount of soil that was being moved was anything to go by, it should be able to withstand the worst of winters.

Off to the east, Thaddeus could see a crew of workmen excavating a small hill. They shovelled piles of earth into wagons that lumbered their loads over to the sides of the road-bed to reinforce the abutments. Half the hill had been hauled away, and the men were still digging. Thaddeus wondered if he and Small should try to pick their way through the excavation, but just then a wagon finally got itself turned around and out of the way, and one of the workers waved at Thaddeus to ride through the small gap that opened as a consequence. He was relieved. If they made good time from here, they could still arrive at their destination with a few minutes to spare.

By the time Thaddeus and James Small finally arrived at the farmer's field, the entrance laneway was jammed with carts, horses, and pedestrians, a circumstance that boded well for the success of the meeting. There were some within the church who maintained that camp meetings were a thing of the past, that the day of the circuit-riding preacher was over, and that people were settling into a pattern of staying put and looking to their own neighbourhoods for their spiritual sustenance, but the presence of so many people so early on the first day seemed to belie these naysayers. In Thaddeus's experience, camp meetings started slowly and gained momentum as they went on, finally reaching a crescendo on the third day.

And when he mounted the speaking platform later that afternoon, he could see knots of tents and campfires around the entire periphery of the field. Whole families had come and appeared prepared to camp out for the duration.

The response to his message was enthusiastic, a sign that the excitement would continue to build until it reached a frenzy of confession and conversion. At the end of his sermon, Thaddeus turned the meeting over to Elias Knight, who would exhort the crowd to come forward until he judged the time was ripe to lead them into a hymn.

Thaddeus's duties for that afternoon were over. He would return to speak twice on the second day, and once more on the third, but in the meantime he was free to circulate through the campground and meet with people individually. Besides, he was hungry, and hoped that somewhere he might find a familiar face and a bowl of soup.

There was the usual mob of peddlers and vendors set up amongst the wagons. Some of them cooked food in quantity over open campfires and served it up to those disinclined to cook for themselves. Others sold trinkets and patent medicines, and, as was usual at camp meetings, prayer books and small Bibles. The scene always reminded Thaddeus of the moneychangers in the temple, and he wondered if the church shouldn't clear these out just like Jesus had; but then he reflected that the crowd had to be fed somehow. There were always a number who needed to be physicked, he supposed, and if a sinner were brought to the Lord during the preaching, who was Thaddeus to say that they shouldn't follow it up with the purchase of a Bible, just to help make it stick?

He walked slowly through the crowd, trying to make a rough count of the number of people in attendance. He first noticed the woman because of her dress. It was a cotton print with a blue background and a scattering of tiny pink and yellow flowers. Long ago he had been paid for a christening with a bolt of cloth that had much the same kind of pattern. At the time, he knew he should have taken it to a store and traded it for something useful like sugar or tea, but something had stopped him. He carried it home to his wife, Betsy, instead, and was rewarded when her eyes lit up. She had fashioned it into a dress for herself, and looked as pretty as a flower in it. Odd that he should remember such a detail after so many years.

Or maybe it was the slight limp that triggered the memory. Betsy had limped a little whenever a storm was coming, a relic of the dreadful bouts of fever she'd suffered. But except for the dress and the small hitch in her gait, the woman walking through the camp meeting was as unlike Betsy as it was possible to imagine. She was very fair, a knot of golden hair showing under her bonnet, and quite small, or at least she seemed so because she was so slight. She was arm in arm with a gentleman who had impressive mutton-chop whiskers and wore a silk hat. They seemed an odd couple to be at a Methodist camp meeting. Their clothes were just a little too fine-looking, their manner just a little grand. They stopped at one of the peddler's wagons and spoke to a man who was hawking patent medicines. Whatever they said appeared to find favour, as some sort of transaction took place while Thaddeus looked on.

A knot of men standing in front of one of the campfires to Thaddeus's right appeared to be deep in conversation, but he noticed one of them glance up at the couple, a sour expression on his face. Thaddeus edged a little closer, hoping someone in the group might mention something about the pair, but at first their talk seemed to be all about the railway.

"They've started work on the bridge already," one man said. "They've brought in a pile driver. It's something to see, I'll tell you. I wasted the whole day yesterday watching them raise a post."

The railway was to run all the way across Rice Lake to Peterborough so that timber and other products from the north could be hauled directly to Cobourg harbour. Thaddeus had his doubts about the project. No one had ever before built a trestle bridge that long. And if frost heave was a problem for a plank road, what would the ice do to the wooden poles that supported the bridge? He didn't want to be caught eavesdropping, however, so he refrained from offering his opinion.

He was about to walk away when he heard one of the men say, "Jack Plews is pretty sour that he lost his land just when it turned out to be so valuable."

Thaddeus knew that this wasn't really any of his business, except that he tried to stay alert to potential sources of contention within his congregation. Generally speaking, neighbourhood issues tended to be petty little disputes that nevertheless could boil up into rancour, poisoning entire meetings and destroying the work that the church had accomplished. He needed to be ready at all times to calm the waters and suggest compromise. He took a step closer, hoping to hear more details of this land sale that was exciting comment.

"I thought he was behind on the mortgage?"

"He was. He thought it was a good deal when the Major offered to buy him out." The speaker gestured toward the man in the silk hat. "And then it turns out that's where they want to put the train station. If Jack had just held out a few more months, he could've got top dollar."

"The Major is pretty thick with Boulton, isn't he? He must have heard where the station was going to go and that's why he bought it."

The first man shrugged. "I don't know what anybody can do about it. Jack sold it fair and square, didn't he?"

"Yeah, he did. But it still doesn't seem right somehow."

"I expect when the dust settles, you'll find that a lot of people have made good coin selling land to the railroad. And none of them will be the ordinary farmers like Jack."

The men were slowly moving off in the direction of the platform as they talked. Thaddeus could scarcely follow them without it being obvious that he was listening, so he let them go on and walked toward the gate instead.

"Mr. Lewis!" He was hailed by a friendly-looking man who had set up a camp just inside the entrance to the grounds. As Thaddeus walked over to it he caught the aroma of cooking and noticed that steam was wafting up from the iron pot hanging from a makeshift tripod.

The man held out his hand. "Leland Gordon," he said, "and this is my mother, Patience Gordon. We haven't met you yet, but I'm the lay preacher at the Sully meeting. We'll be seeing you there in a few days, I expect."

The mother, Patience, was ancient, her back so bent that she could scarcely lift her head to greet him, but her face broke into a wreath of smiling wrinkles. "I hoped we would get a chance to hear you speak today," she said, "to try you out a bit before we heard you at our own place."

"And how did I do?" Thaddeus asked with a grin.

"Splendidly. I could hear every word. I must say, we have all been happy to have you come to this circuit. The last man we had was a little dry."

Thaddeus's predecessor had been Calvin Merritt, who was known to have a weak voice, to perspire heavily, and to stutter in moments of stress.

"We all serve God in our own ways," he said. "Some of us have been blessed with better lungs, that's all."

"We have stew," Mr. Gordon said. "Would you have a bowl?"

Thaddeus accepted gratefully, and leaned against the Gordons' wagon while he ate his late dinner.

"This is a grand turnout for the meeting," Old Mrs. Gordon said. "Mind you, it's been so hot I expect everyone jumped at the chance to camp out; but still, you must be pleased."

"I am. It's a grand occasion to meet you all. And, as you say, it's perfect weather for an outdoor meeting."

"Is it the comet, do you think, that's causing the heat? Some say it's an omen."

A strange ball of light had first appeared in the evening sky at the beginning of the month, near the southern part of the Great Bear, its long brilliant tail trailing behind it. Its appearance had caused a great deal of speculation and not a little alarm.

"No, from what I've read it's a perfectly natural occurrence," Thaddeus said. "Soon it will travel on to another part of the heavens and then we won't be able to see it so easily. I doubt it's a harbinger of evil times to come, but no one seems to know if it affects the weather or not. I suppose it's possible."

"It would be nice if it gave us a mild winter," the old woman said. "My rheumatism would thank it."

Just then, the woman in the familiar dress caught Thaddeus's eye again. He watched as the couple walked past the Gordons' camp, in the direction of the entrance gate.

"Who is that?" Thaddeus asked, hoping that the Gordons could supply him with a few more details about the pair. "I heard someone call him 'the Major.'"

Now that he could see the woman more closely, his impression was confirmed that, although the pattern of her dress was similar to Betsy's, the material was of a far finer quality, and had been fashioned into a skirt with several flounces — more stylish, he supposed, than the plain dress his wife had made.

"The Major and his wife?" Mrs. Gordon said. "I must say, I'm surprised to see them here. Not their sort of thing at all."

"What is he major of, exactly?" Thaddeus asked. The man's coat was well cut and of a good-quality broadcloth, but he was in ordinary street clothes, not a uniform that would denote a commission in any of the British regiments stationed in Canada.

Gordon laughed. "Oh, I don't know that George Howell is really a major of anything. That's just what everyone calls him. He was in the British Army years ago, or so he says, and came out here to settle in the thirties. He has a farm south of us, but he doesn't seem to farm it, hard work being beneath him and all. I rent a couple of his fields for wheat."

"Now, now, it takes all kinds. There's no call to be uncharitable," Old Mrs. Gordon chided.

Thaddeus knew the type. A large number of English settlers had immigrated to the district in the 1820s and '30s. Cobourg itself, and much of the land around Rice Lake, was full of them. The English farmers who had come from small holdings in the old country made a great success of their Canadian farms, but some of the settlers had been half-pay officers unable to live in England on the pensions they were awarded in the wake of the Peninsular War. These former military officers were unsuited to pioneering, and many of them fled to the haven of government appointments and favours. Those left behind on their bush farms seemed to have survived on little more than boxes from home and loans from their neighbours, all the while sniffing at the "Yankeefied manners" that flavoured Upper Canada.

Leland Gordon was unchastened by his mother's words. "I've nothing against Ellen Howell," he said. "She's pleasant enough, and neighbourly, but the Major seems to think we should all be tugging our forelocks when he passes by. It's a good thing he's seldom home. I can ignore him on the few occasions when he is around."

"I feel sorry for her," Mrs. Gordon said. "The English seem to want to stick to themselves, but with the Major gone so much, she seldom sees anybody."

Thaddeus was curious. "If the Major doesn't farm, what does he do? Something in the government?"

Gordon shrugged. "No, some sort of business, he claims, although I've never heard what exactly. He seems to travel in some pretty high circles — well, high for around here, at any rate. Mayor Perry is a friend, apparently. D'Arcy Boulton. He prefers to associate with people like that — or with other Englishmen who used to be somebody."

Thaddeus knew the names. D'Arcy Boulton was a lawyer who had settled in Cobourg and built a large house, a mansion, really, that was called "The Lawn." You couldn't spend much time in the area without hearing about D'Arcy Boulton. *I wonder what the Howells are doing here?* he thought.

A British officer who hobnobbed with the mayor of Cobourg and the Boultons was most likely to be an Anglican, and Thaddeus knew there were not many of those present. Almost every other denomination had been drawn to the campground, whether out of a genuine interest or the promise of a fine entertainment, but the movers and shakers of business and government usually disdained Methodist affairs. Especially Methodist Episcopal ones. It didn't matter one way or the other why the Howells had come, he supposed, but he had to admit he was curious.

He had just handed his bowl back to Mrs. Gordon when a commotion erupted at the gate. Three wagons arrived at once and were jockeying to gain entrance to the grounds. One of the horses balked and stood stubbornly at the gate, blocking the way of the other two, who were growing restless at the delay. As Thaddeus hurried toward them, one of them reared and whinnied.

Thaddeus grabbed the halter of the first horse. "Come on, girl, come on," he said softly, and then slowly led her through the gateposts and into the field.

"Thank you," said the man who was at the reins. "She's an ornery beast. I couldn't get her to budge."

"Sometimes they just need a little coaxing. Where are you from?"

"Bailieboro. We heard about the meeting and decided to come along." The man's brow furrowed and he looked a little worried. "We're not Methodists, though, we're Presbyterians. I hope you don't mind that we're here. Everyone seemed very excited about the meeting and we don't get much edification where we are."

Thaddeus beamed at the man. "You don't have to be a member of our church to come to any of our meetings. We're very happy to share the Word with anyone who cares to hear." He was delighted. Bailieboro was a long way away, but news of the meeting had obviously reached beyond the Hope Circuit. Bishop Smith was right. There was a lot of support in this district.

People continued to pour into the farmer's field for the rest of the day. Thaddeus was particularly pleased to hear that a number of the Wesleyan Methodists from nearby Alderville had chosen to attend, not only many of the Indians who attended the school there, but their teachers as well. Besides the Wesleyans, there were apparently contingents of Baptists and Lutherans, along with the usual groups of backsliders and nothingarians who had come along merely for the outing.

Well, Thaddeus thought, now that they're here, I'll give them a preaching they won't forget.

Over the course of the second day, droves of people came up to the platform and fell to their knees. After a hurried consultation amongst all of the speakers, it was decided that the circumstances called for extra prayer meetings. As a senior preacher, and one of the most popular speakers, Thaddeus was asked to lead these.

He chose a corner of the field well away from the distractions of the main platform. As news of the informal meeting spread through the campground, he was gratified to see a number of people streaming toward him. One young man, who had spread a blanket out and sat on the ground directly in front of Thaddeus, spoke up: "Could you talk to us about Baptism, sir?"

Those sitting around him nodded in agreement. Many of the camp meeting converts were apparently anxious on this account, having never encountered an opportunity to formalize their membership in any church. Thaddeus agreed, but delayed the start of the meeting until it appeared that everyone who was interested had found a place to sit where they could easily hear him. To his surprise, the woman with the flowered dress slipped to a place beside the Gordons. What was her name? Howell. Ellen Howell, that was it. There was no sign of her silk-hatted husband.

Thaddeus stood up a little straighter, and quietly cleared his throat once or twice while he waited for the crowd to settle. He was showing off a little, he knew he was, but he wasn't entirely sure why he was so anxious to make a good impression.

Just as he was about to begin speaking, he became aware of a stir at the back of the crowd. A late arrival, a small man with grizzled hair and a Bible under his arm, jostled others as he stepped closer to the front.

There were a few mutters of complaint, but Thaddeus ignored them, instead inviting everyone to join him in singing "Come, Let Us to the Lord Our God," feeding the lines to those who didn't know the hymn and counting on the Methodists to carry the tune.

As the last notes died away, he began to speak.

"The Gospel of Matthew tells us, *Jesus came and spake unto them, saying 'All power is given to me in heaven and in earth. Go ye therefore and teach all nations, baptizing them in the name of the Father and of the Son and of the Holy Ghost'.*"

Out of the corner of his eye, Thaddeus could see the man with the Bible attempting to gain the front row, to the annoyance of the people he was pushing out of the way. This sometimes happened when someone was seized by the Holy Spirit and was moved to come forward and confess for all to hear. But generally not so early in the meeting, and this man didn't have the usual rapturous appearance of the suddenly saved. He just looked determined to get closer.

Thaddeus ignored him and continued. "And the Gospel of John confirms the direction: *Jesus said 'Verily, verily I say unto thee, Except a man be born again, he cannot see the Kingdom of God. Except a man be born of water and of the Spirit, he cannot enter into the Kingdom of God.*"

"Born again of water!" The man's voice floated over the crowd, and Thaddeus suddenly knew who he was and what he was trying to do. He was a disrupter — someone who had come along to do nothing more than disrupt the Methodist meeting with some other creed's point of view. And since he had been speaking specifically about the rite of baptism, Thaddeus knew that this man must come from one of the denominations that supported full immersion.

"*Shush!*" one woman shouted in the man's direction, but a murmur rippled through the rest of the worshippers. This was entertainment that they had not anticipated, and they were eager to hear how Thaddeus would respond.

He decided to meet the challenge head on, and instead of continuing with the words that Jesus spoke to his apostles, went instead to a verse from Numbers. "*But the man that shall be unclean and shall not purify himself, that soul shall be cut off from among the congregation, because he hath defiled the sanctuary of the Lord. The water of separation hath not been sprinkled upon him. He is unclean.*"

"You must read your Bible more carefully," the man shouted. "Pay special attention to the passages concerning John the Baptist."

"I would be happy to," Thaddeus said, and continued with the verses concerning the baptism of Christ. "The water is symbolic of the new life that God grants us as we join the church community," he explained to the rapt faces in front of him. "It is representative of your covenant with God."

The gathered crowd appeared content with this, but the Baptist (for he must surely be a Baptist) took no part in the singing and praying that followed.

Just as the meeting was ending, the man stepped forward a pace or two and spoke again. He hoisted the Bible he was carrying into the air so all could see, and then he laid it next to his heart. "I love this book above all books," he said, "and I esteem it above all others. It is the Book of Books. My good friend here," the man went on, "relies upon the King James version of this Book of Books, as I am convinced that he knows nothing of Greek or Latin."

Several heads turned toward Thaddeus to ascertain whether or not this was true. He shrugged. There was no disputing the fact that he knew no classical languages.

"I, however," the man said, "thank the Good Lord that I have the knowledge to read the original Greek and Latin for myself, and I can tell you that *this* Bible, this *Protestant* Bible, has been translated wrongly."

A gasp went up. This was heresy.

"I challenge you to meet with me and I will prove to you that immersion is the direct and only mode of baptism established by Our Lord Jesus Christ."

At this point Thaddeus responded. "That's a very interesting proposition," he said. "I would be delighted to meet with you in debate. But I suggest that our meeting should not take place in some corner somewhere, but rather in full view. With witnesses."

The crowd murmured their approval of this plan.

"I will be at the hall in Cold Springs this coming Sunday, and I would be more than willing to give you a place on my platform; provided, of course," here Thaddeus fixed the man with a stern stare, "you can give proof to your claims. Do I understand you correctly? You are saying that you will prove that Our Lord intended baptism to be a rite of full immersion?"

The man hesitated a little in the face of this direct challenge. "I will try to prove it," he said.

Thaddeus grinned. "Oh yes, sir, you can try all you like. I look forward to it. Next Sunday. At the Cold Springs meeting."

The crowd gave a collective gasp and then erupted in cheers. This was so much more than they had bargained for, a battle of preachers with themselves the referees. The Baptist minister looked a little crestfallen. He had no doubt hoped that a debate would take place on the spot, but Thaddeus had far too much experience to fall into the trap. If he engaged in argument at this point, it would appear that he had lost control of the meeting. Besides, news of a lively debate would spread through the neighbourhood and perhaps draw far more people.

He ended the meeting with a prayer, as planned. Having failed to stir any trouble, the Baptist minister wandered off at the end of it.

The rest of the crowd pushed forward to speak to Thaddeus, to shake his hand, some of them just to reach out and touch him. Knowing how important this personal contact was, he tried to take the time to speak to each one. And when they had all drunk their fill of him, he looked for Mrs. Gordon and the woman in the flowered dress, but they were nowhere to be seen.

II

Martha Renwell was delighted when her grandfather wrote and asked if she could come to Cobourg to keep house for him. He'd taken an appointment on the Hope Circuit, he said, but had an assistant and so would not be absent for any long stretches of time. The letter went on:

> As it happens, my assistant's family lives next door, and will be on hand should any emergency arise while I'm away. Mrs. Small has agreed to see to the heavy laundry, and Mr. Small will keep the kitchen supplied with kindling, so even though it's rather a large house, Martha wouldn't be obliged to do anything that she doesn't already do at the hotel. If you could spare her, it would be a great help to me, as I believe I have already amply demonstrated that I'm hopeless at housekeeping.

Her father was dubious about the proposal.

"You're only fifteen," he said. "And you'd be on your own while he's off down the road somewhere. Are you sure you want to do this?"

She was sure. For one thing, she missed her grandfather. She had lived with Thaddeus and Betsy from the time she was a baby. For most of her childhood, Thaddeus had been close by — he had not preached after her grandmother grew so sick — and Martha was used to taking her problems to him, to discussing the things that puzzled her and the subjects that she wanted to know more about. It was only after Betsy died that Thaddeus had returned to his old life of riding circuits for the Methodist Episcopal Church, and even then she sensed that he had gone reluctantly. He had promised her once, when she was very little, that he would never be far away, and when he left for Yonge Street he had assured her that it was a temporary posting. But then he had accepted this new appointment. She had been profoundly disappointed when she heard about his decision, but now it appeared that he hadn't forgotten her after all.

It wasn't that she was unhappy in Wellington. She loved her father and adored her stepmother, but now that she was finished with school, she was finding her days long and not a little boring. There was the constant round of cooking and cleaning and changing of linens attendant on the keeping of a hotel, of course, and she tried to make herself as useful as she could. But under her stepmother Sophie's hand, the Temperance House Hotel was superbly organized. Every day Martha would complete her assigned tasks in short order and then start looking for ways to keep herself busy.

She spent hours walking the shore of Lake Ontario, picking her way over the rough stones and marvelling at the things that washed up on them: driftwood; pieces of ship's tackle and lengths of rope; broken crockery; occasionally an apple or an orange, rotting and sodden from its time in the water. When the weather was too inclement for her to spend time outside, she would read. Newspapers were stacked up in the parlour for the convenience of the hotel guests, and she would go through these from front to back. Occasionally, one of the guests would leave behind a book. Martha would read it before her father had a chance to mail it back to its owner. Sometimes there was no forwarding address for the person whose book they thought it was, and these relics she kept, to reread when there was nothing else.

She envied the boys she had shared a classroom with. Most of them hadn't even completed the basic education offered at the village school, but left at eleven or twelve or thirteen, some of them to help their fathers farm, but others because they found employment at the mill or on one of the ships that carried goods and passengers back and forth along the lake. She understood that these occupations were not open to her. They required physical strength and a fortitude that she was told she didn't have, although she felt herself to be nearly as strong as any of the boys, and just as ready for a challenge.

Some of the girls left early, too, either because they were needed at home or to work as hired help on one of the local farms until they were old enough to get married and have families of their own. It seemed that women were destined to cook and sew and clean, even if they did it as a business and not just on behalf of their own families — Sophie in the kitchen at the hotel; Meribeth Scully, the seamstress at the dry goods store; Mrs. Crawford, who ran a boarding house near the harbour.

Martha wanted something more. She just didn't know what it might be. But of one thing she was sure: she stood a far better chance of finding it if she went with Thaddeus than if she stayed home. It wouldn't quite be the same kind of adventure as sailing on a ship or working at a mill — it would be more cooking and cleaning when you got right down to it — but the unexpected seemed to happen to her grandfather wherever he went, and if Martha lived with him she could be a part of whatever thrilling circumstance came his way.

Thaddeus was in a fine mood as he trotted his horse home toward Cobourg, elated not only by the success of the camp meeting and anticipation of the forthcoming debate, but by the unfamiliar wad of extra money in his pocket. As soon as the meeting ended — "one of the most successful in recent memory," as everyone agreed — he and Small worked their way through their regular schedule of appointments, not only to further introduce Thaddeus to the Methodist meetings, but to let everyone know that the coming Sunday's service would offer something special. "You would do well to come," Thaddeus told them with a sly smile. "It should be most entertaining."

They all seemed to agree. The news of his confrontation with the Baptist minister had travelled ahead of him, and there were numerous requests for extra meetings, as well as a wedding and two funerals for people who, as far as he knew, had not been members of the Methodist Episcopal Church during their lifetimes. But the families wanted the best for their loved ones, and were willing to pay for it. And pay for it they did, in a motley collection of currency. The Province of Canada was making efforts to standardize its money, but the legislation had yet to be decreed. In the meantime, everyone was anxious to get rid of any currency that might not be accepted after the law passed. An easy way to dispose of it was to throw it into the collection plate. Thaddeus wasn't particularly worried by the number of American coins and Halifax shillings he had been given. There were plenty of Canadian changemaker banknotes, as well, and, in spite of what the government wanted, he fully expected that foreign currency would continue to circulate the way it always had.

He was in a mood to celebrate, just a little. The collection money went, of course, to the church's central conference, but any extras — the fees for baptisms and weddings and funerals — was his. Or rather, in the case of the wedding, Martha's, he supposed. Traditionally, wedding fees had always been handed to the minister's wife to use as she saw fit. He saw no reason why Martha, as his housekeeper, wouldn't qualify for the same consideration. He had no need of anything for himself, but there was enough extra money in his pocket that he decided to request a luxury. A chicken dinner. Roast chicken with floury dumplings like Sophie made on special occasions at the hotel. He'd ask Martha about it when she arrived that afternoon.

When Martha stepped from the steamer to the dock, Thaddeus realized that she had grown at least an inch since he'd last seen her, and that she had put her hair up in an arrangement that made her look far older than fifteen.

She was a pretty enough girl, who looked remarkably like her mother had at the same age, but it was the way she carried herself, he realized, that turned young men's heads and drew old men's smiles as they walked down the pier toward town. She was so *assured*. He hoped that he wasn't about to be faced with a stream of would-be beaus to chase off the doorstep, but as they walked through town arm in arm, he realized that Martha gave none of the gawkers any encouragement. This was a relief, since the problem of male admirers hadn't occurred to him when he'd asked her to come.

While they waited for her trunk to arrive, he gave her a tour of the house. She immediately made some practical suggestions to streamline her tasks, pointing out, for example, that the kitchen table should be moved over by the window.

"It's smack dab in the path between the stove and the pantry," she said. "You have to walk around it all the time. Besides, the sunlight will pour in through that window in the morning. Breakfast will be more cheerful if we're sitting there."

She wrinkled her nose at the heavy, dusty curtains in the parlour.

"I'm not sure I can do anything about those," Thaddeus said. "The manse is furnished by the congregation."

"Well, at the very least I can take them outside and give them a good airing," she said, and then moved two stuffed chairs to the other side of the room.

Martha found the manse furnishings old-fashioned and fusty, but she was so delighted to be with her grandfather again that she resolved to make whatever domestic improvements she could and stay mum about any remaining shortcomings. In the meantime, she was determined to earn her keep and look after his every comfort.

"Of course I can make dumplings," she said when Thaddeus brought it up to her over supper. "Chicken and dumplings it is. And shortcake for dessert, if you like, if I can find something nice to go with it. Is there a good market here?"

"We'll find out tomorrow. I need to go to the bank, anyway. Then if you want to stock the larder, I can help carry the packages." He reached into his pocket and counted out a handful of coins, then shoved them across the table to her. "This is yours, by the way."

"Mine? You mean for housekeeping?" She was taken aback by what a small pile it was. She would have to be very careful indeed to stretch this over a whole week. Maybe a chicken dinner wasn't possible after all.

"No. I'll give you the housekeeping money after I go to the bank. This is yours, personally. It's from a wedding. Wedding money goes to the preacher's wife, except in this case it goes to the preacher's granddaughter."

She was astonished. "Mine? Mine for whatever I want?"

"Yours for whatever you want," he said.

And suddenly the pile of coins that had seemed so small a moment before became riches beyond belief. Martha had never had any money of her own, other than a few pennies given to her here and there for candy or ribbons. She scarcely knew what she could buy. She would take some time to think about it, she decided. It would be foolish to spend it just for the sake of spending it, when there might be something she truly wanted later. In the meantime, she could revel in the fact that she had it at all.

The next morning, after breakfast, Thaddeus fetched down his coat and gave it a thorough brushing, then carefully wiped the mud from his boots. He looked at Martha a little sheepishly. "I don't want anyone to wonder what such a pretty girl is doing with such a seedy old coot," he said.

She laughed. "Oh go on, you're so handsome, everyone will think you're my beau, of course."

The sun shone down brightly as they walked into the heart of the bustling town. Cobourg's prosperity had grown from the long wharves that formed a safe harbour for the ships and schooners that sailed across and along Lake Ontario, carrying passengers and freight of all descriptions, from the wheat that grew on the upland plains to timber drawn from the back country, as well as the output from the woollen mills and the town's small manufactories. Tradespeople of all descriptions had found a good living in Cobourg, and an astounding collection of businesses maintained shopfronts on King Street, the main thoroughfare of the town. There were several grocers and provisioners, dry goods stores and tailors, and even a bookseller who offered a large selection of reading materials, both books and periodicals as well as stationery supplies.

But the temperament of Cobourg was really set by Victoria College. Founded by the Wesleyans as an unofficial seminary, the college's activities spilled over into the town, and its debates, lectures, and celebrations were enthusiastically attended by local residents. The streets were often full of the young men from the college, who enlivened the otherwise staid demeanour of Cobourg with their lively pursuits. Martha found the bustle very different from the sleepy village atmosphere she was used to.

"How many people live in Cobourg?" she asked as they walked along.

"Oh, I should think maybe five thousand," Thaddeus said. "But I'm not sure how many of them are students."

Even so early in the morning, they encountered a few groups of boys who were running errands in town. As they walked by Axtell's Bookstore, three young men spilled out in front of them onto the plank sidewalk. Thaddeus and Martha had to step aside into the street to avoid them. Rather than apologize, they stopped in the middle of the walk and looked Martha up and down in a very insolent way as she walked by. She responded with a stony indifference. Thaddeus scowled at them.

"You could sour milk with a look like that," Martha remarked.

"They were very rude. They were staring at you."

"Let them stare, I don't care." And then she squeezed his arm. "Don't worry. If they get too bold, I'll let them have it."

They reached a rather imposing building with a small sign that announced the premises of the Northumberland and Durham Savings Bank.

"I won't be long here," Thaddeus said. "I just need to send off the collection money."

She waited just inside the door, a little intimidated by the solemnity of the interior, although she supposed that a bank needed to impart a dignified atmosphere in order to reassure its clients. It was very quiet. She could hear the low murmur of voices and the scratching of pens, an occasional footstep and the ticking of a clock, but none of the sounds from the street outside seemed to penetrate into this sanctum of finance. The quiet was suddenly disturbed by her grandfather's slightly raised voice.

"What do you mean they're no good?"

She took a few steps forward. Even so, she couldn't quite make out the clerk's reply.

"I'm not sure what good that will do," Thaddeus said. "This money came from my congregation. I can hardly go through the collection box and reject what they've offered. It would be as good as calling them thieves."

Another almost inaudible response from the bank clerk, and then Thaddeus strode toward her, obviously exasperated.

Martha waited until they were outside before she asked what the problem was.

"Three of the banknotes were counterfeit," he said. "The bank wouldn't honour them. The clerk said there's quite a lot of bad money around. Somebody's been shoving. The constables know all about it, apparently, but there isn't much anyone can do unless they catch someone in the act."

"It was the notes? The Canadian notes that were no good?" Martha asked.

"Yes. Why?"

"It's just that sometimes we'd get bad money at the hotel, but usually it would be American coins. You really had to watch the nickels."

"Oh well, I'm not out too much. They weren't big notes, just changemakers. The clerk showed me what was wrong with them, but honestly, I can't stand and peer at the money people give. And what am I supposed to do if it's no good? Hand it back and demand better?"

"No, I suppose not," Martha said.

"Still, maybe we'd better forget about chicken for this week anyway. I don't want to leave you short."

"We can use the money you gave me, if you like. I don't need anything right now."

Thaddeus shook his head. "No. That's yours. To get what you want. That's the rule. It always was." He smiled. "But thank you."

They went to the farmer's market, where the stalls were heaped with late summer produce — potatoes, carrots, pears, a few early apples, and in several of the stalls, baskets of blueberries.

"Can you make a pie?" Thaddeus asked.

Martha looked at him with mock scorn. "Of course I can make a pie. Mine is almost as good as Sophie's."

"A blueberry pie would go a long way toward making up for the lack of chicken."

"Then blueberry pie was just put on the menu."

Together they sifted through the baskets until they had a pound of the most succulent-looking berries.

Thaddeus fished in his pocket and handed over a note in payment.

The farmer looked at it closely before he took it. "Sorry to be so suspicious," he said, "but there's been some odd money float through in the last little while. You can't be too careful."

"So I've discovered," Thaddeus said.

"That's what you need to do," Martha pointed out. "Have a look at it first."

The farmer tucked the note in his pocket and made change with coins. "No offence, sir."

"None taken. I quite understand."

They moved from stall to stall. Martha added potatoes, beans, and half a dozen plums to their basket. She was looking over some beets when raised voices at the next stall caught her attention.

"I won't accept this," a man with a long grey beard said to the woman who was tending the stall. "This is bad money. I should know, I work at a bank."

The woman was red-faced. "I'm sorry, sir, I didn't know there was anything wrong with it."

"A likely story," the man huffed, and when the woman offered him coins instead, he grabbed them and stuffed them in his pocket. "Should call a constable," he muttered as he marched away.

Thaddeus walked over to the stall. "We ended up with some forged notes as well," he said. "The bank says there's a lot of it around."

"Just what we need when nobody knows what's happening with our money anyway," the woman said, and then she looked at Thaddeus a little more closely. "You're the preacher! From the camp meeting. The one who's going head to head with the Baptist tomorrow."

"Yes, that's correct," Thaddeus said. "Will we see you there?"

Martha could see that he was pleased.

"Wouldn't miss it for the world," the woman said. "I'm leaving the market early today just to make sure I get home in plenty of time to get gussied up before we head for Cold Springs. I'm looking forward to it. The whole neighbourhood's going, you know — even the ones who aren't Methodist or Baptist."

"You never know," Thaddeus said, "maybe they will be by the time the meeting is over."

This was met with a deep chuckle. "Well, now I know who I'm putting my money on."

The exchange seemed to put Thaddeus in a good mood for the rest of the day, helped not a little, Martha hoped, by the success of her blueberry pie.

III

The next day dawned warm and fair, a promising forecast for a full attendance at the Great Baptism Debate, as Thaddeus had come to think of it. The entire Small family, not unexpectedly, was eager to attend the meeting, even though it was a six-mile drive to the hall at Cold Springs.

"I know James is only assisting," Mr. Small said, "but we'd all like to hear him. I'll hitch up the wagon so we can take all of us. Do you think young Martha would like to come along as well?"

Thaddeus appreciated the offer. He knew Martha would love to "come along," as Mr. Small put it, but better yet, the Smalls could also bring her home again, leaving Thaddeus free to travel west after the meeting.

When Mr. Small pulled the wagon up in front of the manse, Thaddeus was surprised to see that James had tethered his horse to the back of the wagon, and when he had handed Martha in, he clambered up to claim a place beside her on one of the hay bales Mr. Small had laid out for seats.

Thaddeus could see that Martha was less than pleased with this arrangement. She kept inching away from Small, and initiating conversation with one or another of his brothers.

It was still very early when they left Cobourg, but the sun wasn't far up in the sky before its effects were felt, and the women removed their shawls and wraps. As Thaddeus trotted alongside the lumbering hay wagon, he reflected that his choice of Cold Springs as the site for the debate had been a wise one. Their route was far west of the route the railway was taking and they were unlikely to experience any delays from the construction. Not that anyone would be working on a Sunday, of course, but any of the roads in the vicinity of the railway were rough and chewed up from the constant heavy traffic. They would still hit a number of bumpy sections on the way to Cold Springs, but the weather had been so hot and dry that the road had compacted into a surface as hard as granite. They should make good time.

They did, and not just because of the reasonable condition of the road. At each steep incline, the Small boys jumped out of the wagon and pushed, relieving Mr. Small's rather sad old mare of the necessity of hauling the full load. Martha and Mrs. Small cheered them on each time, and Thaddeus had to admit that it certainly sped up the entire process, and probably kept the horse from keeling over.

Between these heroic and rather comical episodes, Thaddeus reflected on the coming debate. He needed to make a good showing in order to keep people's enthusiasm at a high pitch, but he found that he was not particularly worried by this challenge. In fact, he felt energized by it. He had no need for special preparation. He already knew which verses he would cite to refute whatever the Baptist might say, and his logic skills were well honed after the spiralling and spirited discussions that had taken place at Dr. Christie's dinner table over the past two years. And after the dry struggle on Yonge Street, he welcomed the opportunity to address a receptive audience. Only once or twice during the ride did he caution himself against the sin of pride. Even though the Lord had blessed him with an excellent memory and a commanding voice, and he was only using it to further His cause, he should try not to be too confident. The Baptist might have some unanticipated argument to throw in his direction, and he would need to be sharp-witted in order to recognize and counter it, lest it trip up his argument.

As they drew closer to Cold Springs, they began to encounter streams of people — some riding, some in carts, some on foot — joining the main road from the byways and side roads they passed. They stared when they saw Thaddeus and whispered to one another.

"You're famous, Grandpa," Martha called from her perch in the wagon.

"Go on," he said. "They know I'm a preacher, but they're only guessing that I'm one of the speakers today. And I expect they're not even sure which one."

He was pleased, though. His efforts to publicize the debate had obviously drawn good numbers. Now the rest would be up to him.

When they reached Cold Springs, Mr. Small had trouble finding a place to leave the wagon. There were carts and buggies everywhere, and a large crowd of people milling about in the yard. The hall was a small building, capable of holding perhaps forty or fifty people, if they all stood and didn't mind a close proximity with their neighbours. It would be completely inadequate for the numbers of people who had turned up.

James Small climbed down from the wagon and looked around the yard, then pointed speculatively to a huge tree near the fence line of the property. The towering oak cast a welcome shade over a large part of the yard.

"What do you think about setting up over there?" he said. "We'll never get everyone into the hall."

"I think there will be a riot if we don't," Thaddeus replied. It was a good suggestion. The small building would be uncomfortably hot, even if they were able to cram everyone into it. "I wonder if your father could move his wagon over there? It would make a pretty good speaking platform."

"I don't know where else he can put it anyway," Small replied.

Thaddeus left his assistant to organize the wagon while he moved through the crowd, letting everyone know about the change of plans. He spotted Leland Gordon helping his ancient mother down the rough path, and went over to welcome them. The old woman beamed when she saw Thaddeus.

"Looking forward to today," she said. "There's nothing like a good preacher fight."

"I can only hope it remains a war of words."

"I've seen the fists come out on occasion," she said. "I seem to recall that it was most entertaining." She toddled off, cackling a little as she went.

"We're going to move into the yard," he said to Gordon. "Under the tree over there. You might want to steer your mother to a good spot."

"Thanks," Gordon said. "She'll never forgive me if I don't find her a seat in the front row."

"You'd better get moving then. She's left you behind."

Thaddeus joined Small and his brothers, who were chivvying people out of the way so that Mr. Small could drive the hay wagon to the edge of the yard.

"It's a good thing we all came, then, isn't it?" Mr. Small called. "My wagon will make you a grand platform."

Thaddeus waved, and just as he was turning to walk down the path to the hall, he saw the Howell woman walk through the gate, a girl of twelve or so walking sullenly a few steps behind her. Again, it was the blue dress that caught his attention — that, and the fact that, although it was by now quite hot, Mrs. Howell had wrapped a shawl firmly around herself.

"Good day," he said, walking over to her.

She smiled at him.

She had the most pleasant face, Thaddeus thought. The smile started on her lips but quickly reached her eyes. They sparkled with it, and curved upward to form nearly perfect almonds. It made him feel as though he was the one person in the entire world she had been hoping to meet at that exact moment. He felt a little weak in the dazzle of it.

He found himself utterly speechless for a moment, then managed to recover and tip his hat. "Thank you so much for coming. You may want to make your way over to the tree. We're moving the service into the yard. There are far too many people for inside."

She looked around. "I suspect that would be wise. You seem to have drawn quite a crowd. No one wants to miss the debate." Her voice was deep, and she had a decidedly English accent. Thaddeus found the low timbre extremely pleasing to his ear.

"I can only hope that it reaches a satisfactory conclusion," he said.

"For which one of you?"

Thaddeus grinned. "Why, for myself, of course!" and he was rewarded when she laughed, a sound that was every bit as charming as her voice. "I'm Thaddeus Lewis, by the way. Representing the sprinklers."

"Yes, I know. I heard you at the camp meeting. I'm Mrs. George Howell. And this is my daughter, Miss Caroline Howell."

"How do you do, Miss Howell?" he said.

Thaddeus could see that the girl was at that awkward age when children suddenly grow too quickly. Her wrists stuck out a little too far from her sleeves and her skirt had become too short, falling only a few inches below her knees. She ignored his greeting and slid a half-step behind her mother, so that he could no longer see her face.

Mrs. Howell appeared not to notice her daughter's rudeness. "My husband is looking for somewhere to leave our cart. He may have had to go quite a long way down the road."

"We have a few minutes before we're due to start. I'm sure he'll be here in time." Thaddeus hesitated. He wanted to continue this conversation, but could think of no topic that would be natural. Finally he said, "We're going to set up a pulpit of sorts under the tree. Why don't you go and find a good place to sit? He'll find you easily enough."

"Most kind of you. I'll do that." She was about to walk away when a sudden gust of wind caught one end of her shawl and blew it aside to expose her forearm. It was a mass of deep purple bruises, ugly mottled marks a few days old and starting to yellow at the edges. She gasped and quickly pulled the shawl over her arm again, then glanced at Thaddeus to see if he had noticed.

Thaddeus looked at her questioningly.

"I'm a foolish and vain woman," she said with a laugh. "Our old cow kicked when I was milking her yesterday. I hoped the wrap would cover it enough that no one would see."

The bruise didn't look anything like a hoofmark, though, and it was in an odd place to have been reached by the kick of a twitchy cow. Thaddeus was appalled. He had seen odd bruises on women too many times before. It was always a difficult issue to deal with.

Choosing his words carefully, he said, "There are things that can be done about cows that kick. If you need help with it, you have only to ask."

"Thank you," she said, reddening a little. "I'm sure it will be fine. Good luck in the debate."

She moved quickly away, her daughter in tow. Thaddeus watched her as she walked toward the hay wagon, the slight hitch in her gait more noticeable on the rough ground. By this time, the crowd realized that their entertainment had been moved and everyone was jostling to find the best places to stand or sit, bunching toward the front and spilling along the fenceline. Mrs. Howell was quickly lost in the mob of people milling about.

Thaddeus resumed his course for the hall. As a matter of courtesy, he supposed he should consult with the Baptist preacher about the change in arrangements, although he had no intention of doing anything differently should the man object.

There was a crowd of people in the building, as well, jammed together onto the benches and standing up against the walls, fanning themselves furiously against the clammy heat that had built up as a result of so many bodies in such a small space. The Baptist was standing at the far end of the room, where there was a raised section of floor. He drew himself up as he saw Thaddeus coming toward him.

"Good day, sir," he said, civilly enough. "I'm Phineas Brown, by the way." He was sweating heavily.

"Good day. We have quite an audience," Thaddeus replied. "More than will ever fit in here, I'm afraid. I think we should move the whole thing outside."

He almost expected instant disagreement with this plan, but Brown nodded his head. "Yes, of course," he said. "I'm pleased so many will hear the truth."

Thaddeus let the statement slide by. This was not the place to make his arguments.

"I thought we'd set ourselves up under the big tree. We've commandeered a wagon to serve as a platform, so everyone can see. My assistant will lead the prayer and a hymn and then you can speak."

A small frown. This man would like to have spoken last, Thaddeus knew, but after all, it was essentially a Methodist meeting and Brown was present only as an invited speaker. He could scarcely quibble about the order of service.

"If you're in agreement, then I suggest we wait another five minutes or so before we begin. I'll see you outside."

Thaddeus waited by the oak tree until Brown finally joined him, then they climbed up onto the bed of the wagon where James Small was already standing. The crowd hushed and settled as soon as they saw the preachers. Thaddeus spotted Mrs. Howell off to the right of him, near the fence. She was standing with four other women who had managed to group themselves slightly apart from the rest of the assembly, as if there were an invisible line across which no one dared step. There was no sign of her husband.

Thaddeus didn't know why he was so distracted by Mrs. Howell's presence. He tried to shake all thoughts of her out of his mind. He needed to focus on the task at hand.

Small cleared his throat and waited for a moment until he was sure all conversation had died down. "Welcome to today's meeting," he began, when he had gained everyone's attention. "It is exceedingly pleasant to see so many of you here today. Mr. Lewis and I decided that it would be appropriate to hold the service here in the yard, as otherwise not all of you could be accommodated."

There was a murmur of approval at this, and as Thaddeus scanned the front rows he recognized several ministers who had apparently deserted their own services to attend this one. He smiled to himself a little. He stood every chance of luring away their flocks if he was on his game today.

Again, his eye caught the flash of blue to his right. He wrested his attention away, and tried to focus on Small's opening exhortation and prayer, but as he joined in the hymn that followed, his eyes wandered back to the fence again. He could not afford this. He looked for Martha instead, and found her over at the other side of the wagon, where she was sitting with one of the Small boys and two young men whom he didn't recognize. He would keep his eyes fixed on her until it was time for him to speak.

After the closing notes of the hymn had echoed across the yard, the crowd settled themselves with a great air of expectation. Brown stood to one side as Small outlined the parameters of the day's discussion.

"We are afforded a great opportunity today at this gathering," Small said. "Although this meeting was originally called by the Methodist Episcopal Church of the Province of Canada in order to bring its congregants together in worship, it has been agreed that the Reverend Phineas Brown of the Baptist Church be allowed to address you concerning a matter that weighs heavily on his mind."

Thaddeus allowed himself a small twitch of amusement. *Weighs heavily on his mind.* What a clever way Small had put it. There might be hope for the young preacher yet.

"Mr. Brown has been invited today with the permission and full agreement of the Reverend Thaddeus Lewis of the Methodist Episcopals," Small went on.

There was scattered applause from the crowd.

"The subject of today's discussion is Baptism. This rite is a central part of both our creeds, but there is some dispute as to the form it should take."

"Put them in the middle of the yard and let them duke it out." The voice floated over the yard. Everyone laughed. Although it was a disruption, Thaddeus was glad to see that it was a good-natured crowd. He knew that Brown had marshalled his troops in the same way that Thaddeus had, each hoping to lure away the other's followers. There was always a danger of fisticuffs at these things if tempers were running high.

"First," Small said, "we'll hear from Mr. Brown."

Brown stepped forward to scattered applause. "The Baptist Church practises the rite of Baptism," he began. "We do not, however, content ourselves with a half-hearted sprinkling." He spat out the last word, as the insult it was intended to be. "We believe that only full immersion baptism will admit you to the Kingdom of God. We believe that this is what God intends, and that it says so clearly in the Bible. The Bible, which is the Book of Books, and which I love with all my heart." He held the book he was carrying aloft for the crowd to see. "When you open this Bible," he said, "you will note that it says 'The King James Version.'"

The congregation could note nothing of the sort, Thaddeus knew, since the print was far too small to make out from more than a foot or so away. It didn't matter, he figured, since a great number of them could barely read anyway.

"*Version*," Brown repeated, and then he paused to let the ramifications of the word sink in. "This means that King James gathered together a group of scholars and directed them to translate the texts from the original Latin and Greek. Unfortunately, they did not do it correctly."

There was a murmur through the crowd.

"There are three reasons for this mistranslation." The man waved the open Bible in the air. "First of all, King James directed the translation. He gave the outlines of translation to those to whom the work was assigned. He was the king. They would dare not go contrary to his order even if they were disposed to do so. And after all, everyone knows that King James was a sprinkler."

A number of people swivelled around to see how Thaddeus was taking this point. He remained calm and showed no reaction. As far as he was concerned, the Baptist had already hanged himself.

"Furthermore," Brown went on, "the translators were all sprinklers themselves. As a result, the language has been so changed by this influence that it is not to be depended upon."

Thaddeus knew what the next gambit would be. And sure enough, the man made his pitch, repeating the argument he had put forth at their first confrontation.

"My good friend here," Brown pointed to Thaddeus, "relies upon the King James version of this Book of Books. He does not know how to read Greek or Latin."

Thaddeus allowed himself a small nod of the head in response to this.

"I, however, have read the original Greek and Latin texts for myself, and I can tell you that this Bible, this Protestant Bible, has been mistranslated, particularly with respect to Baptism. If you read it in Greek, or if you read it in Latin, it is clear that the Lord Jesus was in favour of full immersion."

There was another round of clapping from the Baptists in the crowd. Brown bowed in acknowledgment, and then he nodded smugly at Thaddeus and stepped back.

Thaddeus was astonished. This was no argument at all. Brown had quoted no verses, cited no authorities, had done nothing but repeat the statements he had made at the camp meeting. This was too easy. Thaddeus felt a twinge of disappointment. He had been looking forward to a spirited debate that would test his skills as both an orator and a logician, not this pale excuse for a debate. Then he recalled his duty, and knew that this day he would bring many to the Methodist Episcopal Church.

He stepped forward, cast a long look around him, resisted the urge to look toward the fence, and then turned to Brown.

"Thank you very much for that insightful summary, Mr. Brown," he said. A handful of people caught the sarcasm in his voice and snickered a little.

"I'm afraid, however, that you have seized the wrong end of the argument. Now, you must understand me clearly. I certainly do not mean to say, or to be understood to say, that the Reverend Mr. Brown is an infidel."

There was a gasp. Thaddeus held his hand up in admonishment.

"No, indeed, I hold him as a Christian brother. But I do believe that he has mistaken his way on the doctrine of Baptism. And I must say that I have never in my life met an infidel who strove to invalidate and render useless the Protestant Bible so much as he does."

He had the crowd's full attention now. This was more like what they were expecting.

"No, I would prefer to believe that Mr. Brown just didn't understand properly what he was saying or doing. He pressed the open Bible to his heart and declared his intense love for it."

"Yes, he did!" someone shouted.

"He said he esteemed it above any other book. That it was the Book of Books!"

Thaddeus paused for a moment to let the tension build before he went on.

"And then he turns right around and claims that this Book of Books, this Book that he loves with all his heart, is nothing more than a mistranslated piece of nonsense!"

There was wild applause at this. Thaddeus waited until it had just started to diminish, just slightly, and then he turned to the Baptist minister. "Well, which is it, Mr. Brown?"

He thought he would be deafened by the roar that went up. He had to admit to himself that it was a lovely piece of rhetoric, and he couldn't believe that any minister who had achieved ordination would not have seen the contradiction in the Baptist's argument. Brown was red in the face, his mouth opening and closing. He wanted a rebuttal, Thaddeus could see, but the crowd wasn't going to let him have it. Neither was Thaddeus.

He held his hand up to quell the noise. He wasn't quite finished yet.

"It is true that I read neither Latin nor Greek, as Mr. Brown claims to. Nor do many of the people here today." He was reasonably sure that a great many of the people gathered in the yard had difficulty enough with English, and he would be astonished if there were more than one or two persons present who were conversant with the classical languages, but the implication that it was a possibility was a compliment to his audience, and they took it as such.

"Neither could the people of England when long ago King James gathered the finest scholars in the land to translate the scriptures into a language that all could understand. These scholars were the most educated minds of their time. They were chosen carefully. They had spent countless years in the study of ancient languages. And God smiled upon their efforts."

Again, Thaddeus paused, and assumed a look of perplexity.

"Mr. Brown thanks God that he can read Greek and Latin for himself. He will not believe any man or any set of men with whom he disagrees, because he knows for himself the Protestant Bible was not translated correctly. He *knows*. And yet, for all his supposed learning, he has not given you one single example of this so-called mistranslation. He has not quoted a single verse to support his argument. All he has done is insist that you believe him because he is wiser than the finest minds in England."

"Good point!" someone shouted. Thaddeus looked down at Martha, who grinned at him.

"You can claim that certain passages in the Bible were mistranslated if you like."

"No!" someone shouted.

"But if some of them are wrong, doesn't it stand to reason that all of them are wrong?"

"No, no!" More voices joined the protest.

"But if some of them are wrong and some of them are right, which ones are which? Mr. Brown claims to know, because he can read Latin and Greek. The question remains: How well? Better than I can, that's true enough. Better than most of us."

Again, the little compliment.

"But better than scholars who have spent their entire lifetimes in study? I think not. I think I know where a mistranslation is most likely to occur."

Another small cheer.

"And yet, Mr. Brown claims to love the Bible above all things. He holds it to his heart and proclaims it the Book of Books. But only some parts of it. The parts he agrees with. Well, I'm sorry, Mr. Brown. You cannot have it both ways."

There was a stirring off to Thaddeus's right. It was Brown, who had climbed down from the wagon and was striding through the crowd toward the gate.

Thaddeus called after him. "I'm sorry, Mr. Brown. I don't understand your argument. Because you have made none."

There was a huge round of applause and a few cheers as Thaddeus drove his point home.

"Let us then look at what this *mistranslated* Book of Books actually says to us, in language we can understand, as provided by King James's best scholars. *'For thou shalt be his witness unto all men of what thou hast seen and heard. And now why tarriest thou? Arise, and be baptized, and wash away thy sins, calling on the name of the Lord."*

The field was his, and now Thaddeus would give these people what they had come for. On and on he went, quoting, explaining, expostulating, until finally, after an exhausting three hours on his feet, he signalled Small to end the service with a hymn.

The crowd sang loudly and enthusiastically. As the last notes died away, many of the attendees surged forward, anxious to speak with Thaddeus, keen to abandon whatever creeds they had followed until then and join with the Methodist Episcopals. By the time he had treated with them all, Ellen Howell had once again disappeared.

IV

Thaddeus saw Martha and the Small family off in the hay wagon before he headed west in the wake of his triumph. He would work his way through Hamilton and Hope Townships, then carry on along the shore of Lake Ontario to Cobourg for a few days rest before he and James traded routes.

For the first hour or so a flush of exhilaration allowed him to ignore his physical discomfort. He had acquitted himself well, although in all modesty he had to admit that the Baptist minister had proved a poor opponent. Still, Thaddeus knew that his efforts could only help the church, and himself, as well. He would have many baptisms to perform and surely many marriages and confirmations and burials would follow. It was a pleasure to labour on such fertile ground. He just wished that the ground he was attempting to sow wasn't quite so rough.

After his elation wore off, he realized that he was very tired. First there had been the journey from Cobourg to Cold Springs before his day had even really started, and then the three hours of standing on his feet, preaching. And now another long ride. When he'd first started the itinerant life so many years ago he had ridden for hours every day, and had sometimes been offered nothing more than a pile of straw as a bed at the end of it. Many a morning had begun with nothing more than a bowl of thin porridge. *Soft in my old age,* he thought, and yet he couldn't help but look forward to completing his round and returning to his comfortable manse in Cobourg.

He had moments when he felt a little guilty about claiming such a large house when his assistant shared a modest cottage with his parents and four siblings. But as the senior man, Thaddeus was entitled to the benefit, and he intended to make full use of it. After years of making do in tiny houses and furnished rooms in other people's homes, he found that he appreciated the space. He would make a start on his memoirs. He would pore through the many years of notes and records he had kept and put them in some kind of order. He would take over one upstairs room entirely as his office, so he could leave his papers and notebooks spread out over a table. And on those nights when sleep eluded him, he could rise, light a lamp, and write the story of his life.

He shifted in his saddle again to ease the ache in his knee. He carried a supply of willow tea with him now, which he brewed up on a regular basis. His son Luke had told him that it seemed to work best when used regularly and not just when his bones were rattled from the long rides. Luke had also given him a small bottle of laudanum for the really bad times, but Thaddeus didn't like to use it unless he absolutely had to. It dulled his wits and made him careless. He needed to stay alert. One mistake with his horse and they would both be out of action. He was fortunate that the good weather had lasted this far into the year, for when the fall rains came, the ride would be muddy and treacherous.

Even so, he much preferred riding alone with no sound but that of the wind and the birds to keep him company. He was relieved to be done with the first difficult week with his assistant. Small felt obliged to supply conversation as they rode, and it had taken only a few hours for Thaddeus to tire of it. Now he could let his thoughts wander without interruption.

He found that they were wandering far too often in the direction of the Howell woman. He wasn't sure why she unsettled him so. It was the dress, he guessed: a token of a lost time, a happier time. A memory he thought had been lost.

He wondered if he should have a word with the husband about the bruise he had seen on her arm. That could be tricky. The Howells were not members of his church. Mr. Howell was, if not an important man, at least a self-important one. He might not take kindly to an admonition from a Methodist saddlebag preacher, someone who, Thaddeus was sure, Howell regarded as a lower order of being. Besides, sometimes confrontation made things worse. But Thaddeus was sure the bruising had not been inflicted by a cow's hoof as the woman claimed. Someone had grabbed her wrist and wrenched it, leaving the unmistakable outline of fingers in a rainbow of nasty marks. For the sake of his own conscience, he needed to try to set things right. In fact, it was his duty to do so.

Perhaps he should ask Leland Gordon about it first. Gordon said he rented land from the Howells. Maybe he would know if there had been other bruises. Or better yet, he would ask Old Mrs. Gordon, who might be more sympathetic to his inquiry. That resolved, he felt easier in his mind, if not in his body.

As he reached each meeting on his western circuit, he found that reports of The Great Baptism Debate had already spread, and that his arrival was eagerly anticipated in every instance. All of his meetings attracted new people. His services were full. Everyone wanted to hear the preacher who had acquitted himself so well, who had marshalled his knowledge of scripture and commanded a large crowd. He allowed himself to bask a little in the notoriety. His only other encounter with fame had been as a result of the apprehension of murderers. This time, people wanted to know him because of the heavenly message he delivered, and not because of some earthly derring-do. This kind of admiration was much more welcome and he allowed himself to savour it.

He scheduled extra meetings for the coming month. Small would have to pick up some of them. He hoped the junior minister could consolidate the gains he'd made, and that the people didn't wander away again when they discovered that they wouldn't be hearing the preacher who had verbally wrestled a Baptist to the ground.

Second only to the talk of his exploits on the speaking platform was news of the local railways. In the western part of his circuit, the conversation was all about the proposed Port Hope Railway that was intended to snake past the western end of Rice Lake to Lindsay and Peterborough. A company had been formed and a charter applied for, with construction slated to begin sometime in the next two years. Even if it was completed, the Port Hope line would face stiff competition from the Cobourg to Peterborough Railway. They both hoped to draw from the same market, and Cobourg had a head start.

Even so, Port Hope was the far more sensible proposal, as far as Thaddeus could tell. The Cobourg railway seemed to be almost entirely dependent on the integrity of the bridge across the lake, and although the contractor, a man named Zimmerman, claimed to have extensive experience with things like bridge-building and had landed contracts for an enormous number of these small railways as a result, Thaddeus couldn't rid himself of the notion that the project was ill-fated, and that the railway mania that gripped the country would all come to naught in the end. No one had been terribly successful at building reliable roads, and he failed to see how iron rails would fare any better. Still, the province was buzzing with plans for small local railways, and a major trunk line was even now slated to inch its way from Montreal to Toronto.

As Thaddeus reached the limit of his circuit and headed east again, the conversation subtly changed. Although he was still welcomed wherever he went, he began to realize that his exploits were rather a nine-day wonder, and more of the discussions he overheard were about the difficulties that the Cobourg railway now found itself in. The problem was not with the bridge, however, but with a tract of land at the village of Sully.

"The railway company's already started building sheds on the land and now it looks like they may not own it after all," one man in Port Britain said. "Jack Plews is taking them to court."

"But I thought Plews was behind in the mortgage and that's why he sold it," Thaddeus said. That was what the men at the camp meeting had thought.

"People say there was some sharp dealing and that D'Arcy Boulton tipped George Howell off about the plans for the land. Stands to reason, given Boulton is a director of the railway company. Anyhow, Plews intends to get some satisfaction."

"Could be Plews didn't really own it either," said one toothless old man who had hobbled into the meeting on the arm of his neighbour and now sat on the bench closest to the window. "Nor Boulton neither, if it comes to that."

"What are you talking about, Walter?" his neighbour said.

"My uncle farmed that land on shares maybe fifty, sixty years ago, but he couldn't never get clear title for it. There was some problem." The old man stopped and mumbled his gums while he thought about this. "Now, I just can't quite remember the ins and outs of it, but any road, he moved on. Nice piece of property, though, right there by the lake."

"Are you sure, Walter? I didn't know your Uncle Albert ever farmed back at the lake." The neighbour was obviously skeptical about the story.

"No, no, t'wasn't Uncle Albert. It was Uncle Lem Palmer. Or maybe it was Uncle Syl. No, it musta been Uncle Lem, 'cause he was married to Aunt Harriet …"

The old man embarked on a long, complicated explanation of his family tree. The others chuckled indulgently, but Thaddeus figured the core point of the story could well be true. Land titles were tricky things in Upper Canada — proving which parcels were grants and which were purchases, which ones had fulfilled the requirements for a patent, and which had been assigned to settlers who failed to clear the requisite number of acres and therefore forfeited the land to the Crown. The Heir and Devisee Commission existed to sort it all out, but often the original records had been lost or destroyed or simply not recorded accurately. Sometimes land passed through two or three generations with no clear title in place, and a grandson might discover that he couldn't get a mortgage on his property because his grandfather hadn't really owned it in the first place.

Thaddeus would be surprised if the railway company hadn't made certain of their ownership before they began to build, but then, he reflected, everything about the Cobourg railway was being done in a hurry and they may not have bothered before they began construction.

In any event, it wasn't really any of his business and he gently tried to steer the conversation back to the original purpose of the meeting. But he did wonder what would happen to the Sully Railroad Station if Mr. Plews could make his accusations stick. He would probably just be paid off, Thaddeus guessed. The railway company appeared to have no end of funds at their disposal, so what was a little extra to make a problem go away? And that, he decided, was probably what Plews was angling for.

The road that wound its way along the shore of Lake Ontario was kept in reasonable repair, and after the conclusion of the meeting, he made good time, arriving back in Cobourg just before suppertime. He stabled and fed his horse, then walked across the yard to the manse. To his surprise, James Small was standing just inside the back porch, a pie in his hand. Martha leaned against the jamb of the door that led into the kitchen. Small seemed flustered when he saw Thaddeus.

"Mr. Lewis," he stammered. "I'm surprised to see you so soon."

"You too," Thaddeus said. Small must have galloped through his appointments and galloped right home again.

"Mother's just sent over an apple pie," Small said, whisking away the cloth that covered the pan and holding it out for Thaddeus to see, as if he had been challenged somehow about what he was carrying and needed to justify his presence.

"Excellent!" Thaddeus said. A pie was always a welcome thing.

"Thank you, Mr. Small," Martha said and reached for the pan. "And tell your mother I'm very much obliged."

Small nodded at her, and then at Thaddeus, before he stumbled out the door.

Thaddeus kicked off his boots and followed Martha into the kitchen. "What was that all about?"

She sighed. "That's twice now he's made an excuse to come over here. It's a nuisance really, except that both times he brought something — first a box of kindling, and now a pie."

"Ah, I see." Apparently James Small had taken a fancy to Martha. "Is this going to be a problem?" She seemed not just indifferent to, but downright annoyed by, the young man's attentions. "Should I speak to him?"

"I don't think so," Martha said. "I haven't given him the slightest encouragement. Nor will I." She giggled a little. "Have you noticed that his Adam's apple bobs up and down when he talks? I can't help staring at it, and then I miss what he's saying to me."

She was right. It did. Thaddeus had become mesmerized by it once or twice himself. He hoped Small wouldn't be too insistent and that there would be no hard feelings over Martha's rejection. It could make their working relationship awkward if Small took offence, or persisted in spite of her discouragement.

"Besides," Martha went on, "he's *old*."

Thaddeus laughed. "He's twenty-three!"

Martha looked at him solemnly. "And I'm fifteen. Far too young to have any young man coming to the door, much less an old one of twenty-three."

"That's absolutely correct, my dear." He knew he was being teased, but he did wonder again if he had taken on more than he bargained for.

"Anyway, I hadn't expected to see you quite so soon," she said. "I was going to melt some cheese on some bread and call that my supper."

"That sounds fine, if we can have some of that pie for dessert."

"I'll brew some tea for you first."

Thaddeus walked over to the kitchen table and pulled out a chair, but was suddenly struck with the realization that something was different. It took him a few moments to work out what it was.

"Did you put different curtains in here?" he asked. The window had been draped in a worn and yellowed fabric that blocked most of the light. Now only the bottom pane was covered, and with a far lighter material.

"Yes. Those came from the back bedroom. They washed up better than the ones that were there, so I switched them. It's lovely in the morning — the sun pours in through that window."

"Good idea," he said. It was something that would never have occurred to him to do. "They look nice."

He sat down and reached for the newspapers that Martha had left on the table. He had seen only one or two papers in the days he had been away, and then he had not been able to do anything more than glance at them. It would have been rude to do otherwise in someone else's home; he was expected to make polite conversation, to comment on the fineness of the meal, and to lead the family in prayer, not sit with his nose stuck in their reading material. Now he looked forward to a steaming cup of tea and a bite to eat, all consumed while devouring the latest news and the commentary on it. It was a luxury to take the papers, but one that he was reluctant to forego.

The *Cobourg Star* had only a brief article on the matter of the Plews lawsuit, stating only the barest of the details. Thaddeus wondered what the Sully neighbourhood was making of the whole affair. George Howell was not a particularly popular figure to begin with, apparently, and his seemingly unscrupulous land deal seemed to have uncovered a tangled web of questions, none of which had been answered by the newspaper. It didn't seem to matter, as far as the town fathers were concerned. Thaddeus discovered in a second article that they were prepared to pour another forty thousand pounds of municipal money into the railway project, and in a third, that they had unveiled plans to build a substantial town hall to reflect the glory that would soon be Cobourg's. This seemed rash to Thaddeus. Better to wait and see whether the bridge fell down and the lines heaved first.

Bemused, he turned to the next page, which featured the international news. Trouble was brewing on the Crimean Peninsula, and it looked as though France and England were prepared to go to war with Russia in a complicated dispute that somehow involved the rights of Christians in Jerusalem. Although this was something that Thaddeus was all in favour of, his understanding was that the city was controlled by the

Ottoman Empire, and he couldn't quite follow the article well enough to discover how so many other countries had become embroiled in the dispute. The Crimea was nowhere near Jerusalem. Or at least he didn't think it was. Just another of Britain's imperial squabbles, he decided, and unlikely to affect Canada. He leafed through the paper looking for reading that was a little less taxing, but he had exhausted the intellectual offerings of *The Star*. The rest of the paper was filled with social news and advertisements.

He reached for the *Toronto Globe*. Tucked beneath it was a small volume. *Uncle Tom's Cabin or Life Among the Lowly*, he read. It was a popular novel, he knew, a tale that exposed the evils of slavery.

"Is this yours?" he asked.

Martha glanced at the book. "Oh, that's where it went. Yes, it's mine now, I suppose. One of the guests left it at the hotel, but we couldn't ever figure out who it belonged to, so father gave it to me."

"Have you read it?"

"About five times. Whenever I get tired of the papers and don't have anything new to read, I go back to my old favourites."

Thaddeus was surprised. "You read the newspapers?"

"Yes, of course. They're here anyway. You needn't bother reading them yourself. Just ask me what you want to know and I'll tell you all about it." She set his tea in front of him.

"Can you explain the situation in the Crimea?"

"Nobody can explain the situation in the Crimea. There is no explanation."

"That was my conclusion as well."

She laughed and returned to cooking their makeshift meal.

He was impressed by her, but he tried not to let it show as he once again buried his nose in the day's news.

V

Thaddeus was surprised by the little twinge of disappointment he felt when he failed to see Ellen Howell in Sully the following week. There was no reason why he should, he told himself. She was not a Methodist. She had been at the camp meeting with her husband, who evidently had business to conduct there. Like many others, she had attended The Great Baptism Debate, he was sure, for the entertainment of it, nothing more. Old Mrs. Gordon said that the Howell farm was south of Sully, but even if she lived in the village itself, he couldn't expect to see her flitting about on the very day he happened to be there. And more to the point, why had he been hoping to see her at all? Yes, of course, there was a concern about her circumstances, but no more so than any number of other people, some of whom were actual members of his congregation. He would address the question of the bruised arm if he could, but it wasn't really an overwhelming concern. He didn't know why he kept thinking about it.

This was his first visit to Sully since the debate at Cold Springs, and he was pleased to see that here the effect of his triumph had not yet worn off. The meeting was full, but Thaddeus estimated that approximately half of the new faces attended out of curiosity, and he was sure that when they found it less exciting than the debate they would wander away again. A handful of the new attendees, however, seemed genuinely interested in joining the church on a permanent basis, and he hoped that he could safely deliver them into the arms of full membership. He made a point of greeting each person warmly. Honestly, he thought, he had enough sinners and backsliders to keep him more than busy. He needn't go looking for trouble with the Howells when he had so much work right in front of him.

Still, after the meeting was completed and he made his way to the Gordons for his dinner, he resolved to ask about the bruise if the opportunity should arise.

It was a long time coming. The table talk over dinner was all about Jack Plews and the railway. According to Old Mrs. Gordon, half of her neighbours were annoyed with Plews for instigating the lawsuit and the other half with George Howell for sharp practice in the first place.

"Everyone's afraid the dispute may delay the completion of the line," she said. "They can see all the money flying away."

"Surely it won't come to that?" Thaddeus said.

"Oh no, I expect the railway company will just make good on the difference in price," Leland Gordon said. "But they'll do it with investor money. In the end, it's the shareholders who will pay."

"In the end it's always the people who pay," Old Mrs. Gordon pointed out, and Thaddeus could think of no argument to counter this, but he was distressed that even here, in this remote village, all anyone could think of was how rich they were about to become.

"I was at a meeting in Port Britain last week," Thaddeus said. "There was an old, old man there who claimed that Plews couldn't have had title to the land in the first place. He said there was some problem that prevented his uncle from buying it years ago. Of course, the old fellow couldn't remember which uncle it was, so nobody took his story very seriously."

"I don't see how that could be," Leland said. "Plews had been on the property for five or six years, and it had always been farmed before that. If there's a problem, wouldn't it have turned up before this?"

"I'm not so sure it hasn't," Mrs. Gordon said. "There were some disputes here a few years ago." She began to chuckle. "Well, maybe not so few. I forget how old I am sometimes. But I remember my father talking about one of them." Her face creased into a thousand wrinkles while she tried to recall the details. "It might have been Margaret Dafoe's family." She turned to her son. "You remember Margaret. She married a Palmer."

Gordon shrugged a little. What was so clear in his mother's memory had never registered with him. *It's the way of old age, I guess,* Thaddeus thought. *I must tell Martha to ignore me if I start talking about people she's never heard of.*

"Any road," Old Mrs. Gordon went on, "it must have been sorted out somehow, because I don't remember hearing anything more about it."

"I don't understand how you could get a mortgage on a piece of property you don't own," Thaddeus said. "There would be nothing to secure the loan."

"I expect you can if you get it from D'Arcy Boulton," Mr. Gordon said darkly. "Let's not forget who most likely engineered the whole purchase in the first place."

The talk turned then to the excellent turnout at the local meeting, and how Thaddeus's fine showing during the debate had engendered so much interest in the church. It wasn't until he was about to leave that he ventured to introduce the topic that remained uppermost in his mind.

"I have something to ask you. It's a bit of a delicate subject, and I don't know if I'm speaking out of turn."

"Oh, Mr. Lewis, I doubt you could ever speak out of turn," Mrs. Gordon said. "Go ahead. Ask away."

"It's about Major Howell's wife. I noticed a very nasty bruise on her arm the other day."

Mrs. Gordon seemed to grasp what he was asking right away. The women always did. "And you're wondering how it happened?"

"She claimed that a cow kicked her, but it didn't look like it to me. It looked like the sort of bruise that would be left by someone wrenching her arm. Violently."

"And you're asking who might have done that?" Leland said. He thought for a moment before he shook his head. "I haven't seen any other marks, but it's not like I see her every day or anything. I go there only when there's work to do on their fields. Even then, I wouldn't see her unless she asked me to split some wood or do some other chore for her."

"You probably wouldn't see anything anyway," Mrs. Gordon said. "In my experience, women try to hide those kinds of bruises. They don't want anyone to know."

"And that's the problem," Thaddeus said. "I'm by no means certain, and unless it happens frequently, it's very difficult to come up with enough evidence to make an accusation. And sometimes bringing it up only makes matters worse."

Leland looked dubious. "I don't like Major Howell, but he doesn't strike me as the type. Too much of a gentleman — in his own estimation if in no one else's."

"Sometimes those who profess to be gentlemen are the worst offenders," Thaddeus said. "In any event, I thought I'd just mention my concerns, and perhaps you could keep a little closer eye on things, when you're there. Even so, I'm not sure what I could do. They aren't members of our church, after all, but perhaps I could ask their own minister to intervene if there's a problem."

"That would be the Anglican man, Reverend Barris, if it comes to that," Mrs. Gordon said. "That's where people like the Howells go."

"Should we be concerned about the girl, as well?" Thaddeus asked. In his experience, violence in a family was seldom limited to one member. Most often, everyone felt the brunt of it.

"Now, that I really couldn't imagine," Leland said. "The girl follows her father around like a puppy. She seldom seems to notice anyone else. I doubt she's ever said more than two words to me. Only occasionally do you see her with her mother, and when you do it's clear she doesn't want to be there. The Major seems to be the only human being she can be bothered with. She wouldn't be like that if he was beating her, would she?"

Thaddeus wasn't so sure. These cases were so complicated. Sometimes the victims were the staunchest defenders of the abusers. "Well," he said finally, "I'd appreciate it if you could keep your eyes open. And let me know if you see anything."

As he rode away from the Gordon farm, he puzzled over what possessed men to use their fists on their wives, and why there were so seldom any repercussions as a result of it. Except in cases of extreme injury, the law took the view that a husband was within his rights to raise his hand against anyone in his family, but why it should countenance even that was beyond his understanding. The Church declared that the Lord had given men dominion over women, but to protect them, not abuse them. He couldn't imagine any circumstance that would ever have inclined him to strike his wife, and he had never disciplined his children with more than a word. He had scarcely disciplined them at all, truth be told. He was never at home to do it. He had left it all to Betsy.

If the Gordons were correct in their assessment, it seemed unlikely that George Howell was a brute who beat his wife. But why would Ellen Howell manufacture such a flimsy story about the bruise on her arm unless she was attempting to hide its true origin? It was his duty to interfere if he thought she was in danger, but in all honesty he couldn't say that was the case. He had made his inquiry, and done what he could. Now he needed to put the woman firmly out of his mind so he could concentrate on the extra meetings he had scheduled in the wake of the debate. These had resulted in a far more hectic schedule than he had bargained for.

There was little enough time to spare before his next appointment, but Thaddeus couldn't resist stopping for a few minutes at the shore of Rice Lake to watch the crew working on the bridge. Nor was he the only one who was curious. Several small boats full of sightseers bobbed in the water close to the construction barges. And farther out, Thaddeus could see the steamship chugging its way across the lake to the Sully dock. Passengers hung precariously over the port side, craning their necks in order to gain a better view of the work in progress.

Massive logs marched in a line toward Tic Island, the jumping-off point for the long stretch of bridge that would cross open water, and another huge timber was being pulled out of the lake and slowly inched to a vertical position as he watched. As soon as it was in place, the steam pile driver pounded it in, bark flying with every blow. The noise made at each hammer stroke shattered the lakeshore's serenity and drowned out any sound made by the wind or the water.

Hundreds of these wooden stilts would be needed to form a framework for the trestles, and as substantial as the timbers were, Thaddeus failed to see how they would ever hold up something as heavy as a locomotive, or how they could ever resist the heave and pull of ice and current. Not to mention the inherent dangers of human failure, which had been amply demonstrated just a few months previously when forty-eight people had been killed in Connecticut.

The newspapers had been full of the details of the accident. A train travelling at the reckless rate of fifty miles an hour had plunged into Norwalk Harbor from a swing bridge opened to allow the passage of a ship. The driver of the locomotive ignored the signal to stop and noticed the open stretch of water only a few hundred feet before he reached it. He activated the brakes and slammed the train into reverse, but it was not enough to stop the forward momentum of the train. The engine flew across the gap and slammed into the opposite abutment, then sank in twelve feet of water, the cars behind it falling down, one after the other, to crush the ones before them in turn, until, finally, one of them broke in two, leaving the front half hanging over the near abutment while the rear half remained on the track. The loss of life had been terrible, and many questions were being asked about the qualifications of the drivers, the adequacy of the signalling system, and the safety of rail travel in general.

There was a comparable section of swing bridge included in the design for this project. A similar accident could happen just as easily here, but no one ever seemed to mention this. Thaddeus was fairly certain that no one would ever be able to coax him aboard the train that would cross this bridge, no matter how big the timbers were.

Enough gawking, he finally said to himself. *You're no better than the idlers on the lake.* He kicked his horse into a sedate trot, a gait that should get him to his meeting on time but that was still slow enough that he could drink in the lovely view along the shore. Rice Lake was dotted with islands — Tic Island across from Sully, where the rail line would run;

a little farther from shore, Spook Island; to the west, Sugar, Sheep, and Black Islands; and in the distance, Cow Island and the bluff of land where long-forgotten tribes had buried their dead under mounds of earth. It was almost a shame, he thought, to spoil so pretty a scene with piles and trestles.

He had not travelled far along the lakeside trail when he noticed a skiff heading toward the shore. It would reach land west of the village, he judged. He would have assumed that it was one of the spectators tired of watching, or a fisherman who had caught enough for one day, and not thought anything further about it, except for a flash of blue that caught his eye. Blue made him think of Ellen Howell. He attempted once again to shove any thought of her aside. Just because he saw someone dressed in blue didn't mean that it had anything to do with the Howell woman. This was obviously someone else, someone who had a dock or a landing farther down the shore and who had merely been out for a ride on the lake on a spectacularly lovely September afternoon.

Still, he took careful note when he passed the section of shore where he was sure the boat must have landed, but he could see nothing through the trees and bushes that clustered along the bank.

VI

Thaddeus was well over on the western border of his circuit, at a women's meeting in Wesleyville, when he heard about the murder on Spook Island.

"A murder? Really?" he asked the local lay preacher.

"There's no mistaking it for an accident," the man said. "The dead man has a gash in his head and a bullet in his chest. No one seems to know who he is. They couldn't find any papers on him."

The men at the evening meeting were buzzing with speculation about it, too, and Thaddeus had no small task to settle them down sufficiently to focus on interpreting the Bible verses he had chosen.

By the time he returned to Cobourg, details of the murder had reached the newspapers. Martha had been expecting him home that evening, and had a stew simmering on the stove, the table set, and the week's newspapers stacked beside his plate.

"Sit down," she said. "I'll have your supper in two minutes."

In spite of the fact that he was curious to see what the papers had to say, he was also very hungry and pleased that

Martha had a meal ready for him. He had to stop himself from bolting it down as soon as she set it in front of him. The best compliment for the cook, he knew, was to take the time to savour each mouthful, and after the first few bites, he found this no hardship. Whatever flavourings Martha had used imparted a rich, redolent tang to the dish. It was some recipe learned from her stepmother, he was sure.

"What did you put in it?" he asked. "This is delicious."

She smiled. "Not telling. Cook's secret."

"If you'd just fill me in, I could pass the information on to some of my congregation. They don't stint on the servings, but they seldom add much of anything besides salt to their dishes."

"If you did, my reputation as a good cook would be destroyed. Anyone could do as well in the kitchen. My position as your housekeeper might be in peril."

"Oh, I doubt that," he said, grabbing a piece of the crusty loaf Martha placed on the table. "I'd still need somebody to wash my socks."

"If you're not careful, I'll send your socks to Mrs. Small to be boiled along with the sheets," she retorted. "See how long you last then."

"I retract my request. I'll pester you no more about what delicious things you put in my dinner."

Soft, dry socks were one of the few comforts he had always insisted on. His outer clothing was frequently wet through from rain or sleet or snow; he could make one shirt do for a week or two, except in the summer when it became soaked in sweat; and his boots were generally caked with mud or covered in dust. These things he could put up with. But not socks that had been boiled with lye soap and dried to a rock-hard finish. His wife, Betsy, had always washed his in rainwater and vinegar and had taught Martha to do the same. She knew how fussy he was about it, and apparently had no compunction about using the threat of boiled socks as a way to score conversational points. He loved the fact that she could banter with him this way.

He finished his stew with a satisfied sigh, then carried the papers through to the parlour, where he discovered that the most comfortable chair had been moved next to the butler's desk, itself now positioned on the opposite wall from where it had previously stood. It made sense to have the chair next to the desk, he supposed. The lamp could be placed on its top, high enough to cast a circle of good light for reading.

He sat down and opened the *Cobourg Star*, which had much the same information about the murder as he had gleaned from the excited chatter at the meeting. A body with a bullet in it had been discovered on Spook Island by a local fisherman. There was a delay in reporting the discovery, apparently, as the fisherman was concerned that he might be considered a suspect in the case.

However, the fisherman's father persuaded him to contact the local constable and report the death. The coroner called the usual inquest, but at the time the paper went to print there were no results from this. Nor had the deceased been identified, as he carried no papers in his pockets.

"You're reading about the murder?" Martha asked as she joined him in the parlour, book in hand. "There's not much information in the paper, but then I suppose they have to wait until everything is confirmed, don't they? Not like the gossips at the market."

"What are they saying at the market?"

"That it was all just silly. There was no trouble finding people to serve on the jury. Everyone was clamouring to be picked. The problem was getting them all over to the island."

Regulations stipulated that when an inquest was called, the jury must view the body in the circumstances in which it was found, so that they could take careful note of details like how it was lying, what it had in its possession, and any extraneous details that might prove to be important evidence. Although any sensible person might think that it would be wise to limit the number of people who had access to a murder scene, there were frequently a large number of spectators at these investigations, and jurors were instructed to watch them with great attention, "in case the murderer is in attendance and gives himself away by word or action." In Thaddeus's opinion, it was far more likely that enthusiastic gawkers would simply trample evidence into the ground.

"Apparently, no one wanted to give up their boats," Martha went on, "because they all wanted them themselves — so they could go and stare. The coroner had to offer twice over the going rate to rent them."

Thaddeus snorted. He could well imagine the scene, boat owners torn between seeing the spectacle for themselves and making an opportunistic penny.

"Well, they got them all over there eventually, but on the way back some of the people had to share a boat with the corpse. They weren't so cheerful then."

"What did they find on the island?" Thaddeus wanted to know. "Anything that might provide a clue?"

Martha gave him an odd look. "You're not thinking of getting involved in this, are you? You nearly died yourself the first two times you went off chasing a murderer."

That was true enough. Thaddeus had been close to drowning when he fell through the ice between Kingston and Wolfe Island while pursuing the Isaac Simms case, and had suffered a severe blow to the head and a broken arm in the course of chasing down the truth of the Elliott affair. His role in these cases was common knowledge, and Martha had grown up hearing the stories of his exploits. Thaddeus judged that now was not the time to fill her in on the other two crimes he had helped to solve, the details of which he had told no one.

"Of course not," he said. "I have no reason to be concerned with it at all. It's just that everyone seems all atwitter about it and it's hard not to be at least a little curious."

"Uh-huh." Martha looked skeptical. She let the silence drag on for a few moments until finally she said, "Do you want to hear what else they're saying in the town?"

"Well, of course I do."

She smiled a little sideways cat smile. "Well, there was little question about the cause of death, other than speculation as to whether it was the blow to the head or the bullet in the chest that did him in. They've sent him for an autopsy anyway, and that seems to be the thing that people are grumbling about most."

The number of inquests and autopsies called by coroners had been a sore point for years. They were a great source of income for unscrupulous people who had been appointed to the post, and the costs incurred were borne by the district in which the death occurred. Local governments balked at paying for post-mortems in routine cases, and they were well within their rights to complain; still, Thaddeus figured that a body with a bullet in it was definitely something that needed to be investigated. But then again, he supposed that a gunshot wound was a pretty definitive finding, in which case the autopsy was a little superfluous.

"I expect everyone has a theory about what happened," he said. "In these cases they usually do."

"I've heard everything from robbery to self-inflicted wound," Martha said.

"What? He picked up a gun and shot himself and then just to make sure bashed his own head with a rock?"

"I'm only telling you what I heard."

It was only later, as Thaddeus was preparing for bed, that he considered that a discussion of dead bodies and autopsies and gunshot wounds might not have been the most appropriate conversation to have had with his fifteen-year-old granddaughter. But then he reminded himself she was an intelligent girl with a lively interest in the world around her. It would be impossible to keep the news from her anyway. Besides, he had thoroughly enjoyed having someone to talk it over with.

Over the next few days, more details of the crime became public knowledge. A number of people had appeared as witnesses at the inquest, and apparently they had no qualms about repeating their testimony to whoever would listen. As he worked his way through the circuit, Thaddeus couldn't help but overhear tidbits of information. He tried to discourage this gossip, but he wasn't surprised that the imagination of the community had seized upon so thrilling an occurrence.

The island had been scoured for clues, he heard at a prayer meeting in Precious Corners. A piece of paper had blown inland and caught on a bush. This proved to be a banknote in the amount of five dollars. No one seemed to know if it truly had anything to do with the dead man, but the general consensus was that he must have been robbed and that the lone note had blown from a bundle of many with which the culprit had escaped.

A man at the service in Baltimore reported that several footprints had been found in a patch of mud by the shore. According to the chief constable, these indicated that at least three people had been present on the island, probably at the same time.

"It only stands to reason," he said to the group of men that were hanging on his every word. "The prints were all in the same spot, and although the outline had degraded somewhat, they had all degraded to much the same extent."

As to the size of these footprints, no one could be certain, except that one of them appeared to be quite large and one of them quite small. At other meetings, Thaddeus heard that the murdered man remained unknown; that the chief constable knew who he was, but was keeping it secret; that the murder was a complete mystery; and that everyone knew who had done it. But at no time did he hear any speculation as to what the man had been doing on the island in the first place.

The closer Thaddeus drew to Rice Lake, the surer the informants became, until in Gores Landing he overheard one of the men who had been on the jury and was holding forth prior to the meeting. The man claimed he had all the details and was more than willing to share them.

"It was Donald Dafoe found the body," he said. "He was out fishing near the island, and pulled in such a lovely pickerel that he decided on the spot to go ashore and cook it for his supper. It was then that he discovered the body. He didn't touch it or anything. He skedaddled home and told his father about it."

"Why didn't he send for the coroner?" another man asked.

"That's what the coroner wanted to know," the juror said, "but we both know the answer. He was afraid that he would be blamed for the death. His father pointed out to him that if he didn't report it, and it came out later that he had been on the island that day, he would probably end up being blamed anyway, so he might just as well go tell somebody."

His father's advice had been wise, as it turned out. After only a short deliberation, the jury agreed that the unidentified body had been the victim of foul play at the hands of a person or persons unknown, and the coroner directed the chief constable to make further investigations, as to both the identity of the victim and the possible culprits.

But it wasn't until Thaddeus rode in to Sully that he heard the most astonishing news, and he heard it from the Gordons.

"They've arrested Ellen Howell."

Thaddeus was so flabbergasted, he was sure that his hearing had temporarily ceased to work properly.

"How could Ellen Howell have had anything to do with this?" he blurted out. But then he stopped before he said anything more. He didn't really know anything about the woman, and he knew from experience that murderers don't wear their intentions for the world to see.

"It's both of them," Leland Gordon said, "the Major *and* his wife. They've taken Mrs. Howell to the gaol in Cobourg."

"And the Major?"

"Well, there's the problem," Mrs. Gordon said. "No one knows where he is."

"I don't understand," Thaddeus said. "Why do they think the Howells did it?"

"So far it's all pretty circumstantial," Leland said, "but solid enough to warrant the arrest. Apparently witnesses saw the Howells in the right place at more or less the right time."

"It's sickening, it is, to see how ready people are to believe it," Mrs. Gordon said. "And all because of the railroad land. They'd like to see the Major get his comeuppance. But in the meantime, there's poor Mrs. Howell in a gaol cell in a strange town."

Thaddeus didn't like the notion of so fine a lady as Ellen Howell sitting in such a rough place, either. Gaols were full of drunks, and worse.

"Do you think I should visit her there, when next I'm home?"

Mrs. Gordon beamed, and Thaddeus realized that they had been hoping he would offer to do something of the sort.

"If I give you a bit of money, could you take her something extra to eat? Something that's a luxury. Something they wouldn't serve her in gaol." Mrs. Gordon's face turned a little red then. "Not that I know what kind of food they serve in gaol, but you know what I mean. I just can't imagine how awful this must be for her."

"Of course," Thaddeus said. Mrs. Gordon's kind offer was the perfect excuse to go to the gaol. Not that he really needed an excuse, he told himself. He was a minister. No one would question his attendance. But then again, it might seem odd as Mrs. Howell was not a Methodist. And then he wondered why he was going to such great lengths to rationalize his actions. He would go to the gaol because Mrs. Gordon had asked him to deliver some food, that was all.

Mrs. Howell herself might well be puzzled at his presence, and if it turned out that she had no interest in his company, he would leave it at that.

The courthouse was some distance from the centre of town, in what had once been called Amherst back when Cobourg was known as Hardscrabble and there had been two separate villages. Amherst had been chosen as the district town, but Hardscrabble had grown faster. Now Cobourg's limits sprawled to encompass them both.

Like all monuments to government authority, the building was imposing, a two-storey edifice with a portico supported by majestic round pillars and a grand stone staircase that led to the front doors. It was not up these stairs that Thaddeus proceeded, however, but around the side to the gaol entrance.

He explained his errand to the gaoler, who inspected the parcel Thaddeus carried before escorting him through a heavy oak door to a corridor of cells. There was an unpleasant smell of old urine and something worse and someone was shouting, "Lemme out, Keep, you old devil you!"

"Shut your trap, Amos!" the gaoler shouted back. "We'll get you out soon enough." He turned then to Thaddeus. "Sorry. Old Amos ends up here drunk every Saturday night and wakes up mad every Sunday morning. We'll let him out tomorrow in time for work. Then he can do it all over again next week."

The gaoler stopped at a door at the end of the corridor. "We put her down here so she's away from the others," he explained. "It's got a solid door, too, so nobody can peer at her when she's … well, you know."

He slid open the small wooden hatch through which food was served.

"You have a visitor," he said, and then he turned to Thaddeus again. "I'll wait down the hall a bit. I can only give you a few minutes. We're just locking down for the night."

Thaddeus peered through the wicket. She was sitting at the head of a rude cot, huddled into the corner with her eyes closed.

"Hello, Mrs. Howell," he said.

She opened her eyes and looked at him then, although she didn't move from the position she was in. He found her shadowed face difficult to make out. Little light penetrated into the narrow cell from the small, high window above her head.

"Oh," she said. "It's the preacher."

"Patience Gordon sent some food. Some apples and cheese and white bread."

She stirred then and sat up straighter. "That was good of her."

"She's very concerned. As am I."

"Are you here to pray for me?"

"Only if that's what you want."

She didn't answer for a moment, then stood and came closer to the hatch. Thaddeus could see her more clearly then, and was shocked at her pallor and the lines that had etched themselves around her eyes and mouth. All the radiance that had shone so naturally from her face had vanished behind a mask of worry.

"I would take all the prayers that anyone offered," she said, "but I fear they'll do no good."

"God always listens," Thaddeus said, "no matter what has happened."

"Then pray for my soul. I fear my body is forfeit. There's nothing I can do to save it."

Thaddeus tried to choose his next words carefully. He wanted to hold to the notion that this woman could have had nothing to do with anything so vile as murder, yet he knew too well that evil often comes in a pleasant form. "If you have done this thing, then you must answer to God. If you haven't, then you need someone to speak for you."

"What good would that do?" Her mouth twisted into a half-smile. "I'm hanged already, as far as the law is concerned."

"Facts can be made to say many different things. And the law is a twisted thing."

She met his gaze fully for the first time since he had arrived. "You're a very clever man, Mr. Lewis, who makes a good argument when the occasion calls for it. But I don't think you can help with this."

"You're right in that I know nothing of the law. And you need a better mind than mine. Do you have a barrister?"

"I have no money for one. They tell me that if I'm put on trial, they'll prevail upon some local man to speak for me, but that I shouldn't expect to see him until then."

It would be a half-hearted defence, Thaddeus knew. In all likelihood the barrister would be unfamiliar with the evidence and resentful at having to take the case in the first place.

"What about your husband's associates? They tell me he's well connected. Couldn't your friends help?"

"My friends are like me, Mr. Lewis, poor women with little in the way of resources. As for my husband's acquaintances,

I'll tell you what they're worth. You are the first soul to come near me since I was arrested. You and, in a second-hand way, Patience Gordon, I suppose."

It didn't surprise Thaddeus that none of her English friends were able to help, but he did wonder why none of George Howell's business contacts had seen fit to assist in any way.

"Will you let me make some inquiries for you?" he asked. Surely someone Howell did business with could be persuaded to help.

She didn't answer directly, but hesitated for a moment, then said, "You could do one thing for me."

"Yes?"

"Apparently I'm to appear in front of the magistrates on Wednesday, to determine whether or not there will be a trial. I would find it a comfort to see a friendly face there, and there's little prospect of any but yours."

She looked lost again, and bewildered, and suddenly Thaddeus could think of nothing he wanted to do more.

"I'll be there."

The papers were full of the story again the next day, and after supper Thaddeus spent a long time poring over the articles. Most of them were just rehashes of the information that had already been printed and was common knowledge in the district, but the *Cobourg Star* reported that the identity of the murdered man had finally come to light.

His name was Paul Sherman, and his usual place of residence was near the town of Burlington, west of Toronto. According to his family, he had travelled to the Cobourg area in order to conduct some business. When he'd failed to return home on the expected day, his family had contacted the local police.

"It wasn't unusual for him to be gone longer than expected," his widow was reported to have said, "but we read about the Rice Lake murder in the papers and were uneasy about his welfare on that account."

Sherman's brother travelled to Cobourg and made the identification. He also, the paper reported, had retained a local barrister-at-law, a Mr. Garrett, to prosecute the case.

That explained why it had taken so long to schedule the committal proceedings, Thaddeus realized. The Crown's case would be strengthened by the attendance of the deceased's family, and as the Shermans were in a position to hire their own prosecutor, the town would then be spared the expense of paying a justice of the peace or a police magistrate to do it.

Other than the victim's name, there was little more to glean from the newspaper reports. Sherman's family had not stated what particular business was being transacted in Cobourg, or with whom. If there was any other evidence that had a bearing on the case, the authorities were keeping it close indeed. The only mention of George Howell indicated that his whereabouts were still unknown.

He must know that his wife had been arrested. The case was getting widespread attention — being reported not only across the province but in some of the American papers as well. Surely Howell would do the honourable thing and come forward. But then, Thaddeus reflected, he was also wanted for murder. Unless he had a reasonable alibi, coming forward would only serve to put him in a cell beside his wife. But letting her stand trial alone seemed so craven. Thaddeus didn't know if there was a genuine case against Ellen Howell or not, or if she was merely the means for luring her husband out of whatever hidey-hole he had bolted to.

He would have to wait until Wednesday to find out.

The night before the committal, he turned in early but didn't sleep well, tossing and turning as he tried to anticipate what he might hear, and what he might do as a result.

After he heard the prosecution evidence the next day, Thaddeus had to admit that, had he been a judge, he would have reached the same conclusion as the court. The case was laid out piece by circumstantial piece — the witnesses who testified that the Howells were seen at Rice Lake that day, that they had rented a boat, that a blue dress with a bloodstain was found in a washtub at the Howell farm — until altogether it was a great mound of incriminating details that pointed straight at the Howells.

It was only the prosecution's version of events, he reminded himself. No doubt there were questions that had not been asked, explanations that had not been given, but these were difficult things to lay hold of when only one side of the argument had its say.

Thaddeus went to the gaol immediately following the proceedings, but was turned away, even when he announced that he was a minister. The local Anglican man was there, he was told, and one preacher in a day was enough. Thaddeus left, fuming and determined to do something, if only he could figure out what it would be. He had no money to put toward a defence, nor did he know of anyone he could call upon. It was also unlikely that a collection around the neighbourhood would be successful — Ellen Howell was well enough liked by those who knew her, but these were not many, and her particular circle was infamous for its impecuniosities. Besides, there was continued ill-feeling over the Sully station land. The community would be unlikely to help someone they thought might cheat them out of their promised riches.

He wondered if he should try to approach D'Arcy Boulton. Everyone seemed to think that Boulton had used George Howell as a go-between to buy the land for the train station. Boulton was a lawyer and an important man, and his words would hold some sway with a jury. Surely he could be persuaded to defend the wife of a man who had done favours for him. And then Thaddeus realized that Boulton would want to stay as far away from this case as he could. There was too much mud flying already over the land deal. Boulton would do his best to keep any of it from landing on the lawn of his fine Cobourg mansion.

Just as he reached his own door, Thaddeus finally arrived at a decision. It had little guarantee of success, but it was at least a course of action. He would write to his son Luke.

Thaddeus had great respect for Luke's judgment, and although his son did not travel in exalted circles — he was, after all, only a physician in a small town north of Toronto — he did have at least one friend with sterling connections. If Luke knew of someone who might be persuaded to take Ellen Howell's case at a reasonable rate, then Thaddeus would find some way to come up with the money. If Luke knew of no one, or advised him that it was a lost cause, Thaddeus would have to think of some other plan.

That night he dashed off a note.

My dear son,

I find myself in a peculiar set of circumstances here on the Hope Circuit. A local woman who has attended a couple of my meetings has been charged with murder, along with her husband who managed to disappear before he was apprehended.

Thaddeus knew as he wrote it that "attended a couple of my meetings" gave the impression that the woman was a member of his church, and that his concern was ministerial, but he could think of no other explanation for his actions that would make sense, so he let the statement stand.

> *The sum total of the evidence against her is purely circumstantial, including some testimony that is nothing more than remarkably convenient speculation, although I must admit I do not really know the truth of the matter.*
>
> *I attended the committal proceedings and I am uneasy with the fact that the unfortunate woman is in no position to obtain adequate legal representation.*
>
> *I would like very much to provide her with a better defence than she has been offered. Having had so little to do with barristers in my time, however, I am at a loss as to how to proceed. I thought that, due to your more worldly connections, or that of your friend Mr. Biddulph, you might be able to suggest someone with some expertise in criminal proceedings of this sort. I do not know what kind of monies a barrister might charge, or where this money might be found, but I would appreciate it if you could make a few inquiries on my behalf and report your findings and opinions to me as soon as is expedient. If this appears to be a forlorn hope, I would appreciate it if you could advise of that, as well.*
>
> *Your loving father*
>
> *Thaddeus*

He sent the letter off by the next day's post. Now he could only bide his time until he found out what Luke had to say.

PART TWO
The Hope Circuit,
Fall 1853

I

The heat wave finally broke in the last week of September with three days of thunderstorms and heavy downpours of rain. It was Thaddeus's bad luck that it was his turn to take the meetings on the eastern side of the circuit. There was no avoiding the churned ground and deep ruts left behind by construction. Rain pooled in deep, overflowing puddles and the road became a thick porridge-like morass. Thaddeus slogged through it and was late for only two meetings.

Over the course of his travels he heard little new information about the murder from his gossiping congregation, just rumour and speculation. Everyone had a theory as to what had happened, and what would happen next.

"This Sherman fellow probably followed the Howells over to the island and tried to rob them," one man asserted.

The man next to him snorted. "More likely the other way around," he said.

Thaddeus was a little puzzled by this opinion. He knew that George Howell had been accused of sharp dealing, but this statement seemed to imply that he was a common thief. He was loath to inquire what he meant. It would only serve to ignite more conversation, and he wanted to get the meeting underway as soon as possible.

He encountered the same excitement about the case at his next appointment, as well. This was a gathering of women, and they had reached a consensus on motive.

"You saw Ellen Howell's arm that day at the debate," one old woman declared. "I reckon she meant to shoot the Major and hit Sherman by mistake."

The other women nodded their heads in agreement. They were apparently all too familiar with women who might want to take a shot at their husbands.

It wasn't until he was on his way home again that he heard something new, and even then he couldn't see how it would help Mrs. Howell in any way. A strange horse had turned up in the back field of a farm near Brighton, and everyone was sure that it must be George Howell's.

"He probably rode south and jumped a boat that would take him across the lake," one man at the meeting in Baltimore offered. "That's what I'd do."

If that was the case, Ellen Howell had been truly abandoned. Once in the States, her husband could easily disappear forever.

When Thaddeus finally completed his round and returned to Cobourg, he was cold, dirty, and discouraged.

Martha had news, but was wise enough to wait until he had shed his sodden clothing and sluiced himself clean before she gave it to him.

"There's a letter from Luke," she said, handing it to him when he reappeared in the kitchen. He set it down on the table in front of him. He was so relieved to be home that he was unwilling to brook any bad news, at least for a few moments. And he was certain that the letter contained bad news. He had asked Luke to do the impossible, and mustn't be disappointed at the result.

"Aren't you going to open it?" Martha asked.

"After supper."

"Supper's not quite ready." She giggled then. "Or at least no harm will come to it if it boils a bit more. I'm dying of curiosity."

Thaddeus sighed. "Fine," he said. He took a deep breath and tore open the sheet of paper. It wasn't disappointing news, exactly.

Dear Father,

I'm rather flattered that you think I move in such worldly circles — I don't, in fact, know much of anything beyond Yorkville. I did, however, share your letter with my friend Perry, who made some inquiries on your behalf.

As it happens, his distant cousin, a Mr. Townsend Ashby, has recently been called to the bar. The Sherman case has been reported widely here, and he was already familiar with some of the details. He is extremely interested in representing the accused.

I should explain that, at the moment, Toronto is bursting with newly qualified barristers and solicitors, each of them anxious to somehow rise above the rabble and make a name for himself. Mr. Ashby's involvement in the case, whether he mounts a successful defence or not, would be noted in the newspapers and bring him to public attention. For that reason he is willing to waive the usual fee. I am mentioning this, just so you don't make the mistake of feeling too grateful. There is no question that he has an agenda, but as his interests and that of the accused happen to coincide, I see no harm in it. I have met Towns (as he prefers to be called). He is a clever fellow and eager to get going on his first case.

He does, however, have some business details to attend to here in the city before he can make himself available. He is planning to arrive in Cobourg for an initial consultation on September 29th. He will be travelling by steamer. Could you possibly meet him at the dock and perhaps arrange some rooms for him?

Hope you are staying well, now that you're back in the saddle again.

Love,

Luke

"Well?" Martha asked.

Thaddeus shoved the letter across the table to her. He had hoped that Luke might know of an experienced barrister, but he supposed that even someone who was newly qualified was better than someone who had no real interest in the case. And this Mr. Ashby was Perry Biddulph's cousin. If he needed advice, surely he would be able to draw on his connections, even if they were as "distant" as Luke's letter seemed to indicate. No doubt the Biddulph family was full of lawyers.

"Oh good," Martha said when she had finished reading it.

"Good that he's found someone, yes," Thaddeus said, "not so good that he has so little experience."

"No, it's not that. I was afraid that if Luke found someone, he would end up staying here."

"Well, it crossed my mind," Thaddeus said, but not with any degree of certainty. "He is working for free. The least I could do is offer. Would that be a problem?"

"No, of course not, although it might set the neighbours talking, when you're away so much. It's just that ..." she hesitated for a moment. "It's just that it's been kind of nice having the house to myself most of the time. Not that I'm unhappy when you're here," she added hurriedly, "but I don't exactly mind it when you're not, either. It's been nice not to have much of a routine."

Thaddeus could well understand this. She had, after all, grown up at a busy hotel, where each day's tasks were laid out for her every morning, when meals were at set times, where the schedule was public knowledge and strictly adhered to. He supposed her delight in having the house to herself was akin to his own feeling of well-being when he was riding alone from place to place. It appeared that he and Martha were much alike in that respect.

"I understand what you mean. And you're right — it wouldn't be appropriate to have him here, although we should probably invite him to dinner. Would that be all right?"

She smiled. "I can manage dinner as long as I don't have him underfoot every day."

"Then we'll let this Mr. Ashby stay in rooms elsewhere."

"Try Mrs. Baker's. I hear she offers a fair room and board and it's close to the courthouse."

And with the practical ramifications neatly arranged to her satisfaction, Martha rose to dish up their somewhat overcooked meal.

Thaddeus had no difficulty identifying Towns Ashby as soon as he stepped from the steamer to the dock. He was a tall, thinly built young man in a finely cut coat opened to reveal a waistcoat that was a little more garish than those normally seen in a place like Cobourg. It was something more suited to the drawing rooms of the city, Thaddeus thought, at some event like the soiree that his son Luke had attended one time. Ashby was also the only passenger who didn't alight and immediately set off for the town. He stood looking around the wharf with an expectant air.

Thaddeus stepped forward. "Mr. Ashby? How do you do? I'm Thaddeus Lewis."

Ashby responded with a wide grin and doffed his hat, revealing an unruly mop of black hair. "I'm so pleased to make your acquaintance, Mr. Lewis. Thank you so much for meeting me." He offered his hand in a firm shake. "My luggage has yet to be unloaded, if you don't mind waiting for just a moment." And then, before Thaddeus had any opportunity to say whether he minded or not, "I'd have known you anyway, you know. Luke will look just like you twenty years from now."

"More's the pity," Thaddeus joked.

"Oh, I don't know," Ashby said. "He's quite presentable. At least, my cousin Perry seems to think so."

The young man didn't elaborate on this odd comment, and just then the porter set a small leather-bound trunk onto the dock.

"I can carry the trunk, if you would be so kind as to take my valise," Ashby said.

When Thaddeus picked it up he was surprised by the weight of it.

"I tucked in a few law books — easy reference for those cases in precedent that I don't quite have at my fingertips yet. I'm too newly qualified. Can you manage it?"

"Of course. I didn't expect it to be so heavy, that's all."

They flagged down a wagon. After they loaded the luggage the driver looked at them for directions.

"I'm told that a Mrs. Baker offers clean rooms at a fair price," Thaddeus said. "Would you like to inspect them?"

"How kind of you to think of it," Ashby said. "I'm sure they're lovely, but I asked around before I left Toronto and found that the Globe Hotel comes highly recommended. I thought perhaps I'd take a room there. If it proves unsatisfactory, I can always fall back on Mrs. Baker's establishment."

Thaddeus was astonished. The Globe Hotel was touted as the finest hostelry between Kingston and Toronto. It was quite grand, and therefore quite expensive. Apparently this Ashby was accustomed to the best. But he was, after all, a cousin of the Biddulphs, Thaddeus reminded himself, even if the relationship was distant.

"I'm sure the Globe would be most adequate," he said meekly. "I guess the thing to do would be to get you settled there first, but would you care to join us for supper this evening? I could fill you in on what I know about the case. My granddaughter is my housekeeper and she's a fair cook."

"I'd be delighted. You're so kind."

Thaddeus deposited him at the hotel and gave directions to the manse, then went home and told Martha to prepare for a guest.

"What's he like?" Martha asked.

"He seems a very pleasant fellow," Thaddeus replied. "Other than that, I guess we'll just have to find out."

Ashby arrived quite late that evening, long past the usual supper hour. Thaddeus ushered him in and introduced him to Martha. Ashby took her hand and bowed over it, ever so slightly, one eyebrow raised.

Martha's eyes widened a little, but she quickly recovered her self-possession and bade him sit in the parlour until dinner was served.

The only word Thaddeus could think of to describe Townsend Ashby was polished. But it could well be a deliberately assumed manner — there were hints of a more exuberant nature under the veneer, one that bubbled up when something caught his attention and stirred his interest. In the meantime, his affable courtesy and ease of address made Thaddeus instantly comfortable. Ashby appeared not to notice the shabbiness of the chair he was sitting in, or the fustiness of the manse furnishings. He merely leaned back, gracefully folded his legs and beamed at his host.

"I can't thank you enough for making me welcome," he said. "This is my first time in Cobourg, and I must admit I'm a bit lost. You've been so kind."

Thaddeus rather suspected that you could dump Towns Ashby down in the middle of Arabia or any other exotic place in the world and he would immediately find some way to make himself comfortable, but the sentiment was appreciated nonetheless.

"And how are things in the city?" Thaddeus asked, groping for a civilized remark.

"Hectic, as always," Ashby said. "Everyone rushing around trying to do business with everyone else. The prospect of reciprocity has everyone nattering on about new opportunities, and of course, the whole country has gone railway mad."

"No more so than here. The town of Cobourg has invested thousands in a line to Peterborough."

"The feeling in the city is that all those thousands may turn into millions if we have free access to American markets."

"Do you think that's likely to happen?"

Ashby shrugged. "I expect the American government will need some persuading, but there's an insatiable demand for raw materials in the States. The right pressure exerted at the right time may swing it."

"So all this railway construction isn't as foolish as it appears?"

Ashby smiled. "I didn't say that. We'll have to see how it all plays out. Your son sends his best regards, by the way. I ran across him the other day, quite by accident, in one of the pharmacies. He was buying enormous packets of things."

"That's good. That means he's busy."

"Oh, I understand that he has a thriving practice. There are even a few people from Toronto who travel all the way to Yorkville just to consult him. I expect my cousin Perry has sent some traffic his way. Apparently Luke has been the saving of the practice. Christie is such an odd duck."

"Yes, he is," Thaddeus said. "But I like him very much. And he has certainly been good to Luke. I'm not sure what would have happened to the boy if Christie hadn't taken him on."

Ashby gave him an odd look, but before he could say anything more, Martha appeared in the parlour doorway to invite them into the dining room, a room that had seen little use to date, other than as a repository for Martha's mending. This had all now been cleared away. The table was polished to a gleam, and the badly worn rug, the corner of which had tripped Thaddeus the first time he walked across the room, was nowhere to be seen. Martha had gone to a great deal of trouble to impress their guest. Or maybe the improvements to the dining room were just another result of her experimentation with the furniture.

Somewhere in the sideboard she had discovered a matching set of reasonable-quality dishes with which to set the table, a step up from the cracked and mismatched collection of dinnerware they used when they ate in the kitchen. She served lamb chops. They were a little overdone, not surprising since she had been frantically trying to hold their dinner in an edible state until Ashby's arrival. The savoury onion sauce she spooned over them helped disguise the blackened edges. Thaddeus was so ravenous he would have bolted down anything she put on the table. He dove in to the food on his plate.

Ashby was a charming dinner guest, having the ability to appear profoundly attentive to whatever remarks his companions made, whether they merited any weight or not. Thaddeus could see that Martha was flattered when any observation she ventured was taken quite seriously and responded to with consideration. Small talk, including several remarks about the unusually hot summer, occupied the first few minutes of their meal. Thaddeus wondered at the propriety of introducing the topic of murder over the dinner table, but decided that he might just as well, as murder was Ashby's only reason for being there in the first place.

"I don't know whether this has any bearing on the Sherman case or not," he said, "but at any rate you may find it interesting in light of what you were saying about the railway turning thousands into millions. There was some sharp dealing with regard to the sale of some lands that one of the stations is to be built on."

Briefly, he outlined what he had heard about Jack Plews and the land at Sully.

Ashby absorbed this for a moment and then he said, "This could well be more than a simple case of an argument gone wrong then, do you think?"

"I wasn't at all sure that's what it was to begin with."

"You could be right," Ashby said. "An argument is the simplest explanation, and all too distressingly often the simplest thing is what, in fact, occurred, but that scenario doesn't offer our client much of a defence. If you have any other theories, I'd like to hear them."

"I'm not sure I'd call them theories," Thaddeus said, "but there are some very peculiar aspects to the case that puzzle me."

"My grandfather has quite a history of sorting out puzzles, you know," Martha said as she passed a dish of mashed parsnip.

"Yes, I did know that," Ashby said. "He's been involved in several rather thrilling adventures, hasn't he? I've heard all about them."

"From my son, I expect," Thaddeus said.

Ashby waved a languid hand. "Yes, some from Luke, although the topic rather embarrasses him, but I've heard from other sources as well."

Thaddeus wondered what other sources could possibly have any information about his past history, but Ashby didn't seem inclined to elaborate. Instead he said, "So, what can you tell me about the woman who has been accused?"

"I don't know a great deal about Ellen Howell at all. She attended a couple of my services, but it was in the company of others, and purely, I'm sure, for the entertainment it afforded. And anything I know about her came via her neighbour, although I have no reason to believe that the information is inaccurate in any way."

"So you have no particular interest in this woman?"

"No, not really, except that I hate to see anyone subjected to trial without adequate counsel. Especially when it's a capital offence."

"Fair enough," Ashby said, and turned his attention to the delicate dissection of a chop.

Thaddeus was grateful that the young barrister didn't belabour the point. If pressed, he would have a great deal of difficulty explaining his interest. He wasn't sure what it was himself.

"She's English, but has been here for a number of years," he went on. "The Howell farm is just south of Sully, which is on the near shore of Rice Lake. That's where the railway will cross if they ever manage to build the bridge. She's liked well enough in the neighbourhood, although her particular class of English settler tends to consider itself of a finer cut than the ordinary farmers around them. Everyone refers to Mr. Howell, her husband, as "The Major." Thaddeus shrugged. "I'm not sure if he really was ever a major or not. Apparently he puts on a few airs, but no one takes it very seriously, and that's their way of showing him up."

And then he stopped, momentarily embarrassed. He knew nothing about this young man who sat across from him. For all Thaddeus knew, Ashby himself came from that same background and might take offence at his remarks.

However, "I see," was his only response, and he appeared in no way put out, but returned to carving away at another thin slice of lamb. He was taking an enormous amount of time to eat his meal. Thaddeus had dispatched his in short order and Martha appeared to have finished, as well, but Ashby's plate was still half full of food. Martha took a slice of bread and made a great business of buttering it while Thaddeus toyed with a spoonful of potatoes, both of them waiting for Ashby to catch up. He seemed in no hurry, and frequently placed his knife and fork on the sides of his plate when he spoke, a habit that further delayed the completion of the meal.

"Why don't you just tell me what you've heard, whether it's confirmed or not?" he said. "I have the basic facts from the news articles, but I'd like to get an idea of the lay of the land, so to speak. What is Mrs. Howell's explanation of what happened?"

Thaddeus was happy to oblige, not least because as long as someone else was talking, Ashby would continue to work away at his dinner.

"She offers no explanation at all. She seems to think that the whole affair has been decided already, and that her days on this Earth are numbered."

"Really? Now that's interesting."

"She claims not to know the victim, and denies ever having been on Spook Island where the body was found, but other than that, I don't believe she's provided any details that would either prove or disprove the allegations."

"And the blood-stained dress?"

"I don't know," Thaddeus said. "I don't think she said anything about it."

Ashby must finally have noticed that the others were waiting for him to finish his meal, because he let silence fall as he scooped up the rest of the food on his plate, then laid his knife and fork across it to signal that he was finished. Martha rose to clear the dishes away and returned a few moments later with a pudding and a carafe of coffee, instead of the usual pot of tea she and Thaddeus normally shared after meals. She must have decided that a city person would prefer the more exotic beverage.

As soon as they finished dessert, Ashby reached for his valise and pulled out a stack of papers.

"Would you like to use the parlour?" Thaddeus asked. "There's a good writing desk there."

"Oh no, I'm fine here, if you don't mind me commandeering your table," Ashby replied. "There's room to spread these papers out, and I must admit I wouldn't mind getting Miss Renwell's opinion of the case. I'll willingly forego my brandy and cigar so that she can remain with us."

Thaddeus didn't bother to point out that there weren't any cigars, or brandy either, and that this was a Methodist household where Ashby would be unlikely to ever be offered such things, but he was pleased that Martha wasn't being chased away. She had as good a grasp of the case as he did, and might well remember some detail he had forgotten.

Martha looked astonished. The law was men's business, as a rule, and ladies were seldom invited. Nevertheless, she smiled a little and said, "I'd be happy to consult, if you give me but a moment. I'll just clear away the dishes."

"Well," Thaddeus said as soon as Martha returned and took her seat, an eager look on her face. "Where do we start?"

"Let's just recap what we know to date," Ashby began. "What I could gather from the papers is this: Mr. and Mrs. Howell were seen in the village of Sully by a number of steamer passengers and a few of the villagers, but they weren't seen to board the boat. Instead, they rented a small skiff and went out on the lake for the afternoon. No one saw them return."

For some reason, Thaddeus found that he was reluctant to mention that he had seen someone in blue rowing for shore that same afternoon. After all, he wasn't at all certain that it had been Ellen Howell. It could have been anyone else. There were any number of people on the lake that day.

Ashby went on. "Some time later, a Mr.," here he stopped and shuffled through his notes again, "Donald Dafoe discovered a body on Spook Island, which, I take it, is in Rice Lake?"

"Yes. More or less halfway across at that point, and set a little away from the other islands."

Ashby nodded. "Mr. Dafoe delayed reporting the discovery until his father persuaded him that it would be in his best interest to do so. A contingent of local law enforcement went to the island to confirm the report. As Dafoe said, there was a dead man who had been both shot and whacked on the head. Nothing was found in the deceased's pockets, but there was a banknote stuck on a bush. The police then questioned the neighbours, who reported having seen the Howells that day, one of them having rented out his boat to them, but this gentleman was unsure who returned it or when. Based on these accounts, the chief constable proceeded to the Howell farm, where he discovered a blue dress soaking in a washtub. The dress has a stain on the skirt, which the constable concluded was a bloodstain. Mrs. Howell was arrested on the spot. Mr. Howell would have been as well, except that no one seems to know what's become of him. Is that correct?"

"Yes, that's correct."

"I take it that Mrs. Howell didn't offer any information about where her husband might be, and that the authorities are finding that omission a bit suspicious."

"Apparently, he travels a great deal on business, so it isn't unusual for him to be away."

Ashby frowned as he reread his notes. "The dead man was subsequently identified as Paul Sherman, who had travelled to Cobourg on business and never returned home. So according to the prosecution, the Howells rented a boat, somehow encountered Paul Sherman, did him in, and rowed for home, at which point Mr. Howell skedaddled, leaving the missus to face the music."

"I'm afraid that's it in a nutshell," Thaddeus said. This was hopeless. The evidence against Ellen Howell, as circumstantial as it might be, was sure to hang her. Why had he bothered dragging a lawyer all the way from Toronto for such a lost cause?

Ashby noticed Thaddeus's gloomy face and smiled. "Don't worry. I have to look at the facts of the case in the same way that the prosecution does. Then I have to see if I can find an alternative explanation."

"Of course." But Thaddeus had no hope that there might be one.

"I think there are a number of questions we need to ask. First of all, how many other people would have been out on the lake that afternoon?"

"Quite a few," Thaddeus said. "There were all the barges and skiffs involved in the bridge construction, just for starters, and several small boats full of spectators watching the work. There might have been a few others, besides all the people on the passenger steamer, but I would think that Donald Dafoe, the man who found the body, had to be one of them."

Ashby was astonished. "You were there that afternoon?"

"I just rode by. I was on my way from Sully to Gores Landing and stopped to watch them working on the bridge."

Ashby scribbled this information into his notes. "Well, why didn't you tell me this before?"

Thaddeus shrugged. "I didn't think it was important."

Ashby fixed him with a glare. "Everything is important. Every. Single. Thing. Cases sometimes hinge on the most minor of details. Did you happen to remark on anything else?"

Thaddeus hesitated, but just for a moment. This young barrister, was, after all, here to help Ellen Howell. "I saw a boat headed for shore. Whoever was in it might have been wearing something blue. I didn't see where it made landfall. There was too much vegetation in the way."

"And what time was this?"

Thaddeus had dined with the Gordons after the meeting in Sully, and had lingered on the shore watching the pile drivers for a time. "Maybe about three o'clock? But that's a guess."

Ashby scribbled on his papers again.

"I have a question," Martha said. "How did Paul Sherman get to the island?"

Ashby beamed at her. "Excellent question! How indeed?"

"It's just that … the man who rented the boat to the Howells has come forward, but no one has claimed any such thing for Paul Sherman. He wasn't local … he's from Burlington, so he wouldn't have had a boat of his own readily available."

"Precisely. And that's one thing you can do for me, Mr. Lewis. Ask around. See if you can track down where Sherman might have got a boat."

Thaddeus felt thoroughly trumped by his granddaughter. He had been fussing about what they knew and she had gone straight to a very salient point about what they didn't.

"Would it be possible that he swam to the island?" Ashby asked.

"I shouldn't think so," Thaddeus replied. "It's farther than it looks from shore. Most people can't swim anyway, even the ones who live close to water."

Ashby nodded. "Let's set that aside as improbable for the moment then. It begs the question anyway — why was he there at all? What's the connection between Sherman and Howell?"

"According to Mr. Sherman's family, he was in Cobourg on business," Martha said. "I don't know what kind of business would have taken him to Spook Island."

"And what exactly does Mr. Howell do that would have taken him there?" Ashby added. He beamed at Martha again, who ducked her head a little, but was smiling.

"All I know is that he travels on a regular basis," Thaddeus said. *So many questions,* he thought. *Questions that he himself should have been asking long since.* He was beginning to think that he was losing his touch, had become suddenly lacking in that ability to connect seemingly unrelated information and circumstances into a picture that made a whole.

"But he was around enough to make himself unpopular with the neighbours?"

"No, not exactly. He wasn't generally well liked, but I think it was because of his manner rather than any specific point of contention until he was blamed for sharp dealing in connection with the train station at Sully."

"Ah yes, the land deal. Do you know any of the details?" Ashby's pen was poised over the paper, ready to record them.

"It's a one-hundred-acre parcel that was being farmed by a man named Jack Plews. He fell behind in the mortgage, at which point Mr. Howell bought him out. It was only after Howell gained control of the land that it was announced that the railway company wanted it for a station."

"And who held the mortgage?"

"A local lawyer and a friend of Howell's," Thaddeus said, "D'Arcy Boulton, who also happens to be on the Board of Directors of the railway company."

Ashby's eyebrows shot up. "A Boulton? Oh my, my, my, this is getting interesting. I expect everyone assumes there was collusion?"

"What's collusion?" Martha asked.

"It means they put their heads together and hatched a shady deal," Ashby replied. "I don't know for sure if the deal has anything to do with the murder, but it certainly makes an interesting starting point, doesn't it?" He tapped the table with his pen for a moment. "So, here's what we need to do. Mr. Lewis, I need you to find out what this Mr. Plews was doing on the afternoon of the murder, and where Paul Sherman obtained the boat that took him to Spook Island. I'll interview Mrs. Howell tomorrow to see if she can shed any light on her husband's business enterprises. And I'll stand a couple of rounds at the Globe and see if liquor loosens some tongues."

Thaddeus was glad to see that Martha wrinkled her nose in distaste at this ploy, but he had to admit that it was probably a sound strategy on Ashby's part. The Globe Hotel was a favourite haunt of Cobourg's business community. More deals were made there, they said, than in any office in the town. As a Methodist minister, Thaddeus would find it difficult to access those circles and he certainly would never "stand a round or two" of drinks. Ashby must have deep pockets indeed, if he could afford to drink at the Globe.

"What can I do?" Martha asked.

"It would be useful to know what the community is saying about the case. Often someone lets slip a key piece of information without realizing it. Have you heard anything at the market, or at teas or parties, or anywhere really?"

Martha knitted her brows while she thought about this. Finally she said, "I don't attend parties, and I don't like gossip. But I can't help but overhear what people are saying while I'm running errands. Generally, they seem to think Mr. Howell is guilty, and that Mrs. Howell just happened to be there."

"I would suspect that's probably true; however, it won't make any difference in terms of how the prosecution proceeds."

"What do you mean?" Martha asked. Thaddeus was just as anxious to hear the answer.

"The law is quite clear. If two or more people form a common criminal purpose, they are all guilty of every crime committed by any one of them in the execution of that purpose. That is what my opposing counsel will assert — that the Howells were engaged in a criminal act that somehow went awry, and that, therefore, Mrs. Howell is as guilty as her husband."

"Even if she didn't actually do anything?" Martha asked.

"Even so," Ashby said. "It's only if one of them committed a crime foreign to the common purpose that the other would be innocent of it."

Thaddeus was puzzled. "But what was the common criminal purpose? Nobody knows what any of them were doing on the island."

"And that is what I will attempt to show in court," Ashby responded, "that the Howells had no criminal purpose, and that, therefore, Mrs. Howell's culpability is divorced from her husband's."

"But only if she didn't do anything," Martha pointed out. "We don't know that for certain."

"Precisely!" Ashby said and gave her another approving look. Thaddeus was taken aback. He had assumed that Ellen Howell was innocent and that this fresh-faced young man would somehow prove that fact to the court. He hadn't considered any other possibility. He was jumping to conclusions again, only in reverse, he realized. He had a long history of believing in the guilt of people he didn't like. Now he was believing in the innocence of one he did.

"What happens if you discover that she's guilty after all?" he asked quietly.

"It makes no difference. We'll give her a grand defence anyway," Ashby said with a wave of the hand. When Thaddeus looked dubious, he went on. "You have to understand my role here, Mr. Lewis. It doesn't matter if she's guilty or not, my job is to provide the best defence I possibly can, within the framework of the law as it is written."

Thaddeus thought that it mattered a great deal, at least to him. But he wasn't about to argue with a lawyer. Not even a newly qualified one.

"I don't suppose there's any question of arranging bail for her?" he asked.

"We'd have to ask a superior court judge for it, and that would take some time. And some money. Unless you can persuade someone to post bail for her, I expect she's stuck where she is. I'll make some inquiries, though. And make sure she's being properly treated, that sort of thing. Oh, and Mr. Lewis, you might also stop by the Howell farm if you could and have a look around."

"Wouldn't it have been searched already? When they arrested Mrs. Howell?" Martha asked.

"Yes, it would have. And I don't really expect to find much of anything, but you never know. They might have missed something. And they didn't have your grandfather to do the searching. From what I hear, he has a habit of finding things that other people can't."

Ashby started stacking the papers he had strewn over the table. "For now, keep your ear to the ground," he said, "and write down anything you hear, no matter how unimportant it might seem. And keep mum about anything you find. I don't know what the prosecution has up its sleeve, and I don't want to tip them off."

"Don't they have to tell you about whatever evidence they have?" Thaddeus asked.

"No, they don't. But I don't have to tell them anything either." He turned to Martha. "Do you suppose you could track any relevant articles that appear in the newspapers regarding the case, so we have as complete a history as possible? And if you can find any back copies, you could save those as well. I need to return to Toronto tomorrow, so I won't be on hand to do it myself."

"Of course," she replied. But after all her talk about not wanting anyone underfoot, Thaddeus thought she looked a little disappointed that Towns Ashby was leaving Cobourg so soon.

II

As he rode north the next day, Thaddeus reflected that in some respects he was grateful that the excitement over The Great Debate had died down as quickly as it had. As he predicted, attendance at meetings had fallen off by half, allowing him to revert to the more leisurely pace of his original schedule. He would have plenty of time to make the inquiries Ashby had requested of him, without missing or being late for any meetings. No one had ever complained in the past, but Thaddeus was aware that, at times, he had been sailing close to the wind in terms of the amount of time he spent doing other things when he was supposed to be ministering. This time, he judged, he could give his full attention to the class meetings he had arranged, stop by the Howell farm for a good look around, and still reach Sully in time to preside at that evening's women's meeting and ask some questions about boats.

It was easier now to focus his flocks on their prayers, too, and that saved time. Immediately following Ellen Howell's committal, all the talk had been of the evidence that had been presented, but now, with no new information to feed the rumour mill, people turned their attention to other matters. Other than the usual discussions regarding successful births and impending marriages, the conversation was dominated by the slow but steady progress of the rail line and the spectacle of the trestles that stretched four abreast out into Rice Lake.

Thaddeus was particularly pleased to note that news of Townsend Ashby's involvement was not yet common knowledge. The young barrister would be far more likely to pry loose the information he was seeking if no one knew why precisely he was asking. Liquor was a befuddlement that loosened men's tongues, but not if they were too watchful in the first place.

Thaddeus was bemused by Ashby, and not a little impressed. This might be the young barrister's first criminal case, but he had seemed well-prepared, with a number of relevant points to investigate and an engaging manner that would serve him well in a courtroom. Whether or not all this would be enough to win the case remained to be seen. He was astute enough — he had certainly zeroed in on Thaddeus's reasons for retaining him in the first place — but he was circumspect enough not to comment on them. "So you have no particular interest in the woman?" he'd asked. Thaddeus was sure Ashby had noticed his discomfort. He must have wondered.

And in all honesty, if Thaddeus looked at the situation from an outsider's point of view, it must seem very strange that he had gone to so much trouble for a woman who wasn't even a member of his church. But no, he decided, the fact that she professed another faith was irrelevant. It was the injustice of an accused having a poor defence that bothered him, that was all. And the fact that she had apparently been abandoned by her spouse, a man who might well have been treating her roughly. His stomach churned whenever he thought of the bruise he had seen on her arm.

He had forgotten to mention the bruise to Ashby. The young lawyer claimed that every detail was important, that even the smallest thing could tip the balance either way. Thaddeus would have to start writing things down. He was just so rattled by this case that his memory was becoming faulty, and he was losing his ability to concentrate on the bigger picture.

Lost in his thoughts, he suddenly realized that he had already reached the general vicinity of the Howell farm. He wasn't sure exactly where the laneway might be, but as luck would have it, an old farmer driving a hay wagon trundled toward him as he was stopped, puzzling, in the middle of the road.

"You look lost," the farmer said.

"Not lost, precisely. I'm looking for something. You don't happen to know which is the Howell farm, do you?"

"Why do you want to know?" the man asked. "Here to gawk? Or to steal?" Then he took a closer look at Thaddeus. "Oh, you're the preacher. You're the one who talked down the Baptist."

"That's right," Thaddeus said. There were advantages to being quasi-famous. "I've just come from Cobourg. I spoke with Mrs. Howell. I thought perhaps I should check on her house."

"Good idea," the man rumbled. "You never know who's about, or what they might take when nobody's looking. Not like the old days when you could leave a cabin for weeks and no one would touch a thing. Other than the coons, of course. They're always a problem. And the mice."

"Do you know where I might find the laneway?"

The man gestured in the direction from which he had just come. "On up a ways. You'll see a big oak tree and a broken-down fence. Just follow the track. It's a long way in, though, and no guarantee you'll find anybody when you get there. The girl won't talk to anybody. Skedaddles as soon as you get close."

For a moment Thaddeus failed to understand what the old man was talking about and thought perhaps he was a little senile.

Then he remembered Ellen Howell's daughter. He could have kicked himself for not thinking of her long before this, but he had seen her only once, the day she had accompanied her mother to The Great Debate. Had she really been left alone on such a remote farmstead while her mother languished in a cold cell? Surely someone had offered to take her in, or at the very least dropped in on her now and then to make sure she was all right.

And how very odd that her mother hadn't asked after her well-being. Ellen Howell hadn't mentioned her daughter at all.

Thaddeus thanked the man and continued down the road. He rounded a bend and found, just as described, a gigantic oak and a section of rail fence that was in rather desperate need of repair. Leland Gordon had said that Major Howell wasn't much of a farmer. If the state of his fences was any indication, he certainly wasn't interested in keeping livestock, at any rate.

The winding lane was crowded on both sides with lilac, sumac, and weed maple, all of it smothered with wild grape. No one had bothered to slash the intrusive growth back from the edges of the path in a long time. It would not be many years before it choked the laneway entirely. As he advanced a little farther, the lane widened out a bit and the fences had been shored up on either side to enclose several cleared fields. Leland Gordon's work, no doubt. Beyond this, it didn't look like anyone had paid any attention at all to the state of the holding.

Thaddeus knew he was close to the house when he smelled woodsmoke. As he rounded yet another turn in the path, he saw a small, squat building that appeared to be a rude settler's shanty that had been improved in a haphazard fashion. A room had been added to one side and a shed built at the back, but the basic log structure was still clearly visible. He rode farther into the dooryard and called out. There was no answer but the plaintive bellow of a cow, and off in the distance the yelp of a dog.

Behind the house a privy leaned at an alarming angle, surrounded by untrimmed nettles and stalks of goldenrod. Beyond a square of kitchen garden was a small barn, little more than a drive shed, with a hole above the carriage door where the wind had ripped the boards away. It was a grim holding, slowly falling into ruin, and at complete odds with the prosperous public face the Howells presented.

He called again, but was answered only by the cow. She was standing behind the barn, in obvious distress, in a small field hemmed in by the outbuildings and the slope of the hill that rose steeply from the meadow. Thaddeus went through the gate and pushed open a Dutch door that led into the back of the barn. One side of the building had been fashioned into stalls of a sort. There was a metal bucket in one of them. Thaddeus turned to discover that the cow had followed him in, hoping, he expected, that someone would relieve the pressure on her bulging udder. He stood aside and she walked into the stall. He grabbed the bucket and a three-legged stool he found beside the door. It had been many years since he had milked a cow, not since he had been a lad back on his father's farm, and even then he hadn't done it often. Milking was women's work. Generally men were too ham-fisted to achieve the sure and regular strokes that reassured the cow and made the milk flow.

It took him a few minutes to get the rhythm, but then the warm, frothy milk began to squirt into the bucket. Fortunately, this cow wasn't a kicker, no matter what Ellen Howell claimed.

He stopped when the pail was half full. The cow seemed content, and the milk would give him an excuse to enter the house, should anyone happen along and challenge him. He turned the beast out into the meadow again and walked to the back door of the house.

"Hello?" he called. There was no answer, so he pushed the door open.

"Hello?" he said again. What was the girl's name? Mrs. Howell had told it to him at the debate, but he met so many people that day that it wasn't surprising he couldn't remember it. He would have to ask the Gordons.

He made only a cursory inspection of the cabin. The stove was quite hot, and there were dishes still on the drain board by the pump. It was clear that someone had been here recently. More than just been here — lived here. If the old farmer was to be believed, it was the Howell girl, but why on earth did she run off whenever anyone approached? More to the point, how did she know when there was someone coming down the lane?

He set the pail by the sink and left, shutting the door carefully behind him. Ashby had instructed him to take a good look around, but he could scarcely snoop through the house in the face of such obvious habitation. He would have to find answers in some other way.

Even so, he scanned his surroundings again before he headed back down the laneway. There was nothing to see but the weathered buildings huddled under the tree-covered hill. Again he could hear the bark of a dog, but the sound was muffled. *It must be a long way off,* he thought.

To his surprise, the old farmer had pulled to one side of the road fifty feet or so from the entrance to the lane. Thaddeus waved a greeting at him and rode on.

"Caroline. Her name is Caroline," Leland said when Thaddeus reached the Gordon house in Sully, "although I've never addressed her as anything but 'Miss Howell.' She's never been exactly friendly."

"An old farmer I met on the road said she runs and hides whenever anyone comes near."

"She's been doing that ever since her mother was arrested. Ma did some baking the other day and I took a loaf of bread and a pie over to her. We figured that might be something she didn't know how to do for herself, you see. She was nowhere in sight, so I just left it on the table."

Thaddeus was pleased that the Gordons had at least thought of the girl, which seemed to be more than either of her parents had done, or himself for that matter. And maybe other neighbours had reached out to her, only to be ignored.

"How does she know when someone's coming?" he asked. "She'd obviously been there, but hid well before I got to the end of the lane."

"It's the dog. Just an old mutt, but he won't leave her side. I expect he knows someone's coming before they even turn in and he barks to let her know. That lane is so long, she'd have plenty of time to hide."

Thaddeus thought the barks had come from a long way away, but as he thought about it, he realized that the sound had been muffled. It could have come from behind a closed door inside a building. Where had the girl been? The house consisted of nothing more than a couple of rooms and a shed. He hadn't searched them, but he was sure the barking hadn't come from inside the house. The barn was a simple wood-shed, not nearly as large as the drive shed at the manse. And he hadn't heard anything while he was inside milking the cow.

It was puzzling, but since there had been little to see other-wise, Thaddeus doubted that it had any relevance to the case. He'd report his lack of findings to Ashby, and in the meantime get whatever information he could from the Gordons.

"You don't happen to know what kind of business Major Howell is in, do you? Or where he goes when he goes away?"

"That's the question everybody's asking," Gordon said, "including the chief constable. Some say it's something to do with promoting railway bonds, but to tell you the truth, I know so little about that sort of thing I'd be hard-put to tell you what it's all about — or how anyone makes a living from it. Why do you ask?"

"I've found a barrister who's willing to represent Mrs. Howell. He's set up all kinds of inquiries, but I'm not sure which ones in particular will serve to help her case. Neither does he at this point. I'm just looking for whatever information I can find."

Gordon looked relieved. "Ma and I talked about trying to find someone, but we were a little afraid of the cost."

"As was I. He's working for free. He's just graduated and thinks being involved in a high-profile murder trial will cement his reputation." Thaddeus shrugged. "I figured it was better than court-appointed."

"Well, it's certainly better than we managed."

And Thaddeus was reminded once again of the essential goodness of people like the Gordons, who were willing to consider helping a neighbour even when the neighbour wasn't very neighbourly.

Martha saw her grandfather off in the morning, then set about tidying up from the dinner party the night before. She had been too keyed up to wash the dishes or shake out the tablecloth after Ashby left, deciding instead to bid Thaddeus good night and go to bed. She lay awake a long time, though, going over and over the rather stupendous events of the evening.

She had never before encountered anyone quite like Towns Ashby. There had been many gentlemen travellers who stayed at the Temperance Hotel in Wellington — businessmen, salesmen, well-to-do farmers, representatives from the

Agricultural Society. They had paid no attention to her, other than to ask her to fetch them a clean napkin or a fresh pitcher of lemonade — except for that one occasion when she had been airing the beds on the second floor and had been cornered by a paunchy, red-faced man who claimed he wanted to show her something, and would pay her a pound if she let him. She had grabbed a bolster and raised it as a weapon.

"If I scream, my father will be here in thirty seconds," she said. "Do you really want everyone to know what you just said to me?"

Then she had backed away from him slowly, until she was close to the door. Keeping her eyes on the man, she reached behind her and wrenched it open. Then she threw the bolster at him and ran down the stairs.

She hadn't told anyone about it. She figured it was all just a little pathetic. Like the boys at school who had sometimes followed her down the street in a pack, making comments and elbowing each other until the day she reached down and picked up one of the road apples some passing horse had dropped. She spun around and threw as hard as she could, and was rewarded when the nugget landed squarely in the middle of Harry Pitt's forehead. They hadn't been so bold after that, and she had ignored them from then on.

She hadn't ever had anyone actually *bow* to her before, like Ashby had done. It had been very slight, and extremely elegant. At first she was amused by it, then a little intimidated, a feeling that intensified during dinner as he and her grandfather discussed the Howells, and Ashby so slowly and deliberately ate his food, delicately dabbing his mouth with his napkin and laying his knife and fork down between bites. Towns Ashby was a cut far above the farmers and shopkeepers and blacksmiths she normally encountered. He was aptly named, she decided. He had town manners. A city shine. Not that she was a bush girl by any stretch of the imagination, but she had grown up in a village, not a city, and she hoped that she hadn't seemed like too much of a country mouse. She mustn't have, she finally concluded. Otherwise he would never have included her in the after-dinner discussion about the case. But she resolved that should he ever come to dinner again, she would try to copy his manners, and not wolf down her food quite so hastily.

When she finally confronted the dinner dishes the next morning, they were caked in a congealed mess from having sat all night. With a sigh, Martha set them to soak, then went into the dining room to clear away the table. She carefully folded the cloth so that she could carry it outside and shake it, but as she was shoving the chair back, her foot bumped against something solid. Puzzled, she reached down to discover a book: *Commentaries Volume I,* by Sir William Blackstone. It must have been in Ashby's valise. He'd taken it out, no doubt, when he removed his notes, and then forgotten that he'd set it on the floor. She leafed through it, stopped and read a paragraph here and there, and then, dishes forgotten, she moved a chair closer to the window where the strong morning light would make it easier to read.

Both the life and limbs of a man are of such high value, in the estimation of the law of England, that it pardons even homicide if committed se defendendo, or in order to preserve them. For whatever is done by a man to save either life or member, is looked upon as done upon the highest necessity and compulsion. Therefore, if a man through fear of death or mayhem is prevailed upon to execute a deed, or do any other legal act; these, though accompanied with all other the requisite solemnities, may be afterwards

*avoided, if forced upon him by a well-grounded appre-
hension of losing his life, or even his limbs, in case of
his non-compliance. And the same is also a sufficient
excuse for the commission of many misdemeanors, as
will appear in the fourth book. The constraint a man
is under in these circumstances is called in law duress,
from the Latin* duritis, *of which there are two sorts:
duress of imprisonment, where a man actually loses
his liberty, of which we shall presently speak; and
duress* per minas, *where the hardship is only threatened and impending, which is that we are now dis-
coursing of. Duress* per minas *is either for fear of loss
of life, or else for fear of mayhem, or loss of limb. And
this fear must be upon sufficient reason.*

This was followed by a long phrase in a language that
she couldn't read. Latin, she suspected, but she would have
to ask Thaddeus when he returned. She thought it must
reiterate the concept expressed in the paragraph: that killing someone in fear of one's life was an adequate defence
under the law. She wondered if it could be argued that Mrs.
Howell had been in fear of her life. Or even Mr. Howell, she
supposed. If one of them had shot Paul Sherman because
they were both being threatened, then surely the exonera-
tion would extend to the other as well.

She discovered that it might not be nearly that simple
a little further on in the book. "*But though our law in general considers man and wife as one person, yet there are some
instances in which she is separately considered; as inferior to
him, and acting by his compulsion. And in some felonies, and
other inferior crimes, committed by her, through constraint
of her husband, the law excuses her: but this extends not to
treason or murder.*"

Martha was a little taken aback by this passage. A woman could be excused, apparently, for obeying her husband in committing a crime unless it was one of the ones that could get her into the most trouble. Then she was on her own.

She hoped that she had misinterpreted the text; otherwise, it hardly seemed fair that a woman was deemed inferior and subject to obedience to her husband right up until the time he told her to kill somebody.

She read on, struggling through the unfamiliar terms and foreign phrases, trying to understand. Thaddeus knew a great deal about a great many things, but she judged that this was beyond even her grandfather's expertise. She would have to take her questions to Ashby, if she got the chance.

The sun was high in the sky by the time she put the book down, her eyes tired from reading, her mind whirling with questions. She was about to go to the kitchen to attend to the still-unwashed dishes when there was a knock on the front door.

And there, on the porch, stood Towns Ashby, as if she had conjured him.

He tipped his hat. "Miss Renwell, I'm sorry to disturb you, but in the process of packing my things I discovered that I have misplaced one of my books. I wondered if you, by any chance, had run across it."

"The Blackstone? Yes, it was by your chair. Please come in. It will only take a moment for me to fetch it. I'm afraid I took the liberty of reading a little of it."

He looked surprised. "Really? I would hardly call Blackstone a suitable book for a morning's light entertainment. I could barely get through it myself." He stepped into the hall, leaving the door ajar behind him.

"I think you'll find that many ladies are interested in more than the latest trashy novels," Martha said. "The trouble is, no one ever gives us anything meatier."

He laughed. "Point taken. From now on I'll endeavour to leave behind only the driest and most uninteresting of my textbooks. Perhaps I can get you to read them and tell me what they say."

She didn't give an inch. "I'd be delighted." She went through to the dining room and retrieved the Blackstone. When she returned, a scowling James Small was standing on the porch.

"Is everything all right, Martha?" he asked.

"Of course. Why wouldn't it be?"

Small shifted from foot to foot uncomfortably. "Well, you know, a strange man at the door, and then he goes inside. You never know. There are a lot of ruffians about. The railway crew and so forth."

Ashby had an amused smile on his face, one eyebrow lifted in question. Just then Martha could have leaped at Small and strangled him by his bobbing Adam's apple.

"Mr. Ashby may be strange to you, Mr. Small, but he's not to me."

"It's just that I know your grandfather isn't home right now. I wanted to make sure you were all right."

"I'm fine, thank you. Mr. Ashby has just come to retrieve the book he left behind last night."

"And now that I have it," Ashby said, taking it from Martha, "I'll be on my way. I have some information for your grandfather, incidentally, but perhaps it would be better if I wrote to him." His eyes slid sideways toward Small. "My steamer leaves shortly, but I'll send a letter as soon as I get back to the city." He tipped his hat again. "Miss Renwell. Mr. Small." And then he exited the door and sauntered away down the path.

"Well, if you're all right, then I'll just go too," Small said, although he didn't move from where he was standing.

"Thank you," Martha said, and closed the door in his face. Then she let out an exasperated sigh. She couldn't believe how fast Small had come galloping across the yard, and how quickly he'd managed to chase Towns Ashby away. She'd wanted to talk to Ashby. She'd wanted to ask him questions about what she'd read. She'd wanted to hear what he had found out about the Howell case. But most of all, she'd just wanted him to stay a little longer.

After a few moments, she allowed herself a peek out the parlour window. Small had finally given up on any thought of being invited in and was loping back across the yard.

III

"I stopped at your farm the other day," Thaddeus said to the figure sitting on the narrow bunk. "I was passing anyway, and I thought it was an opportunity to make sure that everything was all right. I hope you don't mind."

The heavy wooden door to Ellen Howell's cell had been left open, but Thaddeus hesitated to walk right in, leaning instead against the solid oak jamb.

"And was it all right?" she asked.

"As far as I could tell. There seemed to be someone still living there. The neighbours seem to think it's your daughter."

She looked puzzled. "Caroline is still there?"

"I don't know that for sure," Thaddeus replied. "The stove was warm. There were dishes by the pump waiting to be washed. I called, but no one answered."

She appeared to take a moment to digest this information. "How odd."

"I agree," Thaddeus said. "I would have thought that someone would take her in. One of your friends, perhaps, if you have no family here."

"I have no family anywhere," she said, "and my friends, unfortunately, are not well-placed to feed another mouth."

"I must admit, I don't know if they tried to do something for the girl or not. Patience Gordon sent her some baking, but Leland says he can't get close to her. This was confirmed by a farmer I met on the road, and mirrors my own experience, as well. As I said, I called, but my only answers were from a cow and a dog."

Her face cleared then. "Caroline will be fine as long as she has Digger. He won't let any harm come to her."

Thaddeus was astounded by her lack of concern. She hadn't asked a single question about Caroline's welfare, or what arrangements could be made for her. Was she protecting her daughter in some way? If she was, he decided there was no point in asking her about it.

"At any rate, I milked your cow."

She laughed and the warmth came back into her face. "I should like to have seen that," she said. "The famous preacher with his face stuck in a cow's flank. I'm surprised you know how."

"It took me a while to get the hang of it again," he admitted. "It's been a long time."

She stood. "I'm allowed to take my exercise in the hall," she said. "Would you walk with me?"

Again, Thaddeus noted the small hesitation when she stepped through the door. Not a limp, exactly, just a stiffness. She noticed his concern.

"It's an old injury," she said. "When I was a child we lived on an estate in Norfolk. We children had ponies, and used to dare each other to jump the fences. I mistimed things one day. The pony crashed into the fence, then crashed into me. The pony was fine. I broke my leg. It didn't heal properly and I've been left with a slight limp ever since."

Thaddeus fell in beside her as she headed down the hall. It would have been natural for him to offer his arm, but he felt awkward about it as she had made no move to take it on her own.

"Father got rid of the ponies after that," she went on. "For the longest time I thought it was because of my accident, but then he started selling other things as well. Eventually everything was gone. Anyhow, the damp of this place aggravates the stiffness. Under normal circumstances, it doesn't give me that much trouble."

"Mr. Ashby is looking into the possibility of getting you out on bail," Thaddeus said. "It may be that you won't have to stay here until the trial." Although where the money was to come from, Thaddeus had no idea. How much would they want to ransom an accused murderer? Quite a lot, probably.

"I must thank you for finding Mr. Ashby," she said. "I'm not sure how much help it will be, as I can shed no light on what happened, but I must admit that it's comforting to have him on my side. I had no idea how daunting court would be."

So she hadn't told Ashby anything either.

"He told me that he's working pro bono, which is a great relief. I know he hopes to establish his name with this case. In all honesty, I don't see what good it will do him if he loses, but so long as he doesn't send a bill, I don't suppose it will do me or mine any harm."

"It would be a completely unfair trial otherwise," Thaddeus said.

"I suppose you're right. They'll hang me anyway, you know, but at least it will be *fair*." She emphasized the last word, drawing it out and tingeing it with irony.

"Don't count him out yet. By all accounts he's a very enterprising young man."

They had reached the end of the hall and turned to retrace their steps.

"Is there anything I can do for you in the meantime?" Thaddeus asked. "Is there anything you need?"

"Yes."

Thaddeus held his breath and hoped that her request would be within his means to deliver.

"Time hangs heavily on my hands. It is far too dark in here to read, even on the sunniest of days, but I am not allowed a lamp or a candle unattended. I believe they would allow you one. Do you think that you could, just occasionally, read to me for an hour or two? My friends are too far away to come, and I'm not entirely sure that the gaoler can read at all. I have no one else to ask, other than the local Church of England man, and I can tell, just by looking at him, that he'd take his selections from religious sources." She stopped, and looked a little shamefaced. "No offence meant by that, but I'd prefer something lighter."

"What would you like to hear?"

"Something that would remind me of home. Some Jane Austen, perhaps. Maybe one of the Brontes. Something entertaining and full of romance."

"Count on it. I can come tomorrow. After that, I'll be off on my wanderings again, but only for a few days, and then I can come back."

He was rewarded with a smile that seemed to light up the entire hall.

Thaddeus stopped at the bookseller's on his way back to the manse. Once inside the shop, he became mesmerized by the long shelves of books, in particular by the section that contained volumes of philosophy and theology. He wondered that there were enough people in Cobourg to sustain a large selection of such heavy material, but then he realized that many of them were introductory texts, aimed, no doubt, at the students of Victoria College. The more advanced books would appeal to the professors, he supposed.

There were several shelves set aside for fiction, and this seemed to be more in keeping with the general tenor of the town. He lingered for a moment over a collection of Edgar Allan Poe's stories. Once, long ago, he had read and enjoyed Poe's *Murders in the Rue Morgue*. Then he realized that macabre stories about death would hardly be a comfort to someone in a gaol cell awaiting trial for murder. Besides, they were to his taste, not hers. She had asked for something romantic.

He found several Jane Austen novels on the shelf. He finally picked out a volume called *Mansfield Park*. She said she'd like something that reminded her of home, and in leafing through the volume he found several passages that described the English countryside. He handed over a few coins he could ill-afford, tucked the book under his arm, and went home.

Martha's eyes lit up when she saw what he had in his hand. "Is that for me?" she asked.

"Oh. No, I'm sorry, it isn't." Thaddeus should have realized that Martha would want to dive into the book. He was about to tell her that she would have to wait and then he realized that there was no reason the book couldn't be shared. "But you can have it for all but the few hours that I'm reading it to Mrs. Howell."

"Why can't she read it herself?"

"It's too dark in the cell, and she's allowed no light."

Martha had an odd look on her face. "That's awfully nice of you." Then she heaved an exaggerated sigh. "I can see now what will happen. I'll be right at a thrilling bit and you'll want to rip it out of my hands and take it away."

Thaddeus laughed. "And I'm afraid if that happens you'll have to wait to see how it all turns out. But you won't have to wait long. I can spare only an hour or two here and there."

"I'd like to start reading right now, but not necessarily the book in your hand. There's a letter arrived that I would have torn open and read long since except for the unfortunate fact that it's addressed to you."

"From Ashby?" Thaddeus said.

"I expect so." She pointed to where it was lying on the kitchen table. "He said he would write."

Thaddeus pulled out a chair and sat down. Martha hovered behind him.

"I hope you're not going to read over my shoulder," he said.

"Maybe you should read it out loud. Then I won't bother you." She took a chair next to him.

Thaddeus unsealed the letter and spread it out. There was no salutation; none of the niceties of normal correspondence. Instead, Ashby jumped straight to the subject at hand: "I must say there are rather a jolly lot of drinkers in Cobourg and they do appreciate a fine brandy. One night in the saloon at the Globe Hotel and I'm quite sodden from drink."

"I hope some of them had some useful information to impart," Martha muttered. "Otherwise, it sounds like a foolish way to spend your time."

"Do you want to hear what he has to say or not?"

"Sorry. I'll be quiet from now on."

Major Howell, or rather I should say Mister Howell, as he doesn't appear to have been anywhere near the British army — is quite well known at the Globe. He appears to be on good terms with most of the leading citizens of the town and is particularly noted for his willingness to assist in delicate business matters. As is already general knowledge, Howell purchased the land at Sully at the instigation of Mr. D'Arcy Boulton, who in all probability also furnished the wherewithal to complete the purchase.

"Who is D'Arcy Boulton?"

"Shush."

"Oh, all right."

Although the recent land purchase itself appears to be perfectly straight-forward, there has in the past been a cloud over the title, as is the case with several other pieces of property in the area. The difficulty dates back many years, in fact to the very first settlement and the rather chaotic manner in which land was handed out. The Court of Heir and Devisee has allowed the titles to pass a number of times in the meantime, but I'm curious enough about the original problem to dig a little deeper. I will let you know when and if I discover anything of interest.

Other than being a go-between for the local movers and shakers, it appears that Mr. Howell dabbles in currency exchange and the sale of railway bonds, both Canadian and American.

I met with Mrs. Howell, but she said absolutely nothing that will shed any light on the situation. As far as she is concerned, she was minding her own business when the constables came and arrested her. She seems quite resigned to being found guilty.

I will be returning to Cobourg the middle of next week, and am anxious to hear what, if anything you've discovered in the meantime. There is no need to meet the steamer — I can find my way to the Globe without assistance — but I would like to meet with you and your granddaughter again, at which point we'll decide where we go from here. I would, of course, be delighted if Miss Renwell could be persuaded to furnish another excellent dinner.

The letter was signed, but with such a scrawl that Thaddeus recognized only the initial *T* and a capital *A* in the middle.

"Oh dear," Thaddeus said.

"What?" Martha had taken the letter from him and was rereading it avidly.

"Do you remember the first time we went to the market?"

"And you ended up with a pocketful of bad money?"

"Yes. That was right after the camp meeting. The first time I ever laid eyes on the Howells. I remember thinking they didn't fit in very well. They were all over the site doing some sort of business. I didn't pay much attention at the time. Now I wish I had."

Martha looked up from the letter. "Do you think it's Major ... sorry, Mister Howell, who's been passing counterfeit money?"

"I don't know what to think. I'm not even sure what 'currency exchange' is. But remind me to tell Ashby about it."

"I think we should keep a list of the things we need to tell Mr. Ashby," Martha said. "I'll go find some paper and ink." And she jumped up and went into the parlour, still clutching Ashby's letter.

The next morning Thaddeus tucked the copy of *Mansfield Park* into his pocket, careful not to disturb the hairpin Martha had left on page fifty-five as a bookmark.

When he arrived at the gaol he showed the keeper his book and asked for a light. After a moment's hesitation, the keeper allowed "as to how it would be all right" and fetched a small lamp for him, then let him through to the cell block. Ellen was at the end of the hall, and walked to meet him.

"Mr. Lewis. As promised!"

"And, as promised, with a book in hand."

She smiled as he held it out for her to see.

"An Austen! Oh, well done!"

He felt a flush of pleasure in her approval, wondering at himself even as he did so.

There was nowhere to sit but in her cell. Thaddeus set the lamp on the small table by her cot and took a seat on the wooden stool that had been drawn up to it.

"Shall we begin?" he asked when he was settled, his feet tucked under the stool to give her more room.

She sat on the end of the cot and waited expectantly. He opened the book and began:

> *About thirty years ago, Miss Maria Ward of Huntingdon, with only seven thousand pounds, had the good luck to captivate Sir Thomas Bertram, of Mansfield Park, in the county of Northampton, and to thereby be raised to the rank of a baronet's lady, with all the comforts and consequences of an handsome house and large income. All Huntingdon exclaimed on the greatness of the match, and her uncle, the lawyer, himself, allowed her to be at least three thousand pounds short of any equitable claim to it.*

The first chapter seemed to concern the quite different fortunes of Miss Maria Ward's sisters, which were not nearly as advantageous in nature. One sister in particular brought disgrace upon herself by marrying a mere Lieutenant of the Marines.

Thaddeus wasn't at all sure that he liked the tenor of this story, in which one's fate was dictated by the amount of money one was able to either inherit or marry. His own father had been a hard-working farmer, prosperous enough and well respected, but neither Thaddeus nor his fifteen brothers and sisters had received any great advantage because of it. They had been expected to make their own way and decide the course of their own lives. Nor had it occurred to any of them that they were inferior in any way because of it.

He soon, however, became engrossed in the story of the disgraced sister's little girl, who was summarily plucked out of the bosom of her family and brought to Mansfield Park. But even then, her circumstances made her in no way equal to her cousins.

> *"There will be some difficulty in our way, Mrs. Norris,"* *observed Sir Thomas, "as to the distinction proper to* *be made between the girls as they grow up; how to pre-* *serve in the minds of my daughters the consciousness* *of what they are, without making them think too lowly* *of their cousin; and how, without depressing her spirits* *too far, to make her remember that she is not a Miss* *Bertram. I should wish to see them very good friends,* *and would, on no account, authorize in my girls the* *smallest degree of arrogance towards their relation; but* *still they cannot be equals. Their rank, fortune, rights* *and expectations, will always be different.*

What nonsense, Thaddeus thought, to take a child into your household and treat it differently from the rest. His own daughter had married young, in haste, and perhaps unwisely, but in those dark days after she had been murdered, he and Betsy had endeavoured to provide a real home for her baby. Martha had been as their own child, and he knew that she had always regarded them as her parents, even after her real father finally came back.

Ellen Howell, however, appeared to hear nothing amiss in the premise of the story. While the first chapters unfolded, she sat very upright on her cot, but as the story deepened she closed her eyes and leaned her head back against the wall. She was so close that Thaddeus could see the fine lines that etched the skin beside her eyes and at the edges of her lips. He could hear her slow, steady breathing. He would glance up and watch her mouth form into the slight upward curve of a smile at the words he spoke to her.

After a time, his knee began to hurt from the tucked-up position of his legs, and he stretched them out to ease the ache. The cell was so narrow that his foot brushed against hers. He pulled it back hastily, but she appeared not to notice.

He gathered himself and read on. The story progressed in such a way as anyone could have predicted — the little girl was miserable and much put upon by the Bertram family, with the exception of one son, who, much to Thaddeus's amusement, was to be given a church and a ready-made congregation, an appointment which apparently was within Sir Thomas Bertram's purview to hand out to anyone he pleased.

"Was Mansfield Park the sort of place you grew up in?" he asked at one point.

She sighed, but didn't open her eyes. "Oh no, nothing so grand. My father had no title, just a smallish estate inherited from his grandfather. The rents were never enough to cover our expenses, though we lived quite simply. There were three of us girls, and no male heir." She opened her eyes and looked at him then. "You've just read about what it can be like in England. With no money and few connections, our prospects of good marriage were slim, and father had little means to provide for us otherwise. The estate was in rather perilous debt and father hoped Canada would restore our fortunes. The land was so cheap, you see. Surely it would be no time at all before we made great riches and could go back home to live in a much finer style than we had ever dreamed of before."

Her voice trailed off. Thaddeus had no need to hear the rest of the story. It was a common enough tale. No one had told the English that two hundred acres of Canadian bush was very different from two hundred acres of settled English countryside, and that they would be expected to work their land themselves. It had been a rude awakening for many of them.

Clearing a bush farm would be a daunting prospect for a family with no sons. No doubt it had worn the father out, and the girls had been left to marry whoever was willing to provide for them. George Howell must have seemed a good choice. He was, after all, the same class of people Ellen had been used to. It may not have turned out to be a very good match after all, given her current predicament.

Thaddeus was about to continue reading when Ellen spoke again. "I never thought I would be called upon to milk a cow, or to bake bread, or to scrub a floor. It was quite a shock, for my sisters and me, when we realized that if we didn't do it, no one would. It seemed so degrading."

It would, he supposed, if you were brought up with the notion that labour was something to be despised. How foreign these English settlers must have found it here, where "hard-working" was a term of the highest praise.

It would have been a natural thing to ask her then how she had met her husband, but this was a subject that Thaddeus felt disinclined to discuss, and not only, he realized with a start, because her husband had landed her in such a mess. He let the moment go by and started reading again, and a few minutes later the gaoler appeared in the doorway to announce that it was time for him to go.

"I won't be back for a few days," Thaddeus said to Ellen. "But when I return to Cobourg, I'll come again and read some more if you would like me to."

"I would like that very much," she said. "Thank you, Mr. Lewis."

IV

Thaddeus spent the next three days in the eastern part of his circuit, where there was little opportunity to ask any questions that might further the investigation, but quite by accident he overheard a potential answer to one of the questions Ashby had asked, reported with a great deal of tut-tutting at a women's prayer meeting. Three Indians from the village on the far shore of Rice Lake were harvesting the wild rice that had given the lake its name when they discovered a small skiff tangled in the reeds and grasses. They recognized the craft as belonging to a man who lived near Gores Landing, and towed it back to him.

It was only after a few days of reflection that the owner, a Mr. Greeley, realized the significance of this and reported it to the local constable.

"I didn't think nothing of it when I found the boat was gone," the man said. "I thought mebbe it had just drifted away, or someone had borrowed it and would bring it back sooner or later. It was only after I pondered for a bit about when it went missing that I thought mebbe it might have something to do with the murder."

"That would have occurred to anyone else right away," one of the women said. "But Harry Greeley never was too well endowed in the brains department. It's a wonder he thought of it at all."

There was no telling, of course, whether or not this was the boat that had taken Paul Sherman to Spook Island, but Thaddeus figured the timing was right, and the discovery seemed to suggest that Sherman had been following George Howell and not the other way around. After all, Howell had rented a boat. Sherman, if it was Sherman, had simply taken the first one he ran across.

At least Thaddeus would now have something concrete to report when Ashby returned that evening.

He arrived home to discover that Martha had rearranged the dining room.

"How did you manage to move the sideboard?" he asked. It was a solid, carved piece that was far too heavy for one person to shift.

"Mrs. Small gave me a hand," she said. "I pulled it out to clean and by the time it was far enough from the wall to dust behind, it was halfway into the room anyway."

She had also dressed her hair in a new arrangement of braids and knots.

"What do you think?" she asked when he commented on this.

"I think you're pretty no matter what you do with your hair," Thaddeus replied. "Didn't that take an awfully long time to do?" The style looked complicated and time-consuming.

"Yes, but don't worry, I didn't skimp on any chores."

"I can tell that by the fact that you dusted behind the sideboard." He wasn't at all sure that the extravagant hairstyle was appropriate for a fifteen year old, but he had no basis, really, on which to make that assessment. For the millionth time he wished that his wife Betsy was there. She would have known.

Martha had organized dinner on the assumption that Ashby would arrive at the same late hour as before. Much to her chagrin, he knocked on the door at five o'clock.

"I've been informed that reasonable people eat their suppers at five," he said. "I must apologize for arriving so late the other night."

Not knowing what time supper would be served, Martha had concocted something she called "ragout of beef" which could simmer on the stove until it was wanted, but there were still last-minute touches that she hadn't completed. Thaddeus thought she did an admirable job of hiding her annoyance.

"Food will be a few moments yet," she said. "Do come in. And no talking about the case while I'm gone." Then she disappeared into the kitchen.

Ashby handed his hat to Thaddeus, then they both settled themselves in the parlour.

Ashby smiled. "Well, we've been given our orders. Now I don't dare tell you anything until Miss Renwell returns."

"Yes, we'll have to discuss other topics. Otherwise I'll never have comfortable socks again."

"How goes the railway? It was all anybody could talk about at the Globe the other night."

"As far as I know, it goes apace," Thaddeus said. "It's a dreadful nuisance for anyone attempting to travel the roads near the line, but I haven't heard of any particular delays. There's been another bond issue go out, which the people of Cobourg are snapping up at a great rate. Forty thousand pounds worth, or so I'm told."

Ashby looked concerned. "You haven't bought any of them, have you?"

Thaddeus laughed. "Ministers don't have money to invest in anything other than the necessities of life. Why do you ask?"

"Just some things I've heard. It's the sort of enterprise that the big players will make a great deal of money from. I'm not so sure it's a good deal for the small investor."

"But I thought the bonds were guaranteed by the government?"

"And I expect those members of government who invested will see to it that their returns are paid. As for the rest," he paused and shrugged his shoulders, "I don't know if the principal will ever be repaid, never mind generate any interest. And the municipalities that invested will have to hope that the promised prosperity actually materializes. Otherwise the taxpayer will be left to pony up."

If true, this was bad news indeed for the town of Cobourg. All their plans for a grand new hall in the centre of town depended on everybody getting rich from the railway.

"The only person who appears to be guaranteed of anything is the contractor, Samuel Zimmerman," Ashby went on. "He seems to have tied up the agreements for an enormous number of these smaller projects, all with clauses that allow him to charge extra for unforeseen difficulties in construction. Gossip has it that difficulties will be encountered in every single one of them."

"But why would anyone agree to such an open-ended contract?" Thaddeus asked.

"Because Zimmerman somehow has the ability to expedite their charters in the first place. No Zimmerman, no railway. And he floats his negotiations on a sea of champagne. The company directors sign on in a golden haze, then he does what he wants with them."

"And if the directors refuse to pay the extra charges?"

"They don't get control of the line. Zimmerman doesn't have to turn it over until he's been fully compensated."

"Champagne and greed are a bad combination, aren't they?"

"Believe it. And should you happen to have a little extra money, there are far better investments, trust me."

Thaddeus had many more questions he wanted to ask Ashby, but Martha appeared in the doorway to announce that their meal was ready. She must have finished her preparations in record time. They filed into the dining room and Ashby pulled out a chair for Martha before he went to his own, then he took his seat and waited while Thaddeus said grace.

Martha served them from a covered bowl that Thaddeus was pretty sure was meant to be a soup tureen. She passed Ashby a plate, and his face lit up when he took his first bite of the ragout.

"This is delicious. Much better than the fare at the Globe. You'd better be careful, Mr. Lewis, or the hotel will try to steal your cook."

Martha blushed, but all she said was "Thank you."

"I made a good choice when I asked her to keep house for me," Thaddeus agreed, determined to give credit where it was due. "She's a fine cook."

Martha blushed even redder.

"Well, now that we're all in the same room, I can fill you in on what I've discovered," Ashby said, getting down to business right away. "As I indicated in my letter, Mrs. Howell had absolutely nothing to contribute to my understanding of the case. In fact, she almost seemed uninterested in anything I had to say. I came away with the impression that she's protecting someone, and that she's willing to go to any lengths to do so."

"Her husband?" Thaddeus offered. "Maybe she knows where he is and is afraid to say a word in case she gives something away."

"Maybe." But the young lawyer looked unconvinced. "I keep coming back to the funny land deal, although I'm still not sure what the connection is. The title seems to be clear enough as of the present. In the past, the difficulties appear to have been a little more than the usual contention over whether or not settlement duties were carried out. The thorniest of these cases often concern the districts where there was confusion over how many acres the land agent could claim as his own. I don't know whether or not this is one of those cases, or how it ties anything to Paul Sherman, but I have a colleague who has agreed to dig back through the registries to see what he can find. With any luck, I should have an answer before the trial begins."

"There was an old man at one of my meetings who said his uncle farmed that land years ago, but that he couldn't ever get clear title. He seemed to think that Jack Plews didn't own it in the first place, because of the prior difficulties. And an old woman in Sully said she could remember several disputes in the neighbourhood."

There was something else that Patience Gordon had told him, but Thaddeus couldn't quite retrieve the conversation from his memory.

"The general consensus around here is that the railway company will just pay off whoever owns the land so they can go ahead and build their station," Martha said.

"Yes, that's what I've been hearing, too," Thaddeus said. "It would be rather a lot of money by ordinary standards, but everyone seems to think it's nothing at all for the company. And I don't see how it could be enough to justify murder."

Ashby shook his head. "People have been killed over the matter of a few pounds, you know. It happens all the time.

But it does raise the question of someone besides Mr. Howell having a motive for murder, provided, of course, that Paul Sherman can somehow be tied to ownership of the land. After all, Howell and Plews already have their money from the sale, and sorting out the title is the railway's problem."

"Even if you can find someone with a motive, don't you have to prove that this someone else actually shot Mr. Sherman?" Martha asked.

"No, actually. In this particular instance, the rule in Hodge's should apply."

"Which is what?"

"The case against Ellen Howell rests on the premise that she and her husband went to Spook Island with criminal intent, and that the murder was committed in the course of enacting this intent."

Martha nodded with impatience. Ashby had already explained this.

"This is based purely on circumstantial evidence. The rule says that the court can convict only if the evidence is consistent with the guilt of the accused and inconsistent with any other rational conclusion based on fact."

"So if we can find someone else who had a good reason to kill Paul Sherman, that would be enough to prove Ellen Howell's innocence?" Thaddeus said.

"Well, not entirely," Ashby said. "Circumstantial evidence can consist of many things. Motive is certainly important, and in this case George Howell doesn't appear to have one. He had opportunity — he was there on the island with Sherman — but I'm not sure the opportunity was exclusive. There were many other people on the lake that afternoon. Any one of them could have put ashore, or even, I suppose, have fired the shot from a boat."

He stopped for a moment as a thought struck him. "I wonder no one heard the shot? Noises echo across water in a way they don't on land. Unless the wind was blowing in the wrong direction. You don't happen to remember what the wind was like that day, do you, Mr. Lewis?"

"No, I don't," Thaddeus said, "but it doesn't matter. There was work being done on the bridge. The crews were putting in the log supports with a pile driver. I remarked at the time on what a racket they were making."

"Excellent. Remind me to write that down later."

No writing at all would take place unless Ashby started to eat a little faster, Thaddeus thought. He had been so busy talking that he had taken only a few bites of food from his plate.

"As well, a jury would have to consider whether or not Howell had the means to commit the crime," Ashby went on. "No one knows if he had a firearm with him, so I expect a certain amount of doubt could be raised over that. And although he is certainly a bit of a shady character, there is no history of violence."

The taste of Martha's excellent supper suddenly turned sour in Thaddeus's mouth. The livid marks on Ellen Howell's forearm were a sure sign of violence. The Gordons didn't seem to think that they had been inflicted by her husband, but Thaddeus could think of no other explanation for what he had seen. Reluctantly, he told Ashby about it.

"Really?" Ashby thought for a moment. "Were you the only person who saw the bruises?"

"Patience Gordon noticed them. And a number of other people did as well."

"Still, that's no proof that Howell would kill a man. It's not good news as far as our defence goes, but there's a lot of difference between raising your hand to your wife and actually killing a man."

"Not really," Martha interjected. "If you can hit someone you love, what are you capable of with someone you don't?" She looked at her grandfather, as if she expected him to protest this statement. "We need to anticipate what the prosecution will say," she pointed out. "I expect they would have rather a lot to say if they thought Mr. Howell was in the habit of beating his wife."

"Yes, Martha, you're quite right," Ashby said. "We'll just have to hope that the prosecution doesn't know about it. Whether or not they do, they certainly will make a great deal about Howell's apparent flight and continuing absence, but really, that and opportunity are the rather shaky cornerstones of the prosecution's case."

"But if you find a connection between Mr. Howell and Mr. Sherman, don't you run the risk of supplying the motive?" Martha asked.

"My goodness, my dear, you could be a barrister yourself," Ashby said with a laugh.

"But really," she insisted, "aren't you taking a chance?"

"Yes I am. But you can be certain that the prosecution is scrambling to find the same thing. I don't need any surprises in court. If I know about it, I can deal with it. And if I'm really lucky, I'll find something they don't."

"I have another piece of information that may or may not help," Thaddeus said. He was beginning to feel a little left out of this conversation. Once again all the really intelligent remarks had been made by his granddaughter. "I have a strong suspicion that George Howell has been passing bad money." Briefly, he outlined what he had seen at the camp meeting. "Afterward, I discovered a number of bad notes in my collection plate."

"Currency exchange," Ashby said, "the perfect way to introduce counterfeit bills without much chance of getting caught. And it would be particularly easy with all the uncertainty over the new currency law. Yes, that would fit with the impression I got of George Howell. Is it possible that Paul Sherman was stung? And that he threatened to expose Howell?"

"But why go all the way to Spook Island to do it?" Thaddeus said. He was getting his stride back. "You could have that sort of argument on the main street of Cobourg and no one would take any notice. In fact, if Sherman wanted to confront Howell, it would be in his best interests to do it in a public place."

"Yes, the island. Why the island?"

Ashby's expression mirrored his puzzlement. He sat, head bowed slightly, lips pursed. Thaddeus wasn't sure whether to break the silence or not, so he reached for a sip of water while he waited for Ashby to work through whatever line of thought had suddenly struck him. The movement appeared to bring the young lawyer back to the present. He looked up at Thaddeus, then at Martha, then down at his plate, as if he had only just noticed the food that was there. He grabbed his fork and disposed of his main course in short order, delicately dabbing at his mouth when he was finished.

Martha carried the dishes into the kitchen and returned with dessert — poached pears with shortcake.

"Splendid!" Ashby said, and without delay picked up his spoon and ate. By the time Martha brought the coffee through to the dining room, he had finished and was pulling papers out of his briefcase.

"So where does this leave us?" he asked. "What do we need to know that we don't already?"

"I do have an observation about Ellen Howell's continued silence," Thaddeus said.

"Oh yes?" Ashby stopped fussing with his papers and gave Thaddeus his full attention.

"I went to the Howell farm, but I didn't get much chance to look around. It was obvious that someone is living there, and it appears that it's the Howells' daughter, Caroline."

"They have a daughter? How old?"

"I judge her to be twelve or thirteen maybe. The neighbours say she's very shy at the best of times, but now that so many troubles have afflicted her family, she's grown very reclusive. She runs away whenever anybody approaches."

"Did Ellen Howell say anything about her when you were speaking to her?"

"Not really. And that's what I'm puzzled about. If you had a shy twelve-year-old who was suddenly left alone on a remote farmstead, wouldn't you be asking how she was managing? Or if anybody had thought to look after her? I worry enough about Martha, and she's older and has the Smalls right next door."

Martha wrinkled her nose in distaste. "James pays a little too much attention."

Ashby looked at her and grinned. "Is that the gentleman who came running the other day? He's an admirer, is he?" He glanced at Thaddeus. "There's rather a lot of that going around, isn't there?"

"Not as far as I'm concerned, he isn't," Martha retorted.

Thaddeus was relieved that Martha had not caught the inference. Ashby had obviously formed an opinion about why Thaddeus had been so anxious to find a lawyer for Ellen Howell. And if Ashby had reached that conclusion, who else had as well? Thaddeus felt quite ill, and wondered if he should curtail his visits to the Cobourg jail. But how could he leave Mrs. Howell sitting there friendless and alone? He had promised to return and read to her. He would have to make sure he was absolutely circumspect in all his dealings with her, that was all. His actions must give no weight to any speculation about his motives.

To Thaddeus's relief, Ashby quickly turned the conversation back to the investigation. "Fancy a little list-checking, Miss Martha?"

"I'd be happy to. What would you like me to check?"

"You said that George Howell travels a lot on business, is that right, Mr. Lewis?"

"Yes." And then he realized what Ashby was getting at. "Oh. His name would turn up on the passenger lists, wouldn't it? And it would be interesting to see who else is there."

"Precisely. Maybe we can find a connection to Sherman."

If Howell had crossed the lake, his name would most certainly have been recorded, Thaddeus knew. Even back in '47, when thousands of sick and starving Irish had flooded down the St. Lawrence and along the north shore of Lake Ontario, the steamer companies and immigration agents had recorded names and destinations. It had taken a great deal of subterfuge to get access to them, though.

"I can subpoena the records for the last couple of years," Ashby said. "Then perhaps Martha here would be good enough to go through them."

If it was going to be as easy as that, Thaddeus was grateful that the barrister was involved. He had access to far more useful tools than the average person.

"What do you need me to do?" Thaddeus asked.

"I'm convinced Ellen Howell is protecting someone. You're a regular visitor at the gaol?"

"He's reading to her," Martha said. "Jane Austen."

"Really?" The lawyer's eyebrows lifted in surprise. "How romantic. In between the chapters, see if you can find out what she knows."

"I can scarcely interrogate her," Thaddeus protested. "I'm there as a friend."

"Well, ask her in a friendly manner. Be subtle."

Martha began to laugh. "Oh dear," she said. "Have you read much Austen? It's hardly material that lends itself to the topic of murder."

"Oh." Ashby seemed a little taken aback. "No, I haven't. Oh well, see what you can do."

"It would be nice to know the whereabouts of Jack Plews — the farmer who got bought out — on the day of the murder," Thaddeus said, desperate to steer the conversation away from his activities at the gaol.

"Yes. And whatever else you can find out about him as well."

"I'll talk to Old Mrs. Gordon. She seems to know everything about everybody in Sully."

"Good." And then Ashby froze for a moment, once again lost in thought. "You know, it would be nice if you could get close enough to the daughter to ask her a question or two about what her father was up to."

"I'll try," Thaddeus said. "But I'm not promising anything."

"Take Martha with you. Maybe that will help."

V

Thaddeus had a great deal of difficulty sleeping that night. He would doze off, then come suddenly awake, his mind whirling with the details of the evening's discussion. He would go over and over what they knew and what they suspected, what they needed to find out and what they might never know, but eventually, inevitably, his thoughts would come circling back to Ashby's remarks. "Is he an admirer?" he'd asked of James Small. And then the sidelong look. "There's a lot of that going around, isn't there?" "How romantic," he'd remarked when Martha mentioned what Thaddeus was reading to Ellen Howell.

Was it romantic? Thaddeus had to admit that he wasn't sure.

It couldn't be, he told himself. Ellen Howell was a married woman, and even though her husband had disappeared, leaving her in a mess of trouble, he was, still, in the eyes of God and man, her husband.

Thaddeus had broken many commandments in his time. After his stint in the militia during Mr. Madison's War of 1812, he had disregarded the Sabbath many times, preferring the comfort of a bottle of whiskey to the solace of God's Word. He had once been drunk for a stretch of fifty-one days in a row. He had taken God's name in vain with regularity. He had killed. It had been in war, of course, not a cold-blooded act, but it was killing all the same, a stealing away of another man's life. He'd had no interest in anything but a dissolute life until he'd met Betsy. He had bargained with God so that he might have her.

The one commandment he'd thought he would never break was that of coveting his neighbour's wife. Why would he, when he already had the best wife, the most wondrous wife that a man could have? No one else had ever tempted him, although many had tried.

After Betsy died, he had been in a state of deep mourning for a long time. He had withdrawn into himself and mumbled over his memories. Yes, he had prayed to God as well, but he'd known in his heart that death had been a kindness for Betsy, and believed that one who had been so true and so brave and so loving must surely have been welcomed into heaven. He had mourned for himself more than anything, and had emerged from the dark place he was in only when he was called upon to take some action. It had been his son, Luke, who had awakened him. Together they embarked upon an adventure that had nearly killed them both. Ironically, it had made Thaddeus feel alive again.

But when all the excitement died down, he was left with one indisputable fact — he was lonely. Hints were dropped, after a suitable period of time, of course. He knew his family wondered if he would marry again. It was not so uncommon. He was only fifty-nine, after all, with only a few streaks of grey in his hair. Some people married two or three times in the course of their lives, after their spouses had been carried off by accident or illness. Thaddeus knew that there were any number of widows who eyed him speculatively whenever he walked into a meeting. None of them stirred his interest for a moment, and he ignored them all. He thought he would never want anyone after Betsy.

Until he met Ellen Howell. And Ellen Howell was impossible.

He would pray to God for guidance, except that he already knew what the answer would be. *What God has joined together let no man put asunder.* So many times he'd said these words to fresh young faces standing before him, believing it as he said it, trusting in the sacred sacrament that bound the pair together. And yet, and yet, he wanted to protest, what about the other promises made? To comfort, to honour, to keep in sickness and in health? George Howell had done none of these for his wife. *To be faithful as long as you both shall live.* There was the sting in the tail. He could not argue that dereliction of one part of the sacred vow allowed a disregard for the rest. Otherwise, he was no better than the Baptist minister who wanted to pick and choose his Bible verses.

He must set his feelings aside and treat Ellen Howell as a friend. And even as he decided this, Thaddeus knew what his advice would have been to anyone else: remove the temptation and do not treat at all. But having set a certain train of events in motion, how could he abandon her now? He had to see it through. And then, one way or another, he would put Ellen Howell out of his mind.

The next afternoon Thaddeus brushed down his coat, tucked his copy of *Mansfield Park* into his pocket, and set off for the Cobourg courthouse. In spite of his emotional turmoil of the night before, he found his spirits lifting the closer he got to the gaol. The simple fact was, he enjoyed the hours he spent with Ellen, even though they seldom talked much beyond a discussion of the book. She was good company, even in the odd circumstances of their meetings.

The gaoler let him through, then settled himself in a chair that he had set halfway down the hallway. He looked at Thaddeus sheepishly. "I can't help but hear some of what you're reading. The sound echoes right down the hall. I thought I'd move a little closer so I can get it all."

"That's fine," Thaddeus said. "Are you enjoying the story?"

"Well, now, I have to say I am, sort of, except for the parts I didn't quite catch and some of the words I don't understand. I can't say as to how I've ever heard a story like that before."

"Me neither. But the lady likes it. What's your name, by the way?"

"Clayton Palmer."

"Well, Mr. Palmer, I'll endeavour to speak clearly, so you can be sure to hear it all."

"That would be a fine thing. The rest of the boys in the place want to hear you, too, but sometimes they miss a bit if your voice drops too low."

Thaddeus was suddenly alert. He hadn't realized that everyone else in the cell block could hear him. And if they could hear him, they almost certainly could hear Ellen.

She beamed when she saw his face in the doorway, as if she had persuaded herself that he wouldn't come after all, and was surprised and delighted that he would show up as promised.

"How are you?" he asked.

"In great need of diversion," she said. "The closer it gets to the trial, the more slowly the time seems to go by."

"I'll do my best to keep you entertained today. Unfortunately, I'm off on business again tomorrow."

He was rewarded by a look of disappointment. "Do you think we'll finish the book before the trial?" she asked.

"No. But you can always finish it yourself afterward."

"I doubt that will be possible. Mr. Ashby was here again this morning. He seems quite frustrated that I have no information that he can use to his advantage."

Thaddeus chose his next words carefully. "Whatever information you have will be used in your defence, you know. If you have any, you should vouchsafe it to him. It's not for his advantage, but for yours."

She pursed her lips as she considered this. "No, I rather think the advantage is Mr. Ashby's." And then, before Thaddeus could say anything more, she went on. "In any event, I have none, so it's rather a moot point, isn't it? Are you going to read to me today or not?"

She must know how well the sound carries in here, he thought. She can hear the others as well as they can hear her. He must remember to warn Ashby. In any event, there was no point in Thaddeus trying to shake loose any information — she would remain resolutely mum, especially with the keeper sitting just down the hall.

He opened *Mansfield Park* and began to read.

Up until that point in the book, Thaddeus had been quite scornful of the life it depicted. He found the characters shallow and astoundingly idle. None of them seemed to do much of anything except cater to their own pleasures, so he was somewhat surprised when the younger son, who was destined for the church, proclaimed that it was, in fact, his decision and desire to pursue this vocation, and that the appointment was not merely one of convenience. One of the young women challenged his declaration.

Oh! No doubt he is very sincere in preferring an income readymade, to the trouble of working for one; and has the best intentions of doing nothing all the rest of his

*days but eat, drink, and grow fat. It is indolence, Mr.
Bertram, indeed. Indolence and love of ease — a want
of all laudable ambition, of taste for good company, or of
inclination to take the trouble of being agreeable, which
make men clergymen. A clergyman has nothing to do
but to be slovenly and selfish — read the newspaper,
watch the weather, and quarrel with his wife. His curate
does all the work, and the business of life is to dine.*

Ellen began to laugh. "Oh, poor Mr. Lewis! So this is what people think of you!"

"It's not the same thing," he protested. And then he realized that she was teasing him. "I never quarrelled with my wife."

"Ah, but more to the point, does she have a quarrel with you?"

"She might have, once or twice, when I was being particularly disagreeable. Sadly, she's no longer here to quarrel with."

Her face softened. "I am so sorry," she said, "I didn't know. Is it a recent loss?"

"Six years ago now. I still miss her. It ambushes me at odd moments. She stood by me through some rather desperate times."

And then he realized what he had said. This woman's husband was pointedly not standing by his spouse. He had run off and left her to face the consequences of what he had done. Thaddeus went on hurriedly to cover the awkwardness. "The life of a Methodist minister in Canada is very different from that of an Anglican clergyman in England, you know. There's very little fine dining and not much ease. I always read newspapers, but watching the weather is something I do not for amusement but because I need to know whether or not I'll be able to travel the next day."

"It's not exactly a ready-made income, either, is it? I don't believe such a thing exists in Canada."

"Not for many," Thaddeus agreed. "Most of us are on our own."

And then he returned to reading about the vicissitudes of the landed gentry.

When the gaoler called that their time was up, Thaddeus closed the book.

"I'm afraid I won't be able to come for the next few days," he said, "but I should be back before the trial begins." He needed a day to go to the Howells' farm, and three days after that to cover his share of meetings.

"I'm grateful for whatever time you can spare. I really don't know how to thank you for all that you've done for me."

"It has been my pleasure," Thaddeus said. He felt that he had never spoken truer words.

Martha was thrilled to be going somewhere with her grandfather. She had grown up with tales of his adventures — of the places he had been and the people he had known, of how he had waded through snowdrifts and fast-running rivers, of how he had wrestled hecklers to the ground at camp meetings. He had told her many of these stories himself. But there were other stories, too, told only in hints by her grandmother but in far more detail by her father and her neighbours. These were darker and more concerned with murder and theft and nefarious deeds, and Thaddeus was a hero in every single one of them. She herself had been threatened by a murderer once, but she had been an infant at the time and remembered none of it. And here he was again, in the middle of an adventure, but this time she would march into danger by his side. Not that there would be any danger, she corrected herself. All they had to do was gain the confidence of a wary twelve-year-old, but still, it was a far cry from the constant drudgery of housework or the incessant drone of the classroom.

"If you can find the girl, try to bring her here," Ashby had said. "I'd surely like to talk to her before anyone else does, if only to make her understand that I represent her as well as her mother, and that she needn't say a word if the constable decides to question her."

"Why would they? Everyone in the neighbourhood knows she's still at the farm and no one's asked her a question yet, as far as I know," Thaddeus pointed out.

"Let's make sure we keep it that way." And then Ashby said the most wonderful, most amazing thing: "Take Martha with you."

It was amazing on several counts. Amazing that he would suggest it. Amazing that her grandfather hadn't objected. And amazing that she was no longer "Miss Renwell," but had somehow become the more familiar, more intimate "Martha."

There had been discussion about just how, exactly, they were going to go north. Martha had no experience with horses and Thaddeus was concerned that a novice rider would not last long over such rough roads.

"Perhaps you could borrow the Small's wagon?" she ventured finally, desperate that such an exciting opportunity might be slipping away in the details. "That way if we do manage to persuade the girl to come to Cobourg, we'll have a way to get her here."

Ashby laughed. "Ah, Martha. Practical as always."

Thaddeus was dubious. "The only way that old wagon made it all the way to Cold Springs is because there were a passel of Small brothers to push it up the hills. We'd never make it on our own. I suspect the best thing is to hire the lightest rig and the steadiest horse I can. Then Martha can drive and I can push, if necessary."

"I'll pack some food so we can have breakfast along the way," Martha said quickly, before her grandfather could reconsider his decision.

"Excellent idea. Don't bring too much, though. I'd like to go to the Gordons first and they're sure to want to feed us. I'm hoping I can persuade Leland to come to the Howell farm with us." He turned to Ashby. "The girl knows him. It might make her a little more approachable."

Ashby was ticking items off the list he had written down. "I'll get the steamship lists and have them delivered here. And I'll see if I can light a fire under my friend who's looking into land titles. Let me know as soon as you're back. You know where to find me."

"Yes," Thaddeus said. "In the saloon at the Globe Hotel."

Ashby appeared not to notice the dig, and continued scribbling things down on his list of things to do.

Martha spent the morning fussing over what she should wear. After the excursion to the Cold Springs meeting, her Sunday-best dress had been stained and covered in dust and it had taken a great deal of sponging to get it clean again. She didn't want to run the risk of further damage to it, but at the same time she wanted to look presentable for the Gordons — after all, they were supporters of the church and would be sure to remark on the appearance of their minister's granddaughter, so it behooved her to put her best foot forward. On the other hand, if something exciting happened, she didn't want to be sidelined by worry over whether or not she was going to get her dress dirty.

She had only two others to choose from, her everyday dress or her oldest dress, the one she wore when she was scrubbing the floor or weeding the garden. She tried on the oldest. Maybe it could be gussied up a little so that she looked presentable, but at the same time, it would be unlamented should it become stained or dirty or torn beyond repair. It was a little too short to be proper, she decided, and the bodice was starting to feel tight. She must have grown again. She would have to let the hem down before she could think of wearing it in public. While she was at it, she would open up the darts and let out the waistline as well. But even then, she decided, it was a little too worn-looking to be mistaken for anything but a third-best dress. She would have to wear her everyday and hope that nothing happened to ruin it.

Thaddeus went out right after their noon dinner and it was easy enough to guess where he was going, for he took the copy of *Mansfield Park* with him. Martha was in the kitchen washing the dishes when there was a knock on the front door. She rushed to answer it, hoping it might be Ashby. Instead, it was a young boy who was carrying three leather-bound ledgers.

"Miss Renwell?"

When she confirmed her identity, he shoved the books into her arms.

"Mr. Ashby said to give you these. And don't worry, he's already paid for the errand." And with that, the boy tipped his hat and skipped down the porch stairs.

She took the books to the dining room table and flipped open the topmost. They were shipping records from the steamship companies that most often carried passengers to and from Cobourg. Ashby hadn't wasted any time getting them.

She finished the dishes, then went outside to grub up a few more potatoes from the garden. She had carrots and turnips and a little beef left over from dinner. She would make a pot pie for their supper, she decided, and whatever was left from that they could take on the road with them, along with some bread and cheese. It would be an odd breakfast, but it had the advantage of being eminently portable.

Mrs. Small was outside, too, checking on the state of the linen she had draped over some bushes to dry. She called a hello and ambled over to the fence for a chat.

"You had company, just now," she said.

"Not really. Just a delivery boy. I ordered some books."

"They looked like mighty heavy reading. I thought maybe it was that young barrister at your door again."

Martha liked Mrs. Small well enough, and certainly appreciated that she was willing to do the heavy chores for the manse, but whenever Martha talked to her lately, the woman seemed to be clumsily fishing for details about the Sherman murder.

"No. It was just a delivery boy." Mrs. Small would hear no details if Martha could help it.

"Your Mr. Ashby is cutting quite a caper in town, isn't he?"

"Oh really? Is he?" Information could flow both ways, Martha decided. She was curious to hear what Towns Ashby had been up to.

"Oh my, yes. They say he's standing drinks at the Globe every night." The older woman tutted her disapproval and then eyed Martha closely to see what her reaction to this intelligence might be. "And, of course, the girls are all a-flutter. They say he's from a very good family. He'd be quite the catch for any one of them. Even the Boultons are impressed."

"I'm afraid I have no knowledge of what Mr. Ashby does in his spare time," Martha said. "Our contact with him is purely on a professional level."

"Oh yes, Mr. Lewis has taken a great interest in this case, hasn't he? Finding a lawyer for Mrs. Howell and all. He's a good man, to do that for her. Lots of folks have remarked on the amount of trouble he's gone to for her."

Martha took this to be a warning. She supposed it should come as no surprise that the town was talking about Ashby.

After all, Ellen Howell was big news, and the man who was defending her was handsome and young. What did surprise her was that people were talking about her grandfather and his role in the case. There was an undercurrent to Mrs. Small's remarks that Martha didn't like at all. She wondered if she should say something to him. But how do you tell your grandfather that he's the subject of Cobourg's latest hot gossip?

VI

Light was just breaking across the horizon when they got underway the next day. Martha climbed up onto the seat of the light buckboard rig Thaddeus had picked up from the livery and held her face to the rising sun as they trotted through the outskirts of Cobourg. It promised to be a fine day, warm for the third week of October, and with no sign of rain in the sky. Little conversation passed at first. She and Thaddeus were content in each other's company, and Martha's mind was free to wander.

If only it would. She was unable to tear it away from the unsettling exchange with Mrs. Small, a subject that she thought she had exhausted while trying to fall asleep the night before. She dismissed the gossip about Ashby as no more than he deserved. As much as he claimed that drinking at the Globe was a strategy designed to collect information, she rather suspected that he spent a great deal of time in the town's other drinking establishments, as well. After all, the first evening he had come for dinner he had made a comment about foregoing his cigar and brandy so that they could all discuss the case.

Nor was she surprised, although she was slightly annoyed, at the reference to fluttering girls. Ashby was a good-looking young man who appeared to have a great deal of ready money jangling in his pockets. He could hardly fail to attract female attention. And it wasn't that she was jealous or anything — she wasn't sure she even liked him all that much. He was exasperating at times and not nearly serious enough for a lawyer who was defending an accused murderer. It was almost as though he thought it was a game, and that if he didn't win, well, better luck next time. This wouldn't be much comfort for Ellen Howell. And she wasn't at all sure what losing the case would mean to Thaddeus.

She had a very strong suspicion that her grandfather had a greater interest in the proceedings than merely wanting to see justice done, and it appeared that the Cobourg gossips thought so too. She didn't quite know what to make of this. The notion that her grandfather would behave inappropriately with a married woman was ludicrous. He was the most upright man Martha knew. She had wanted to defend him, to argue that he was, after all, a minister, and was merely offering spiritual solace to a person in dire need of comfort. She would have, if she had been surer of her ground.

He had not confided his reasons for helping Mrs. Howell and Martha had not questioned his motives. She assumed that there was a higher moral or ethical reason for everything her grandfather did. But now Mrs. Small had made her doubt him.

"Do you think Mr. Ashby will win?" she said, suddenly breaking the silence.

"I don't know," her grandfather responded.

"What will you do if he doesn't?"

Thaddeus stared stolidly ahead, obviously uncomfortable with her question. As curious as she was, Martha didn't dare press him for an answer. From the time she first arrived in Cobourg, he had paid her the compliment of treating her like an equal, and she treasured the fact that they could joke so easily with each other. But he was still her grandfather, and there were some things you just couldn't ask.

She would have to trust that he would tell her what was going on when he thought she needed to know. And with that decided, she was able at last to sit back and give herself up to watching the passing scenery.

After a time, Thaddeus brightened up and starting pointing out the sights along the way, the houses that welcomed a Methodist minister, the halls and schoolhouses where he had held meetings.

"Another hour will see us there," he said at one point, and Martha began to look forward to getting down out of the lurching cart. Her legs hurt from bracing them against the buckboard when they jolted over a bump or descended a hill, and her back was starting to ache from sitting in such an upright position for so long. She wondered how Thaddeus managed to endure so much travel. It was no wonder he complained of a pain in his knee at times.

They began to pass heavy wagons hauling gravel and lumber and throwing up dust, and here and there through the trees she could see signs of the railway construction.

"I didn't realize they were so far along," Thaddeus remarked at one point. "They'll be to Sully before you know it."

And then the work would be hidden again by the thickness of the woods and the hilliness of the land, making it difficult to see anything, and she would fall to studying the farms and little hamlets they passed, wondering to herself what it was like to live there.

Thaddeus was quite hungry by the time they pulled into the laneway that led to Leland Gordon's tidy white farmhouse just south of Sully. They had long since eaten the makeshift breakfast Martha had packed, and even the jug of water she had tucked by her feet was nearly empty.

As soon as they reached the yard, the porch door of the house was flung open and Mrs. Gordon hobbled out, smiling in welcome.

"Mr. Lewis! What a pleasant surprise!" she said, "and you brought your granddaughter with you! Come in, come in. Have you driven all the way from Cobourg today? You must be starving and dinner's nearly ready to put on the table. Would you join us?"

Thaddeus shot a wry glance at Martha. He had been right. The Gordons would insist on feeding them. Martha climbed down from the buggy and followed the old woman as she began walking back to the house. Thaddeus led his tired horse over to the water trough and met Leland coming out of the barn.

"Mr. Lewis! This is a pleasant surprise. What brings you out this way?"

Thaddeus quickly explained his mission, then appealed for Gordon's help. "It would be useful to me, Leland, if you could spare some time to come with us. At least the Howell girl knows who you are."

"I'm not sure how much help it would be," he said. "I can't get near her. Nor can anyone else. One of the English families, friends of the Howells, tried to fetch her, but they couldn't find her. They said she'd obviously been there, but she wouldn't answer their calls."

"She wouldn't come out, even for them?"

"No." Gordon was obviously uncomfortable with the topic, and he hesitated before he spoke again. "I'm not saying I know this for a fact, and I'm certainly not sure enough to tell anybody else about it, but I think George Howell is there, too."

When Thaddeus thought about this, he realized that it made perfect sense — Mrs. Howell's lack of concern about her daughter, Ashby's conviction that she was protecting someone with her silence, the Howell girl's sudden disappearances whenever anyone came near. The only thing that was surprising was that no one but Leland seemed to have figured it out.

"Wouldn't someone be watching the place, though? After all, Howell is wanted for murder."

Gordon shrugged. "No one much goes near the place at the best of times, and whenever they do, the dog causes a racket long before they get there. Howell would have plenty of time to get away, especially if he's got a bolt-hole somewhere."

Everyone was sure he had left the country anyway, Thaddeus realized. And there were only a handful of constables for the entire district. One of them might check in at the farm once in a while, but none of them would have time to sit there and wait for Howell to show himself.

"I'm only telling you this, Mr. Lewis, because I've been wrestling with my conscience," Gordon said. "Even if I report what I suspect, it won't bring the dead man back. I'm not sure what's going to happen to Mrs. Howell, but I can't do anything about it anyway, and turning her husband in won't make any difference to her defence — if both were to be found guilty, it would mean two of them would hang instead of just one. I don't like George Howell, but I don't want to be responsible for his death, either. And at the same time, I don't want to put you in unnecessary danger. I have no idea if Howell is armed or not, or what he would do if cornered. You see my dilemma."

Thaddeus did, indeed, and was beginning to have second thoughts about his decision to bring Martha along.

"I've told you this in confidence," Gordon went on. "I would prefer that it remain between us, but if your judgment is clearer on the matter than mine is, then you must do what you have to do. But more than anything, I would like your opinion."

God bless the Methodists, Thaddeus thought, forever willing to wrestle with their souls over questions of right and wrong. He smiled at the worried farmer who looked so earnestly for his advice. "My opinion is that the Sully meeting made a wise choice when they accepted you as a lay preacher. I agree that it's a thorny issue when the law is at odds with your principles, but you already know what the answer is, Leland. You must follow your conscience."

Gordon nodded and looked relieved. "I don't agree with an eye for an eye, no matter what the Bible says. So what are you going to do now?"

"I'm not sure," Thaddeus said. "Maybe I should go away and leave them alone. The lawyer wants to talk to the girl, but he assumed she was alone on the farm, and that her father was long gone. She's unlikely to tell anybody anything if he's still there."

"That's true enough. At any rate, you shouldn't do anything until you've had some dinner. We'd better go in. Mother will be wondering what we're talking about out here."

After Leland fetched a bucket of feed for the horse, Thaddeus followed him into the Gordon kitchen and sat at the table while Martha bustled around, helping to serve up the meal. She couldn't have done anything to recommend her more to someone like Mrs. Gordon. The old woman clucked and fussed and told Martha to sit, but looked pleased at the help all the same.

Thaddeus said grace, and then Mrs. Gordon turned to him. "Young Martha here tells me that you're going to the Howell farm. I'll pack up what's left of our meal when we're done. You can take it to Caroline."

"It was our intention to go when we set off," Thaddeus

said. "I'm not so sure now that we should do that. Leland seems to think that maybe we should leave her be."

Martha looked disappointed. He would be, too, he supposed, if the promise of a great adventure turned out to be nothing more than a long drive, followed by dinner and another long drive.

"If you're going by anyway, you should at least stop in and leave the food," Mrs. Gordon said. "No one seems able to get close to the girl, but you could just leave it in the kitchen for her."

"I suppose you're right," Thaddeus said, and Martha brightened up a little. There was certainly no harm in just stopping by, he reasoned. The girl would probably run off at their first approach, like she'd done before. He could have a look around, and if there was nothing to see, he and Martha could be on their way.

"How is poor Mrs. Howell?" the old woman asked. "The poor thing, stuck in a gaol cell. Couldn't your young barrister get her out?"

"It's complicated. Something to do with having to apply to a higher court. The trial will start in a few days, anyway, so she's already done most of her waiting."

"What are the chances of his winning the case?" Leland asked.

Thaddeus sighed. "It seems hopeless to me, but he remains optimistic. I have no way to judge whether his investigations will lead to a successful defence or not, but at least he's digging around. Or rather, I'm digging for him, I suppose."

"What does he want you to find out?" Mrs. Gordon said.

"Well, for one thing, where Jack Plews was on the day of the murder."

"Plews? I'm afraid you're out of luck there," Leland said. "He's left the district entirely. Gone off west somewhere, to live with his cousin, or so I heard."

"That family always was thick as thieves," Old Mrs. Gordon said. "The Plews and the Palmers and the Dafoes always look after each other."

Martha suddenly sat up very straight and cocked her head to one side. "Is the man who found the body from that same family? The Dafoes, I mean."

Thaddeus had made the connection as well, and looked approvingly at Martha.

"Oh yes," Mrs. Gordon said. "They're all intertwined. The Dafoes and the Plews and the Palmers. One sneezes and the others catch cold."

"The family certainly seems to have had more than their share of difficulty holding on to their land, haven't they?" Thaddeus ventured.

"They certainly have," Old Mrs. Gordon said. "Donald's father lost his farm, and so did his uncle. And then Jack, under very peculiar circumstances, if you ask me."

"Was it the same farm that was lost each time?"

"No, no, different ones, but all in Hamilton and Haldimand Townships. I misremember what the problem was with them. Donald's father, and his uncle, Lem Palmer, and there may have been another one as well. Like I said, they're all so mixed up together it's hard to keep them all straight. Lem's son married an aunt of Donald's, and I'm not sure, but I think another one married Jack Plew's mother. That would make them what? Cousins at the very least. You remember Jack's mother, don't you Leland? She had a lovely voice and used to sing at meeting."

Leland just shrugged and looked apologetically at his guests.

"You don't happen to know when, exactly, Plews went west?" Thaddeus asked.

Leland shook his head. "No. He stayed with his sister for a time after he sold the farm to Howell, I know, but I couldn't tell you when he left the district. I just remember hearing that he had, and I can't even tell you when I heard it. It was probably just something that was said at meeting. I could ask the sister the next time I see her if you think that would be helpful."

"I think it might," Thaddeus said, but he had no idea how. "Thank you."

As soon as they'd finished their meal, Martha offered to help with the dishes, but Old Mrs. Gordon shooed her out the door.

"You folks have a long drive home," she said. "You don't want to be held up any longer than you have to." She turned to Thaddeus, "I hope you realize what a fine girl your grand-daughter is, Mr. Lewis. You bring her back here any time."

"I do realize it," Thaddeus said with a smile. "That's why I asked her to keep my house for me. And we'll come back sometime when we're not in quite such a hurry."

They were just pulling out from the Gordons' lane when Martha caught sight of a lone horseman riding in their direction.

"Oh no. Is that who I think it is?" she asked.

Thaddeus squinted a little and then said, "I do believe that's James. He must be working his way back to Cobourg." He cast his mind over the appointment schedule they had set up. "Yes, that would be about right. He should be heading home about now."

Small must have recognized them, as well, for he kicked his horse into a trot and soon caught up with them. He beamed at Martha.

"I didn't expect to see you."

"It's such a lovely day, we thought we'd drive up this way and visit some old friends," Thaddeus said. He didn't make any further explanation and Martha understood that her grandfather was loath to disclose any details about what they were doing. Small looked understandably puzzled. Part of the reason he had been appointed an assistant on this circuit was so that Thaddeus wouldn't have to travel so much.

"That's a long way for a visit," he said.

"Well, yes, but I've got my granddaughter to drive me home, you see, if I get tired."

That seemed to satisfy Small, even though Martha thought the statement made no sense at all.

"You're planning to return to Cobourg tonight, then?" Small considered for a moment, then to Martha's profound annoyance said, "I can ride at least part of the way with you." He smiled at Martha again. "You'd like some company, wouldn't you?"

Thaddeus looked annoyed as well. The last thing they needed was to land in at the Howell farm with a stranger in tow. But short of telling Small what was going on, Martha couldn't think of any gracious way of telling him to make himself scarce.

Neither, apparently, could Thaddeus.

And then, to Martha's dismay, Small climbed down from his horse, tethered it to the wagon, and scrambled up to the seat of the rig. She was obliged to slide over and crowd into her grandfather so that no part of her would touch Small.

Thaddeus noticed her discomfort and shifted to his left as much as he could in order to give her more room, but it still wasn't far enough away for Martha. Small kept leaning over to her to make some comment about the weather or the road. She was aware of his Adam's apple bobbing unpleasantly every time he spoke.

After an uncomfortable mile or so, they reached the long, winding lane that led to the Howells' dilapidated farmhouse. Off in the distance they could hear a dog barking frantically, but as they drove down the lane, this sound seemed to move farther away until it was no longer audible.

"She already knows we're here," Thaddeus said quietly to Martha. "Keep your eyes open. I have something to tell you later."

"Where are we going now?" Small asked, then his eyes narrowed. "This is the Howell place, isn't it? Does this have something to do with the trial?"

"I'm just making a delivery," Thaddeus said. "If it will put you behind time, I don't mind if you ride on ahead."

"No, no, that's all right," Small said. "I'm not in that big a rush," and he moved another inch closer to Martha.

When they reached the house, she pushed past her grandfather and hopped out of the wagon. Thaddeus handed down Mrs. Gordon's basket of food and then they walked up to peer in through the kitchen window. Martha could see that there was evidence of recent occupation, but no one was there. Neither was there anyone in the barn.

"What about the privy?" Martha asked.

"I doubt she's there, but it would still be best if you checked," Thaddeus said. "I'd hate to startle her in the middle of something."

Martha giggled and was about to head for the precariously tilted outhouse when Small said, "Can you hear something? It seems to be coming from up over the hill somewhere."

They could — the occasional rumble of a cart, or the call of a man's voice, together with the intermittent sound of metal striking rock.

"It must be the railway crew," Small said. "I didn't realize they were cutting through so close to the road."

Thaddeus walked around the end of the barn, gesturing for Martha to come with him. Small made to follow.

"James, it would be most helpful if you stayed with the wagon," Thaddeus said. "The horse is rather skittish, and I don't want him to gallop off if he should become frightened by the noise."

Martha thought this statement was hilarious — the cart horse they had hired was one of the most phlegmatic creatures she had ever seen — but she was relieved that Thaddeus had manufactured a reason to leave Small behind. She hoped that Small would become bored, or realize that he was late for a meeting or something, and ride on ahead without them.

There was little to see behind the barn other than the steeply sloping hill.

"Should we climb it?" Martha asked.

She could see him hesitating, and then he said, "Leland Gordon thinks George Howell is still here on the farm. I have no idea whether he's dangerous or not. I don't like the idea of walking into an ambush."

"Oh." All of a sudden the adventure got very real for Martha and she briefly wondered if she shouldn't wait back at the cart after all. It would depend on what Thaddeus did next, she decided. If he climbed the hill, she would go with him. If he turned around and left, she would follow without a murmur.

"Can you see whether there's a path up the hill?"

She looked carefully, but there were too many trees and bushes to tell. "I can't see anything."

He studied it for a moment more. "I'd hate to come this far and give up. Let's see what we find up there. Keep low when we get near the top."

"Mind the thorns, though."

Thaddeus grabbed an old hay rake that was leaning against the barn and used it to push branches out of the way while Martha slid through the opening. Then she grabbed the other end of it and held the thorny bushes back for him. Once they were past these, the way was clearer. They zigged and zagged up the hill until they crested the rise and discovered that the hill descended again quite steeply. A little pond fringed by cattails was nestled at the bottom in a tiny vale. On the other side of this was a smaller hill, wooded on the side closest to them, but completely bare at the top.

"I didn't realize the track was passing this close," Thaddeus said. "Howell must have sold off the timber for ties and he'll collect a roadway allowance, as well, I expect. He certainly has been playing all the angles."

Three workmen with pickaxes appeared at the summit opposite them. One blond giant of a man swung his axe in a high arc over his head and brought it smashing down into the earth. A second time, a third, a fourth, and then with the fifth blow he lost his balance, his arms flailed wildly, and the point of the axe swung perilously close to his head. Suddenly he just disappeared down into the earth he had been digging. The air was filled with yells and angry barks.

"What just happened?" Martha asked.

"I'm not sure," Thaddeus said. "Stay here and keep your eyes open."

He slid down the hill and picked his way through the marshy edge of the pond, then scrambled up the steep climb to where the workman had disappeared. Just as he reached the top, Martha saw a thin girl with blond hair appear seemingly out of nowhere on the far side of the pond. She began to climb after Thaddeus.

Martha didn't give her grandfather's admonition to stay put a second thought. She slid down the side of the hill and ran through the bulrushes.

"Hey," she shouted at the girl. "Wait for me."

The girl turned but made no attempt to run away. Her dress was filthy and torn, her hair wild, and tears were running down her face.

"I've got to get Digger!" she said and began climbing again.

Martha thought she was referring to the workman who had fallen.

"It's all right," she shouted. "The others will get the man out. They'll get a rope and pull him out."

"Not the man. Digger."

Martha had no doubt that the girl in front of her was Caroline Howell. Who "Digger" was, she had no idea. But she certainly wasn't going to wait to find out. She scrambled up the hill in pursuit of the girl.

Thaddeus arrived at the top of the hill to find five workmen peering over the edge of a large hole. It must be a sinkhole, he figured, the inside of a hill eroded by water until just a crust covered the top. The workmen had been in the process of drawing soil and rock to buttress the line embankments — Thaddeus could see that a portion of the adjacent slope had been dug away already. He approached the hole cautiously and looked in.

He saw a mound of scree, the blond labourer backed up against the side of the hole, and an angry brown dog that barked ferociously at the man's feet.

"Hilfe! Hilfe! Zwerg! Der Teufel!"

The workman kicked at the dog with his heavy leather boot in an attempt to fend it off.

"Hilfe! Hilfe!"

"Does anyone have a rope?" Thaddeus asked.

"Joe's gone to bring his wagon up," one of the work crew answered. "He'll have a rope."

The others stared at him blankly.

It will be tricky, Thaddeus thought, to get close enough to the edge of the hole without further collapsing its crumbling sides. He turned as the wagon came lumbering up. It was one of the square three-wheeled construction carts, cumbersome and difficult to manoeuvre. The sorry beast that pulled it managed to reach the halfway point before it gave up and halted.

"Stop there," Thaddeus called.

"I don't think I can get any closer anyway," the man called back. It took him several minutes to turn the horse and wagon so that it was pointing back down the hill. Then he climbed up to where Thaddeus and the rest of the crew were standing.

"I've got a length of sisal," he said. "It's pretty heavy for the job, though."

"It's better than nothing."

The man nodded and returned to the wagon, where he lifted out a heavy coil of rope and tied it to the back of the wagon.

All the while the dog continued to bark and growl as the man yelled a steady stream of German interspersed with the occasional call of *"hilfe!"*

Thaddeus walked gingerly to the edge. The loose sandy soil shifted under his feet. He took a couple of steps back, then dropped to his knees and crawled over to the hole.

"We're throwing you a rope," he shouted at the man. "Tie it around yourself and we'll pull you up."

There was no answer but a continued guttural invective.

"Are you hurt?"

"Hilfe, hilfe! Zwerg! Der Teufel!"

"He don't have much English," said the worker who had spoken before. "You'll have to talk to him in his own lingo."

"Surely he'll be able to figure out what we're doing when we throw the rope down," Thaddeus said. "You don't have to speak English for that." He grabbed the coil from the wagoner and tossed it over the side. He was relieved to see that it reached all the way to the bottom. "Grab the rope and we'll pull you up," he repeated. "Tug on it when you're ready."

There was a renewed volley of frantic barking as the dog confronted this new menace. It lunged at the rope and grabbed it briefly, growling and shaking it from side to side.

Then it seemed to realize that it was in no peril from the inanimate object and renewed its standoff with the beleaguered German, planting itself firmly between the man and the rope.

"We need to do something about that damned dog," the wagoner said. "Hang on a minute."

He walked back to his wagon, then returned with an old battered-looking rifle. "I'll take care of the beast."

He was just aiming down the hole when there was a deafening shriek and a small body slammed into the man sideways. He lost his footing and fell heavily. The rifle discharged harmlessly into the air.

Caroline Howell had arrived at the top of the hill. She ran over to the edge of the hole and dropped to her knees. "Digger!" she called. "Don't worry, I'll get you."

Martha appeared a few moments later. She was panting heavily from the climb, which hadn't seemed to bother Caroline at all. "She's after her dog," Martha said to Thaddeus.

The animal had stopped growling and barking at the sound of its owner's voice.

"Can you get your dog away from the man in the pit?" Thaddeus asked.

Caroline leaned a little farther over the side. "Digger! Go sit," she said. "Go on! Over there!" She pointed at the side of the hole farthest from the German workman. The dog obediently went to where she was pointing and sat, its tail wagging furiously.

The German didn't wait for any help. As soon as the dog was out of the way, he grabbed the rope and pulled himself up hand over hand, showers of loose soil and gravel cascading over him as he climbed. When he reached the top, his workmates finally stirred themselves and grabbed his arms to pull him out. They stood him upright and helped brush him off, then they all wandered down the hill.

Joe the wagoner retrieved his rope and his gun, glared at Caroline, and followed them.

"But what about the dog? Thaddeus asked.

"It can stay there forever as far as I'm concerned."

Caroline looked at Thaddeus beseechingly. She was very like her mother in colouring, he thought, the same pale hair and high cheekbones, but unlike her mother, there was no sunniness in her face.

"Will you help me?" she asked.

Thaddeus looked over the edge of the pit again. The dog began to yelp and jump up and down, then it leaped up onto the heap of rubble that had fallen and clawed frantically at the side of the hole in an attempt to climb up. All this did was bring down more dirt. After a few minutes it seemed to realize that this was futile. It stopped digging and began running around the pit, looking for another way out. Eventually, it started pawing at the far wall, then dug furiously, dirt flying out behind it.

More scree fell, and now Thaddeus could see a piece of wood — a timber that had been knocked over to lean at an angle.

"Is there a cave or something on the other side of that pile of dirt?" he asked.

Caroline nodded. "We were there when the roof fell down. Digger was on the wrong side."

"I don't see how we're going to get him out from here. Do you think we might be able to dig through from the other end?"

"Maybe."

"Are there timbers along the walls and the roof? Pieces of wood that hold it up?"

"Yes."

Thaddeus wasn't sure he liked the idea of going into a cave that had already collapsed once, but then, he decided, it hadn't been an inherent fault in the construction that had caused the roof to fall in, but rather the railroad crew's excavations. In any event, he figured he stood little chance of gaining Caroline Howell's trust unless he could somehow rescue her dog. Besides, he disliked the idea of just leaving the animal there to expire from thirst. Or to be shot by one of the rail crew who might yet return if it grew too noisy.

"We need to go back to your house and find shovels," he said. "If there's just loose sand and gravel we can probably dig through it."

"I'm not leaving Digger," Caroline said, a stubborn set to her face. "What if the man with the gun comes back?"

The dog seemed to be preoccupied with his frantic digging and was unlikely to draw any more attention, but Thaddeus could understand the girl's concern.

"Martha can stay here. If the man comes back she can tell him to go away. Would that be all right?"

Caroline considered this for a moment, then nodded. Martha knelt down a few feet from the hole so she could keep an eye on the dog.

"If you run into trouble of any kind, give a shout," he said to her. "I'm pretty sure we can hear you from the other side."

"Don't worry. They won't get past me."

James Small jumped up in alarm when Thaddeus came down the hill with an unfamiliar girl in tow.

"Where's Martha?" he asked anxiously.

"She's fine, but there's no time to explain," Thaddeus said. "Right now we need to do some digging."

Caroline found two shovels and another hay rake in the barn, then led the two men over the hill and past the pond. Twenty feet from the crest of the second hill, she pushed through a stand of thick bushes that screened a small hole at the base of a massive black oak. It would be impossible to find, Thaddeus realized, unless you knew exactly where it was. He had to get down on all fours to squeeze through the opening.

He didn't know what he had been expecting — a cavern, maybe, carved out of rock, or a series of honeycombed recesses. But it was not a large hill, and the substrate was loose and sandy, partly held in place by the roots of the tree, and partly shored up with sawn lumber. It was a small space, more like a burrow than a cave, the only light coming from the small opening at its entrance. Thaddeus could see, though, that the supports had collapsed at one end. It was going to be tricky to dig it out without bringing more of it down.

He turned to Caroline. "Can you find a couple of buckets?"

She nodded, and while she was getting them, Thaddeus and Small began tentatively to poke at the mound of soil in front of them. When Caroline returned, they started filling the buckets with dirt.

"Take them outside and dump them," Thaddeus said.

She hesitated. "But Papa said not to leave any sign."

"Sign of what?"

"Any sign that would tell somebody where the door is."

So Leland Gordon was right. Howell had been here all along. Elegant, bewhiskered, silk-hatted George Howell had become a cornered animal cowering in a sandpit.

"I'm afraid we'll have to dump it outside," Thaddeus said to the girl. "There's nowhere else to put the dirt. The cave is pretty much discovered anyway, now that the railway men have broken through the top."

She blinked at him for a few moments, then without a word picked up a filled bucket and hauled it through the opening.

"Papa?" Small said, "Does she mean George Howell?"

"I guess so." Thaddeus wasn't sure what to do about Small. He could scarcely ask his assistant to hide the fact that a wanted man was lurking nearby. He wasn't, in fact, sure what he was going to do himself. As Leland Gordon had pointed out, Howell's apprehension would in no way help his wife. But failing to report Howell's presence could open them all to charges of aiding and abetting. Get the dog out first, he decided. Worry about the rest of it later.

As it turned out, Thaddeus was glad he had James with him. The young man worked steadily, and before long they had reached the section where the timbers had fallen. One of them swung loose at the bottom, its top still embedded in the hill.

"Soon, now. But we'll have to be careful. In fact, we might want to shore this up a bit before we go any farther."

No sooner had Thaddeus spoken when the dog wriggled through the remaining scree to its freedom. When it porpoised through the last inches, its back feet pushed against the bottom of the loose support, knocking it to one side. A pile of soil and gravel and lumber cascaded down on top of James Small.

Thaddeus wielded his shovel frantically to clear the mess of debris away from Small's head, so that at least he wouldn't suffocate before they figured out how to extract him. To his surprise, Caroline grabbed the other shovel and she, too, began to dig, although her efforts had little effect. After a few moments, Thaddeus realized that shovelling was futile — the sand and fine gravel quickly spilled back into whatever hole they managed to make.

"Put your shovel down," he ordered the girl. "We're going to have to pull."

"Is everything all right?" Martha could hear them from her perch at the edge of the hole.

"No. Get over here." And then he said to Caroline, "You take one leg and I'll take the other and then we need to pull for all we're worth."

He wasn't at all certain that their combined strength would be enough, but to his surprise they shifted the inert body a few inches with the first pull.

"Again!"

This time Small moved a foot or so. Thaddeus leaped forward and used his arms as a scoop to remove the debris around his assistant's head. To his surprise, a wad of paper was plastered over Small's face, largely shielding his mouth and nose from the sandy soil. Thaddeus swept it aside. Small began to cough and sputter, inhaling great shuddering gasps of air in between spasms, but the cave was filled with a fine dust that stung the eyes and filled the lungs. Thaddeus knew he needed to get the young man into the fresh air as quickly as possible.

Martha scrambled into the cave and together they scooped more soil away, until finally, with one last heave, they were able to pull Small entirely free. They dragged him over to the fresher air at the opening. Although he had by some miracle been saved from inhaling much sediment, he had a cut on the back of his head that was bleeding profusely. Thaddeus scrambled to retrieve the papers he had thrown to one side and jammed them against the wound.

"Put your hand here," he said to Martha. "Keep pressing down, as hard as you can. We need to get the bleeding stopped."

Suddenly Caroline crawled past them to paw through the fallen rubble. She scooped out several other bundles of paper, then she poked around until she uncovered a leather satchel. She pushed the papers inside it, climbed past them again, and disappeared.

Thaddeus pulled Small to a sitting position, then helped him manoeuvre through the small opening. Finally free of the cloying dust, his breathing gradually became easier.

"I thought we'd lost you there for a minute, James," Thaddeus said.

Small looked around, blinking. "Lost? I'm not lost. I just got tangled in the quilt, that's all."

"What do you mean?"

"I slept in. Couldn't get out of bed. I was too rolled up in the bedclothes."

"Oh my," Martha said. "What's wrong with him?"

Thaddeus knelt down beside him. "Do you know where you are, James?"

"In my house, of course. In Cobourg."

"Look around you." Thaddeus spoke in a gentle voice.

Small did as he was told, and then a puzzled expression crossed his face.

"Where am I? This isn't Cobourg. I have to get home. I need to milk the cow."

This last statement was not as odd as it sounded. The Howells' cow had started a mournful low that was audible from where they sat.

"Listen to me, James," Thaddeus said. "You were buried in a cave-in. You were struck on the head, and that's why you don't know where you are."

"What cave? How did I get here?" Small was still bewildered. "Why does my head hurt?"

"You got a bump, I'm afraid. Martha is trying to stop the bleeding."

His face dissolved into a sappy grin. "Ah, Martha," he said. "Is Martha looking after me? That's wonderful."

"We need to get him to a doctor," Thaddeus said. "Perhaps the best thing to do is to take him back to the

Gordons." Then he turned to Small. "Do you think you can walk, James?"

Small nodded, and together Thaddeus and Martha hauled him to his feet. He could walk only a few paces before he had to stop for a moment to rest, but the downward slope helped and they made good progress until they reached the bottom of the hill, where he sank to the ground again.

"We'll rest for a bit, James," Thaddeus said, "then we'll try the climb."

He seemed to gain a little strength after that, and although the going was slow, Thaddeus and Martha managed to push and pull him up to the top of the hill overlooking the Howells' barn. After another rest, Small insisted that he could manage the descent without help. Thaddeus followed close behind, one hand clutching his coattails, just in case he fell.

Digger barked at them hysterically the whole time they were climbing down, adding his protests to the pleadings of the uncomfortable cow.

"Not very grateful at being rescued, is he?" Martha remarked.

Caroline came out of the house and called for the dog, which obediently ran back to her.

It was only then that Thaddeus realized that James's horse was missing. He pointed this out to Martha.

"Major Howell?" she asked. "If he got clear of the cave-in, he may have come back here."

"It's the most likely explanation." Thaddeus had no doubt that Caroline had been genuinely concerned about her dog, but its predicament had made a convenient diversion all the same. And if Howell had taken the horse, he could be a long way away by now. Thaddeus could only hope that his assistant wouldn't remember that he'd had a horse in the first place.

"Let's get James over to the cart, then see if we can borrow a blanket or something from the house," Thaddeus said to Martha when they reached the Howells' dooryard. "He can lie in the back."

"I'm fine," Small protested. "Really." And in fact, he was able to climb up into the back of the rig by himself, a relief for Thaddeus, who hadn't been sure how they were going to manage it otherwise.

Martha went to the house and knocked on the door. "Caroline," she called.

Silence.

"I need to talk to you."

"Go away."

"Do you have a blanket we can use? Mr. Small is hurt and he needs to lie down in the wagon."

There was no answer, but a few moments later the door opened and Caroline threw two old quilts onto the stoop. Martha took them back to the cart and helped Thaddeus arrange a cushion for Small's head with one of them. She covered him with the other. Then Thaddeus pulled her aside.

"We need to take the girl with us. Maybe it would be better if you talked to her."

"I'll try," Martha said, "but I don't know if I can get her to come."

She walked up to the door again, while Thaddeus waited at the cart. "Caroline?"

There was no answer.

"Can you come out and talk to me?"

"No. Papa said don't talk to anybody."

"Your Papa's gone now. He took our horse and rode away."

"He'll come back."

"No, Caroline, he won't. Too many people know he was here. He'll ride a long way away and he won't dare come back.

You don't really want to be here all by yourself, do you?" There was no reply to this. "I'd be scared to be here all alone," Martha went on. "You never know who might turn up."

"The man's dead. He won't come back."

"Which man? The man who fell in the hole?"

"No. The other man."

"Do you mean the man who's hurt? That's a friend of my grandfather's. My grandfather's been trying to help your mother. She's in Cobourg. You could go see her. You could ask her what you should do."

"Papa told me what to do."

"Yes, but things are different now. Your Papa's gone and he's not coming back."

Suddenly the dog burst through the door. He made a beeline for Martha, barking and snapping. She turned her body away to try to deflect the attack.

"Digger, sit!" Thaddeus commanded, in a voice that was as stern as he could muster.

To his surprise, the dog aborted its attack. It obediently sat, but continued a low growl.

Thaddeus walked over to Martha, ignoring the dog. "Do you feel like you're getting anywhere?" he asked.

"Not really." He could see that she was shaking a little. Thaddeus knew he needed to resolve the situation one way or the other in short order. He was worried about Small's condition, and he was afraid that the dog might yet bite one of them. It was also getting late, and he didn't like the notion of trying to navigate the hilly road to Cobourg in the dark. It was frustrating to have found the girl and then be stymied by something so insubstantial as a cabin door and a scrappy dog. He didn't want to leave her behind, but he would if he had to.

"Caroline!" he called suddenly in a harsh voice. "I don't know what you have in that satchel, but you can't keep it safe all by yourself. Open the door now!" It was much the same voice he had used with the dog. It had much the same effect. The door opened a crack.

"Do you know who I am?" Thaddeus asked.

"You're the preacher who talked the most and won," she said.

It was an unflattering summation of his performance at The Great Debate, but at least she remembered him. "That's right," he said. "Your mother sent me to get you. Come on."

He turned and walked back to the buggy, as if there were no question that Caroline would do exactly as she was told. He motioned Martha to follow. He climbed up and took the reins, but before Martha could claim her seat, Caroline emerged from the cabin, clutching the leather satchel she had rescued.

"Wait," she said. Then she walked over to them, a scowl on her face. "What about Digger?"

"He can come, too."

She whistled, and the dog leaped into the back of the cart, with only a growl or two directed at the recumbent James Small.

"Digger, go sit," Thaddeus said. The dog subsided and Caroline climbed in beside him.

"How do you do that?" Martha asked.

"It's just a matter of using the right tone of voice," Thaddeus said as he flicked the reins. "Maybe you should practise on James."

VII

Small refused to be taken into Sully and insisted that he was recovered enough to ride all the way to Cobourg. Thaddeus wasn't so sure, since his assistant hadn't noticed yet that his horse was missing, but then he decided that Small was a grown man and could make his own choices. Besides, returning to Cobourg was infinitely more convenient for everyone else. And having managed to get Caroline Howell into the cart, Thaddeus was determined not to let her out of it until Ashby had a chance to talk to her. Unfortunately, they were now badly overloaded, and Thaddeus could only hope that the horse was up to the challenge of pulling them such a distance.

The dog growled and barked as they reached the end of the laneway, but fell silent again when they were hailed by the same old man Thaddeus had encountered on his first visit to the Howell farm.

"Why, it's the preacher!" the old man said. "You travel this road nearly as much as I do."

"You go by often?" Thaddeus asked.

"Near every day."

"I wonder if you could do something for me? There's a poor old bossy at the Howells' that's been left on its own. Could you or one of the neighbours see to her? I'd do it myself, but I've got an injured man to get home."

He turned to gesture at James Small, and realized that Caroline was nowhere to be seen. She couldn't have jumped out, he decided, or the dog would have gone with her.

"I'd be happy to look after it," the old man said, his eyes flicking over the dog. "There's no one at the farm? To look after the livestock, I mean?"

"There's not much livestock — only the cow and a few chickens," Thaddeus said. "I don't know whether there's anybody there or not. I just know that the cow needs to be milked and I didn't have time to do it."

The man nodded. "Don't worry, I'll see to it."

"Thank you. What's your name, sir, in case we meet again?"

The man hesitated for a moment before he replied. "Dafoe. Albert Dafoe."

Palmers and Plews and Dafoes. That family always was thick as thieves, according to Patience Gordon. Someone had been watching the Howell farm after all.

Thaddeus nodded at the man and drove on.

As soon as they left him behind, Martha said, "You can come out now, Caroline."

Thaddeus glanced back to see the girl emerge from under the seat of the buggy. She had crawled in behind Small and pulled the satchel after her, dragging one of the quilts over her so she couldn't be seen. She offered no explanation, just plunked the satchel down beside the dog and sat on it again.

It was a long, slow drive home. Small, in spite of his bravado, moaned loudly whenever the wheels went over a nasty rut in the road, which was often. On the steeper slopes, everyone but Small had to climb out of the cart and walk while Thaddeus led the horse to the top. Once or twice Martha ventured a remark in Caroline's general direction, but there was never a response other than a nod of the head, and after a while she gave up. That was fine with Thaddeus. He didn't want to discuss what had happened when he didn't know how closely Small was listening.

The sun had already set when they turned into the manse laneway. Martha jumped down and ran next door to the Smalls to get some help in getting James to his own house. She returned with his mother and two of his brothers, the boys lifting James bodily out of the cart while his mother clucked and fussed around him. Caroline had still not moved from her place on the satchel.

Martha held out her hand. "Are you hungry? I am. Let's go find something to eat."

Caroline ignored the outstretched hand, but she stood up and grabbed the satchel, whistled for Digger, then climbed down to follow Martha into the kitchen. Thaddeus was hungry, too, but his meal would have to wait. He had still to return the horse and cart to the stable, and he needed to find Ashby to bring him up to date on the events of the day. He took the tired horse back to the livery, then walked to the Globe Hotel. The smell of spirits and strong tobacco struck him as soon as he walked in. Every head turned in his direction and he was suddenly aware of his rumpled coat and the mud on his boots.

He found Ashby settled in a comfortable chair, with a glass of brandy in one hand and a cigar in the other, chatting with two similarly supplied gentlemen. Ashby, ever polite, rose as soon as he saw Thaddeus and gestured toward the chair.

"Mr. Lewis! What a pleasure. Do sit down."

"Thank you, no. It's been an interesting day."

"Our little pigeon has flown into the net?"

"Yes," Thaddeus said, "but she could fly right out again at a moment's notice. You should come first thing in the morning."

"I can come right now if you like."

"No. It's been a long day. She's tired and hungry. A good night's sleep will do her a world of good. Tomorrow will be better. I promised you'd take her to see her mother."

Ashby's eyes slid sideways to the two men he had been sitting with. He downed his drink and stubbed out his cigar. "Gentlemen." He nodded at them. "Come, Mr. Lewis, I'll walk you to the door."

They stepped out into the night. As quickly as he could, Thaddeus related what had happened at the Howell farm.

"I'm sure George Howell was there," he said at the end of it.

"I see. And are you planning to do anything with that information?"

"I don't think so. I didn't see him myself. I only heard that he might be there. There was some evidence that he might have been, but I have no idea where he is now, so what good would it do?"

Ashby nodded. "Did you talk to the girl?"

"No. I figured that was better left to you. Besides, I was a little busy."

"Fair enough," Ashby said. "I think it wise if we keep her whereabouts as private as possible for the moment, don't you?"

"I don't intend to tell anyone," Thaddeus said, "but several people know — my assistant and his family, for example." He also wasn't sure whether or not the old man had seen Caroline before she scooted under the seat.

"Ah, yes, the unfortunate Mr. Small."

"Mind you, he may not remember it. He's been a little odd since he got hit on the head. Even so, I don't see how we can keep it secret for long."

"All I need is time to question her before it occurs to the constable that she might have something to say."

"I expect we can manage to keep her hidden until tomorrow morning," Thaddeus said. "Oh ... and when you come into the house, keep an eye out for the dog. He's a bit aggressive, but Caroline wouldn't have come without him."

As predicted, Ashby's knock the next morning set off a frantic round of barking from Digger. Martha ordered the dog to go and sit, and she was surprised when he obeyed her. He seemed to have accepted that she and Thaddeus posed no danger to Caroline, but he continued to growl and mutter at anyone else he saw.

"She's in the kitchen," Martha said when she answered the door. "It might be friendlier if you talked to her there. Follow me."

Caroline was just finishing her second helping of toast. She'd already devoured a bowl of porridge and several glasses of milk. She seemed half-starved, an impression that wasn't helped by the fact that she had nearly grown out of the dress she wore. Her wrists stuck out far past the cuffs, and the skirt was too short, even for a twelve year old. The dress was filthy, as well, and torn from the cave-in. *I'll have to find her something else as soon as I can,* Martha thought. *She looks like a ragamuffin.*

Ashby parked himself across the table from the girl, but pointedly refrained from looking at her. "Is there tea?" he asked.

"Of course. Would you like breakfast as well?" Martha asked.

"Couldn't eat another morsel," he replied. "The Globe's food isn't a patch on yours, but they are generous with the servings." He took a long time over his mug, slowly stirring in sugar and dribbling in milk. He seemed tired, Martha thought, his usual polish worn a little thin. The harsh morning light that streamed through the windows emphasized the dark shadows under his eyes.

Caroline regarded him warily as she chewed the last crusts of her toast.

Finally, Ashby turned to her and spoke. "Do you know where your mother is, Caroline?"

"In gaol."

"Do you know why?"

Her face was stubborn. "Papa said not to talk to anybody about that."

"I understand that," Ashby said. "Did Mr. Lewis tell you why I'm here?"

"To help Mama."

Having evidently decided that Ashby was no threat at present, Digger flopped down in the corner by the stove. He stared at them all for a moment, and then, just slightly, wagged his tail before he laid his head on his paws and closed his eyes.

"That's a nice dog you've got there," Ashby remarked.

"He looks after me."

"And you look after him, too. Mr. Lewis told me you rescued him yesterday."

She nodded. "Mr. Lewis helped. And the other man, too. And Martha."

"We're all here to help, Caroline. Why don't you tell me what happened and I'll figure out what I can do to sort it out."

"Papa said not to."

"Do you know what a barrister is?"

She shook her head.

"That's what I am. I'm somebody who tries to help people in trouble. But do you know what's really great about being a barrister? When people tell me things, I don't have to tell anyone else. Barristers are really good at keeping secrets."

Caroline's eyes slid over to Martha and Thaddeus.

"And nobody else has to hear, either."

"Even if somebody did something wrong?"

"Especially if somebody did something wrong. I can't figure out how to help until I know what happened."

"Papa said don't talk to anybody."

Ashby gave up, rather soon in Martha's opinion. "You're a good girl, Caroline, to do what your Papa said. Let's go see what your Mama says, all right? Are you finished with your breakfast?"

She nodded, but looked at Thaddeus, a question in her eyes.

"Would you like me to go with you and Mr. Ashby?" he asked. "I can wait outside while you see your mother, and then I can bring you back here to Martha. Would that be all right?"

She nodded again and slid off the chair to retrieve the shoes she had left at the back door.

Martha wasn't at all pleased at the notion of being left alone with the dog, but Digger seemed reasonably content to sit by the stove after Caroline had commanded him to stay. His eyes followed Martha as she cleared the breakfast dishes and carried them to the sink. There was a burnt bit of toast on one of the plates, and she was about to dispose of it when she realized that Digger had probably not been fed since the previous day. Most dogs lived on scraps, but if Caroline's half-starved appearance was anything to go by, it was unlikely that there had been many scraps in the Howell household. She rummaged in the pantry, looking for something that she could feed the dog that wouldn't be missed by the household. There wasn't much, but she tore a slice of bread into bits and doused it with milk. It was enough to satisfy the dog's hunger for now, she figured, but surely she could find something that would make it a little more palatable. She did have a small barrel of oysters she'd bought at a good price. She could spoon up a few of them for Digger, she decided, along with a few spoonfuls of the oily liquid they sat in.

She set the dish down in front of the dog. He wagged his tail and looked up at her. "It's all right boy, go ahead, eat."

He devoured it all before she had time to fill a bowl of water for him. He drank deeply, sighed, then turned around four or five times before he settled himself once again by the stove.

Martha washed the dishes, then sponged down the dress she'd worn the day before. It was in a sorry state, covered in dust, wrinkled, and torn along the hem. She'd let it dry, then mend and iron it. She really should sprinkle it with salt and set it to soak, but she still had to look at the passenger lists Ashby wanted her to go through. The trial would begin in a couple of days, and he would need the information as soon as Martha could provide it. She found some paper and a pen and spread the ledgers out on the dining room table, where she would have plenty of room.

The writing in them varied from spidery copperplate to an almost illegible scrawl, long columns marching down the pages. Martha found that she could scan the lists more quickly if she used her finger to scroll down them. She found George Howell's name on the third page of the first ledger she looked at. As she continued to work, she realized that there were several other names that recurred with regularity. Ashby hadn't instructed her to do so, but she began making a note of these names as well as their destinations, just in case the information should prove useful.

She set the work aside when the clock neared eleven. Her eyes were tired and it was time to start cooking their noonday dinner. When she went into the kitchen, Digger jumped up and scratched at the back door, but she didn't dare let him out.

Ten minutes later, Thaddeus and Caroline came in. Digger jumped and spun with joy at Caroline's return, his tail wagging furiously.

"Maybe you should take him out to the backyard," Martha said to her. "He's been inside all morning. I'll call you when dinner's ready."

She nodded and led the dog outside.

"I'd like to head off right after I eat," Thaddeus said. "I need to cover as many meetings as I can before the trial starts. James couldn't have picked a worse time to get himself injured."

"What will you do if he's not able to take over when the trial starts?" she asked.

"The lay ministers will have to fill in. They've done it before, they can do it again. Will you be all right here with Caroline if I don't come back tonight?"

"Yes, of course. She's not much company, but that means she's not much trouble either. And she can look after the dog."

"I'll find a piece of rope she can use as a leash. Fortunately he seems to obey her, but I don't want her chasing all over town if he should happen to get loose."

"How did it go at the gaol?"

Thaddeus shrugged. "Ashby said that Mrs. Howell didn't seem very pleased that her daughter was in Cobourg. She's expressly forbidden him to put her on the stand."

"Did she say why?"

"No, and it's just as well, since he'd already gone in to see her when I remembered that the gaoler's name is Palmer."

"And the old man on the road was a Dafoe. *Palmers and Plews and Dafoes.*"

"All tangled up. Just like Mrs. Gordon said."

"Do you think the gaoler's been listening in on Mrs. Howell's conversations?"

"He wouldn't have to listen very hard. He can hear every word that's said."

As soon as Thaddeus set off, Martha returned to the ledgers. George Howell was listed a total of fourteen times over the previous three years, and on twelve of those occasions he had taken passage to Rochester, New York. He had travelled once to Toronto, and on one occasion the previous May had gone to Burlington, a fact that Martha found intriguing. The dead man had come from Burlington.

D'Arcy Boulton, the Mayor, and several local merchants were listed often, as well — but she supposed that wasn't unusual. These men had many business interests. It wouldn't be odd for them to travel in the course of pursuing them, and the destination was most frequently Toronto, a logical place to go to if one had government business to attend to.

Two of the witnesses who had been on the Rice Lake steamer on the day of the murder had also taken passage on occasion, but to various ports of call and there was no indication of a suspicious number of trips. Of all of the names Martha found, George Howell was the most frequent traveller and the only one who journeyed to a single destination with such regularity.

She wrote a brief summary of what she had found and laid it on top of her notes. She'd give it all to Ashby when he next came around.

Caroline spent most of the afternoon in the garden throwing sticks for Digger to fetch. He did this enthusiastically, untiringly, and, to Martha's relief, without too much barking. After supper the girl went off to bed early, handing over her tattered dress when Martha demanded it.

Martha could tell it had once been a lovely dress; a soft brown check, the material of good quality, fashionably cut and beautifully sewn. But now she decided that no amount of scrubbing was going to remove the grimy marks that stained it, and when she turned it inside out, she realized that it had already been altered many times before — the seam allowances let out as far as they could go, the darts nearly nonexistent, and the hem let down so far that only a small rolled piece of cloth remained to bind it.

She would have to sacrifice the dress she had on at the moment, her third-best, so that Caroline would have something decent to wear. But that would leave Martha with only two — her everyday and her Sunday-best. Mind you, her everyday had taken a beating the day before. It really was suitable now for nothing more than grubbing in the garden, but that meant that she would have to wear her Sunday-best for everyday, and she'd have nothing for special occasions. And then she remembered the wedding money — the coins Thaddeus had given her as her due. There had been two more weddings in the meantime and the little cache had grown while she dithered about what to spend it on. There should be plenty enough for a bolt of cloth. She would make herself a new Sunday-best and relegate her everyday dress to scrubbing and gardening.

She changed, then inspected the dress she had been wearing. She would need to pin it on Caroline to see how much it needed to be taken in, of course, but in the meantime she could start ripping out the hem. Shortening was always more successful than lengthening. When a hem was let out, you had to rub vinegar on the old hemline to disguise the whitened line of the fold.

This constant taking in and letting out was a nuisance, she thought, and yet they all did it so many times. Dresses cut down for someone younger, only to be let out again as they grew.

Suddenly she stopped clipping the threads that held the hem.

Dresses cut down. Thaddeus and everyone else that day had seen someone in a blue dress. Not a single one of them had seen the wearer's face. All they mentioned was the dress.

"Oh my goodness …" She said it out loud to the empty room.

Thaddeus had remarked on his surprise at how shabby the farm was, given the prosperous face the Howells liked to present to the world. Caroline's dress had once been first quality, but now it was old, torn, and too small. It had been altered once, twice, three times, as often as possible, until it was worn out and beyond use.

It must have been Mrs. Howell's to begin with. Appearances were everything to the Howells, so she didn't stint on her wardrobe, but she stretched her money as far as she could by handing her dresses down to Caroline as the girl grew. She must have done the same with the blue dress. And when it was seized as evidence by the constable, Caroline had suddenly been left with nothing to wear but a dress that she'd already grown out of.

It was the sort of detail that would never occur to a man.

If she was right about this, Ashby needed a dressmaker who could tell the court that the blue dress had been cut down to fit someone smaller than Ellen Howell.

Thaddeus wasn't planning to return to Cobourg until the following evening. If Martha waited until then to tell him what she'd discovered, Ashby might not have time to find a willing dressmaker before the trial began the following day. Martha had no idea how fast or in what order evidence might be presented, but she knew it would be better if she could find Ashby at once and tell him herself.

She went upstairs and peeked into Caroline's room. The girl was fast asleep, Digger curled up at her feet. The dog growled a little when he saw Martha, but not loudly, and settled down again when Martha backed out of the room.

She grabbed her cloak and went next door. Mrs. Small answered her knock.

"I'm sorry to bother you," Martha said, "but I need to run an errand in town. I wonder if one of you could sit in the kitchen while I'm gone. Caroline is fast asleep, but should she wake up, I don't want her to find an empty house. I'll only be a few minutes."

"Well, of course, dear," Mrs. Small said. "I'll go right over."

It didn't occur to Martha to have any qualms about marching into the Globe Hotel and asking for Ashby. She had grown up in a hotel, after all. However, her confidence wavered when she walked in the front door. She had expected that it would be much like the Temperance, the door opening to a small front hall with the register sitting on a table. She could ask for Ashby and wait by the door until someone fetched him. She hadn't expected anything quite so grand. She was disconcerted when the heads of so many bewhiskered men swivelled to look her over. She took a deep breath and started walking toward the carved wooden counter at one side of the room. She didn't take many steps before a man intercepted her.

"May I help you?" he asked. Whether he was the owner of the hotel or a just a clerk, Martha had no way of knowing, but it was clear that she would be allowed no farther until she explained her presence.

"I need to speak to Mr. Townsend Ashby," she said. "I'm sorry to bother him at such a late hour, but it's very important."

"I'm afraid Mr. Ashby is not currently at the hotel. Would you care to leave a message for him?"

This was a development that Martha had not foreseen. She hesitated for a moment, wondering if she should scribble down the bare facts and ask this man to pass on the note. But then she decided against it. Hotels had too many listening ears and prying eyes, and she didn't dare risk the information being passed to the wrong party.

"Do you know when Mr. Ashby intends to return?" she asked. She couldn't afford to be away from home for long, but if he was expected shortly, she supposed she could wait for him.

"I'm afraid I have no information as to Mr. Ashby's intentions," the man said, a coolness in his voice. "And even if I did, I would not be at liberty to tell you."

She should have waited until the next day. After all, what was Ashby going to do with the information so late in the evening? In her excitement at what she had discovered, she hadn't stopped to consider that he might not even be there. Annoyed with herself, and more to the point, with Ashby, she thanked the clerk and walked back out into the night. She was followed by an older man with a very bushy beard.

"You might try Musgrove's," he said as he walked past.

"Where?"

The man stopped and looked her up and down in a way that made her extremely uncomfortable. "Musgrove's Inn. Down the street. I could go there with you if you like." And then he winked at her.

She fixed him with what she hoped was her best look of disdain. "You can go to the devil if you like."

He held up his hands in protest. "All right, all right. Just trying to be friendly." And then he walked on.

She hesitated. She knew where Musgrove's was. She had walked past it on the way to the butcher's. It was a tavern that seemed to cater to the rowdier elements in the town. What on earth was Ashby doing there?

Her question was answered a half-block down the street. Two figures came toward her, weaving from side to side, laughing together. When they drew closer, she realized it was Towns Ashby. And a woman.

He halted when he saw her. "Martha!" he said. "Lovely to see you. Is your grandfather with you?" He looked behind her, as if Thaddeus might be hiding there.

"No, he isn't. I need to speak with you. Urgently."

"Aren't you going to introduce me, Towns?" the woman giggled. Her hat had fallen forward over her face, and now she reached up to adjust it. As she did so, her cloak fell open, releasing a waft of scent and revealing the low neckline of her dress.

"No," Ashby said to her. "You shouldn't be here," he said to Martha. He seemed to find the fact of her presence somehow astounding.

"I don't want to be here," Martha replied. "But I need to speak to you. Privately."

"My goodness, that sounds important."

"It is."

He took a deep breath. "Oh, very well. Be a good girl, Lizzie, and leave me alone for a moment, will you? I'll catch up with you later." And he patted her crinolined backside to send her on her way.

Martha was mortified. She could smell the liquor on Ashby, and the cigar smoke, along with a trace of the woman's perfume. Ashby's cravat was half untied, his eyes sleepy-looking and unfocused. She took a step back, not sure that she should deliver her message after all. Would he even remember it later?

But then he seemed to gather himself together.

"What have you found out?" he said. "It must be important if you've gone to all this trouble to find me."

Briefly, and with a great deal of hesitation, Martha presented her theory.

Ashby listened through to the end of her speech without saying a word, and when he did speak, it was in a low voice. "Of course. That's why Mrs. Howell is so unhappy that Caroline's here in Cobourg."

"Yes, she's been protecting her daughter all along."

His face split into a grin. "Martha, you are brilliant! I could kiss you!"

"You'd better not try," she said. "You, sir, are drunk. Good evening." And with as much dignity as she could muster, she turned to march home, only to find herself face to face with a very angry James Small.

VIII

Thaddeus was weary to the bone. He had been tired enough after the long drive to the Howell farm and the even longer ride home again, not to mention everything that had happened in between, and now James Small's injury had upset all of his plans. The doctor assured the Smalls that James should recover without incident, but suggested that it would be a good idea for the young preacher to rest as much as possible for a few days.

Small had agreed to take all of the meetings during the week of the trial, but now it appeared that this would not be possible, and Thaddeus was scrambling to figure out how to cover them. On the day he was injured, Small had just come from the eastern part of the circuit. Thaddeus judged that the meetings there could easily wait a few days for a minister. But the congregations to the west had been neglected in the previous week. He would take the meetings at Cold Springs and Gores Landing, he decided, then work his way south to the lakeside village of Port Granby for the Sunday morning service, with afternoon stops in Port Britain and Wesleyville.

That should put him back in Cobourg in time to consult with Ashby before the trial began the next day. Even after it got underway, he might be able to cover Baltimore and Precious Corners, as well as the two churches in town. Everyone else would just have to wait.

His mental state matched his fatigue. He didn't want to be delivering sermons and leading prayers just then. He wanted to be sitting in Ellen Howell's gaol cell reading *Mansfield Park*. Or sitting at his dining room table with Martha and Ashby discussing evidence. Or, at the very least, slouched in one of the overstuffed chairs in his parlour, dreaming of bedtime.

When he arrived at the meeting in Port Britain he looked for the old man who had rambled on about his uncle's farm at Rice Lake. Thaddeus hadn't been paying much attention at the time, but he was sure the name the old man mentioned was either Palmer or Plews, and he wanted to verify this information.

"Walter's not feeling well this evening," he was told. "He wanted to come, but he just couldn't manage it."

Thaddeus knew how he felt. It seemed to take all of his energy to bring the prayer meeting to a successful conclusion and get back on his horse. The ride to Cobourg seemed to take forever.

He stabled his horse and was just walking across to the manse when James Small and his mother waylaid him.

"I need to talk to you, sir," James said. His mouth was set in an angry line. Mrs. Small was wringing her hands.

"Well, you'll have to wait until I at least take off my hat," Thaddeus said. "Come in."

Their arrival set off a round of angry barks from Digger, who was in the kitchen with Caroline and Martha. Martha's welcoming smile slid into a look of exasperation when she saw that the Smalls were behind her grandfather.

Thaddeus slumped wearily into a kitchen chair beside Caroline, who was unconcernedly munching on an apple. He didn't invite the Smalls to join them and they stood awkwardly by the back door.

"All right. What's going on?"

Mrs. Small spoke first, but what she said made no sense to Thaddeus. "Oh, Mr. Lewis, I'm so sorry, I didn't think. She said she just wanted to run an errand, that's all, and that she'd be right back. As soon as I walked in, the dog started barking and then James came across to see what all the fuss was about."

"What are you talking about? Who went on an errand?"

"Miss Renwell," James said. "I'm sorry. I should have been keeping a closer eye on her."

"You keep far too close an eye as it is, Mr. Small. This is none of your affair," Martha said. Thaddeus could see that she was very angry.

"But it is," Small returned. "We're supposed to be looking after you when your grandfather isn't here. I certainly don't think he would allow you to go chasing around after that lawyer at all hours of the night. And nor should we."

"That's enough, thank you, James," Thaddeus said. "I certainly do appreciate everything your family does for us, but I will take it from here." He held his hand up to Martha, who had been about to say something more. "Enough. You and I will discuss this later. In the meantime, we should let these good people go home and get their suppers."

But James was in full complaint and not about to give it up. "All gussied up she was in her best dress, walking the streets of the town looking for him."

"I said I would take care of this, James. Thank you for bringing it to my attention. I will speak with Martha."

"People are talking enough as it is," Small muttered.

"I beg your pardon?"

Small turned bright red. "I said people are talking as it is."

"About Martha?"

"No. About you. And Mrs. Howell. And the time you spend at the gaol." Small was very flustered, but determined to have his say. "And now you've got the daughter here, and your grand-daughter gallivanting around after this Ashby fellow you hired. You're not doing the church any good, you know. It's hard enough as it is without all this gossip about the minister and his family."

His words fell into a room that became silent except for a low mutter from the dog.

The tense silence stretched out. Finally, it was Thaddeus who broke it. "Thank you for your concern, James. Good night."

Small was left with nothing he could do but take his mother by the arm and return home.

Martha waited until the door closed, then she said, "You look done in. What can I get you?"

"You wouldn't warm up a little milk for me, would you?"

"Of course. I'll give Caroline her supper while it heats. I have something to tell you."

"All right. But I need to sit for a minute."

"Go and sit where it's comfortable. I'll bring your milk through and help you with your boots."

Thaddeus walked into the parlour and sank down in one of the chairs, which unaccountably seemed to be in an entirely different part of the room than when he'd left. He only briefly registered this fact. His thoughts were in turmoil.

Whatever Martha had done appeared to be a minor affair, which he was sure she would tell him all about. Of far more concern were Small's words about Thaddeus himself. He supposed he shouldn't be surprised that his actions had become the subject of speculation. What he was doing must look very odd to an outsider's eyes. And he had no answer for it, no explanation beyond the obvious one — he was in love with a married woman and no good could come of it. Small was right. Thaddeus was doing irreparable harm to the church he had laboured for most of his life.

Wearily, he leaned over and began to loosen his boots. He still had his coat on, but removing it would entail standing up, and he wasn't sure he had the strength for it just then. He gave up on the boots and slumped back in the chair.

He hadn't even been particularly successful in proving Ellen's innocence. Bits and pieces, guesses and assumptions; none of it was enough to build a case on. He had been prideful and vain, and for the most selfish of reasons. He had sinned, if not in deed, then in thought. What had he been hoping in his heart of hearts? That George Howell would be caught and brought to justice, and that Ellen would somehow be magically absolved? And that the way would then be clear for Thaddeus? It was a sneaking, disgusting thought, and yet he had to admit that he had wished it.

Martha came into the parlour and put a mug of milk on the table beside him.

"You still have your coat on," she said. "Here, let me have it."

He shrugged out of it. Instead of taking it to put on the hook by the back door, Martha sat down in the chair opposite him, hugging the coat to her. She watched him warily, and Thaddeus was brought back from the sorry contemplation of his own failings.

"So what's this all about?" he asked.

"James Small spying on me."

"Let's put James's motivations aside for the moment. What happened? Did you go looking for Ashby?"

"Yes, but I had good reason."

She thought he would be angry with her, Thaddeus could see. How could he be angry when whatever she had done paled in comparison with his own transgressions?

"Just tell me what happened."

"I figured out who was on Spook Island with George Howell."

It was enough to grab his full attention. In a low voice, and with one eye on the doorway in case Caroline should appear, she explained the conclusions she had reached about the blue dress. "I knew you wouldn't be back until tonight, and if Ashby is to take advantage of what I discovered, he needed to know about it as soon as possible. Or at least I thought he did."

"Did you find him? What did he say?" And then he realized what Martha had done. "Did you go to the hotel looking for him? Alone?"

"Yes, but he wasn't there. I met him coming along the street."

"What did he say?"

She blushed. "He said I was brilliant and that he could kiss me." She ducked her head in embarrassment. "I'm sure he meant nothing by it. He'd been drinking. And he wasn't alone. There was a woman." Thaddeus could tell from her tone of voice that she knew exactly what kind of woman it had been.

"I asked Mrs. Small to stay here while I was gone, you see," she went on, "just in case Caroline woke up. When James found out where I'd gone, he followed me into town and saw me with Ashby."

No wonder Small was so angry, Thaddeus thought. No girl could be on the street at night in the company of a drunken man and a woman of questionable virtue and not expect to be talked about. And the fact that she was the granddaughter of the man who was already a subject of local gossip would make the information even more titillating. It wasn't the sort of thing that a Methodist congregation would put up with for long.

"I'm so sorry, Martha," he said. "This is my fault entirely. I should never have got you involved in this."

"Don't say that. It's what I wanted, more than anything, to be part of one of your adventures."

"But I've ruined everything. I've disgraced my office. And I've put you in an unspeakable position."

"For all have sinned, and come short of the glory of God."

Thaddeus glared at her. "You're quoting scripture at *me*?"

"Why else did you make me learn all those Bible verses if you didn't expect me to use them now and again?" she said. "So what do you think? About the dress?"

Thaddeus looked at her eager face and in spite of himself began to be drawn into her argument. It made perfect sense. Ellen Howell's damaged leg would make her clumsy in a boat. Caroline "followed her father around like a puppy," according to Leland Gordon. Ellen Howell stubbornly refused to say anything in her own defence and was upset that Caroline had been brought to Cobourg. No wonder Martha had gone running off to look for Ashby.

And then, in spite of his conviction that he had made a mess of things, Thaddeus felt a slight lightening of his mood. Maybe now they had something to work with.

Ashby arrived at nine, an hour later than expected. He went straight to the dining room table and began laying papers in piles across its top. Martha nodded at him coolly, took the chair farthest from him, and gave her attention to the dress she was altering for Caroline, aggressively stabbing the needle in and out of the fabric.

Ashby looked a little surprised at this reception, then smiled to himself. "Miss Renwell," was all the greeting he gave her.

When the papers were arranged to his satisfaction, he began. "Each pile represents a prosecution witness," he explained. "All of the prior testimony is noted, along with the questions we need to ask about it. Now we need to add what we've found out in the meantime."

"You seem well prepared," Thaddeus said.

"Oh, I'll do well enough in cross-examination," Ashby said. "Thanks to you and Miss Renwell, I've discovered some rather large holes in the argument. I hope it's enough, because when it comes to the defence, I don't have many of my own witnesses to call."

"Aren't you going to ask Mrs. Howell to tell her side of the story?" Martha said, without looking up.

"No, I'm not. I can't. The accused is not allowed to testify on his or her own behalf."

Martha frowned. "That doesn't seem fair."

"There are many who agree with you, my dear. It's a great controversy. There are those who claim that the accused will always lie, and that therefore the testimony should be automatically discounted. There are others who say that should he or she be allowed to testify and choose not to, the jury will simply assume guilt because of the refusal. It's a bit of a conundrum."

"And Caroline can't confirm her mother's whereabouts when the murder occurred," Thaddeus said. "Caroline was on the island with her father. She'd be equally culpable."

"What's *culpable*?" Martha asked. She addressed the question to Thaddeus.

"Criminally responsible," he answered.

"Not only that," Ashby said, "but Mrs. Howell has threatened to confess on the spot if I put Caroline on the stand."

"So where does that leave us?"

"Thanks to Miss Renwell, we stand a good chance of getting a jury to discount the eyewitness reports stating that Mrs. Howell was with her husband that day. Especially if Caroline is sitting in court and they can see for themselves how much the two look alike."

"You want her to come to court? What will Ellen ... Mrs. Howell think of that?"

"I don't know. I promised I wouldn't put Caroline on the stand. I said nothing about having her present as an onlooker. I think it's worth the risk."

Worth the risk to win the case, Thaddeus thought. Not so wise a gamble if it ends with a confession.

"The one thing the prosecution doesn't have in this case is a motive," Ashby went on. "They can speculate about robbery, since Sherman's pockets were picked clean, or postulate about some disagreement that turned violent, but they have no evidence to back it up. No one knows why George Howell and Paul Sherman were in the same odd place at the same time. The only potential link we have is the Sherman family's claim about a piece of business Sherman had in Cobourg. I'd surely love to know what that business was."

Thaddeus was once again beginning to feel that the case was hopeless. Everything hinged on bits of information that could be interpreted in any number of ways and he wondered if the young barrister was overly optimistic about what the jury might believe. The law was such an insubstantial thing. It was like wrestling with smoke.

"I did find out that Jack Plews, the man who owned the land that Howell bought, has left the district," he offered, with no hope that the information was useful. "He's gone to stay with family in the west somewhere."

Ashby looked astonished. "No, he hasn't. He's here in Cobourg. I could scarcely get a quiet drink at Musgrove's last night, he was pestering me so."

"Really? The rumour in the neighbourhood is that he's long gone. Come to think of it, though, Leland Gordon did say he'd only heard it, and didn't know for certain. What was he pestering you about?"

"About what would happen to George Howell's property if he and his wife were convicted of murder. Whether or not the land sale might be declared invalid or some such nonsense. I let him run on for a bit, just to see if he knew anything I could use, but when it became clear that he didn't, I shut him up by threatening to send him a bill for legal services."

"I take it there's no chance that could happen?"

"Oh, there's every chance a bill will be sent. But no, a guilty verdict wouldn't impact the transaction."

"Strange," Thaddeus said. But he couldn't quite put his finger on why, particularly.

Ashby turned to Martha. "I know you've been very busy, what with your ... um ... sewing and so forth, but did you have a chance to go through those passenger lists?"

It was such a facetious remark that Thaddeus expected her to glare. Instead, she merely looked at Ashby with a glint in her eye and a half-smile on her lips. "Of course," she said. "Since I seldom frequent taverns, I find I have ample time to complete my work." She shoved her notes across the table at him.

"Oh." Ashby stared at her for a moment before he looked down at the papers, but she didn't notice because she had returned to her hemming. Thaddeus looked pointedly in the other direction. He was staying out of this.

"Well," Ashby said after a moment, "Mr. Howell shows a distinct fondness for Rochester, doesn't he?"

"Fourteen times in the last three years," Martha said without looking up.

"Currency exchange and bad money. That fits. Rochester is a hotbed for counterfeiters."

"Is it really?" Thaddeus asked.

"Oh yes. Notes, coins, bogus railway bonds. Looks as though our Mr. Howell is a shover all right. And well, well,

well, what's this? He went to Burlington six months ago. I wonder why?"

"That's where Paul Sherman was from," Thaddeus said. "That has to be the connection."

"You'd think so, wouldn't you?" Ashby said. "I keep going back to the land title, but I just can't quite put it together. And we're out of time. At this point our best chance is to discredit the witnesses and hope that does the trick." He stared at Martha's notes for a moment more before he said, "You know, I can think of all kinds of reasons why someone would want to kill George Howell. But I can't think of a single reason anyone would want to murder Paul Sherman."

PART THREE
Fall Assizes, Cobourg,
October 1853

I

The courtroom was packed. By the time Thaddeus arrived, all the seats were taken and the aisles were beginning to fill up. He opted to stand against the wall at the side of the room, in a position that might catch Ellen's eye if she looked up. He hoped he was tall enough for her to see him, and that she would know he was there, even if he wasn't sitting right down in the front.

A hush fell over the crowd as Sheriff Ruttan escorted the judge to the dais at the front of the room. Justice Edward Stephens was a dignified and stern-faced man who, Ashby said, was noted for his accurate knowledge of the law and high personal character.

"He'll be fair enough, but he's not likely to put up with any nonsense. We could have done a lot worse."

The crowd sat patiently through two pieces of business unrelated to the murder trial, but became restless when Justice Stephens launched into the disposition of a third. Ashby had warned Thaddeus that this would happen. The assizes were held to deal with a number of cases, but the serious charges were always reserved as the last.

Finally, just before eleven a.m., the bailiff led Ellen Howell to the prisoner's box. As she had the first time, she looked up only briefly, a sweeping glance around the courtroom, her gaze resting briefly on Thaddeus before she bowed her head again.

Then the members of the grand jury were called in to report their findings. As expected, they returned a true bill: the charges against the accused were found to be "warranted and just." Thaddeus thought that this particular part of the proceedings was completely unnecessary. After all, the prosecution's evidence had been gone through at the committal hearing, and if there were glaring holes in the evidence, it should have been revealed then.

There were many who agreed with him and who argued that grand juries were an unnecessary waste of time and money and should be abolished. Maybe they would be one day, Thaddeus thought. In the meantime, he supposed they were all stuck with them, like so much else about the judicial system.

The clerk read the charges. Ashby rose and entered a plea of "Not Guilty" on behalf of his client. This caused no stir in the crowd. They all knew that George Howell was the true culprit, and that Ellen Howell was in all likelihood an incidental defendant. They would have been surprised indeed, had any other plea been entered.

Justice Stephens thanked the grand jury and then dismissed them. By then it was time for dinner, and he called for a short recess.

Most of the spectators rose and exited the courtroom, anxious to once again discuss the case over a meal with their neighbours before the selection of the jury would begin. As soon as the front benches emptied, Thaddeus pushed forward and took a seat right behind Ashby.

"No surprises so far," the young barrister said.

"How long will it take to choose the jury?" Thaddeus asked.

"Not long, I shouldn't think. They just draw cards from those who are eligible."

"But everyone has read the details in the papers already," Thaddeus noted with a sour tone. "I don't see how any of them can be impartial."

Ashby shrugged. "That's the way it is, unfortunately. Technically, defence has the right to reject up to twenty prospective jurors, but I'm not sure what it would gain us, since I'm not allowed to question any of them about what they may or may not have read."

Thaddeus fished in his pocket for the package that Martha had handed him that morning. When he opened it he found four thick slices of bread and butter and a generous chunk of cheese. He held it out to Ashby. "Martha sent us some lunch."

Ashby took one of the slices of bread. "No, I think this lunch was meant for you. Miss Martha seems quite put out with me for some reason. Thank you anyway."

"I don't think she likes the company you keep."

Ashby grinned. "Yes, that was my impression as well. The womenfolk never like it when the men have a little fun, do they?" And then he returned to studying his notes, as if Thaddeus was in full agreement with his statement.

Whatever the outcome, Thaddeus was suddenly glad that the trial would be over in a few days, and that Ashby would leave Cobourg at the end of it. Martha had quite liked the young lawyer, he knew. He was sure it was just one of those ephemeral and fleeting attachments that young girls seem so prone to, and would soon fade away with his absence, and it was just as well. As mature as she looked and as assured as she was, she was no match for a man like Ashby.

Thaddeus was roundly scowled at when, half an hour later, people began filing back into the courtroom. He ignored them. He wasn't going to budge from his seat. Justice Stephens and the Sheriff entered as before. The bailiff came forward with a large basket, and the Sheriff began drawing cards from it.

One by one the local men who were called came forward to state their names and occupations. Most of them were classified as "yeomen" — farmers of small pieces of land that they owned. One was a clerk, another a shoemaker. The prosecutor, Warren Garrett, challenged two of the farmers. Ashby objected to one of the clerks.

"Don't like the look of him," Ashby muttered to Thaddeus as he returned to his seat.

In relatively short order, twelve jurors were selected and Justice Stephens outlined what was expected of them. "Because of the seriousness of the charges, you will not be allowed to return to your homes while the trial is in progress," he said. "Neither will you be allowed to mingle freely with the public, nor talk to anyone from the newspapers."

Thaddeus thought two of the jurors looked a little downcast at this. Opportunistic farmers, perhaps, hoping for a free drink or two as a result of their selection? Their celebrity would have to wait until a verdict had been reached.

Prosecutor Garrett rose and presented a brief outline of the case he intended to prove, followed by Ashby, who, as he had indicated to Thaddeus, stated that the evidence against Ellen Howell was purely circumstantial and should, therefore, be discounted. And then the first witness, Constable Miller, was called to the witness stand.

"Could you describe for the court, please, the events that took place on September fourteenth?" Garrett asked.

"I was just thinking about turning in for the night when Donald Dafoe knocked on my door."

"And what time was this?"

"About nine o'clock. Don said he'd found someone dead over on Spook Island and I should come. I rousted out my neighbour who has a boat, and together with Dafoe, we went to the island. It was pretty dark, but even with just a lantern I could see right away that it wasn't a case of drowning or anything like that. The man had a big hole in his chest."

"And what did you do from there?"

"I sat down to watch over the body and told the others to go back to shore and ride for the coroner."

"Did you check the body to see if there were any signs of life?"

The constable nodded. "I did. He was colder than a day in January."

"Did you notice any particulars about him, other than the wound in his chest?"

"He had a gash in his head, but I don't know what from. Could've happened when he fell. There was blood on the rocks nearby."

"And did you attempt to identify the man?"

"No, sir," the constable said. "I didn't recognize him right off, but I thought it best to wait until Dr. Gilchrist arrived before I started rifling through his pockets. There was no point, you see, he was good and dead already, so what difference did it make if it took a while to figure out who he was?"

"Thank you, Constable Miller."

Thaddeus realized that the prosecutor had led with this testimony in order to establish that the body could in no way have been tampered with before the arrival of the coroner. He could see no way to dispute these facts, and neither, apparently, could Ashby, who declined to question Miller.

The coroner took the stand next, and repeated the same testimony he had given at the committal.

Ashby rose. "Could you repeat your opinion regarding the cause of death?" he asked. "I just want to make sure that I am absolutely clear on the matter."

"The cause of Mr. Sherman's death was a lead ball that entered his chest. Probably from a .625 calibre Baker rifle."

"And not from the wound to his head?"

"No. In my opinion, the head wound was not sufficiently severe to have caused a mortal wound."

"I see," Ashby said, "so whoever struck him on the head was not capable of delivering a heavy blow?"

"Or didn't mean to," the coroner said. "It's impossible to tell."

"And is it possible to tell with which hand this theoretical somebody delivered the half-hearted blow?"

"Not definitively. But from the angle, my best opinion is that it was delivered from behind by someone who was right-handed."

"Thank you," Ashby said, and seemed well satisfied with the answer he had elicited. Thaddeus wasn't entirely sure what the young barrister was up to. A feeble blow could certainly be attributed to a twelve-year-old. On the other hand, it could just as easily point to anyone who hadn't had a clear swing at Sherman. But then he realized that Ashby was making it crystal clear that it had been the gunshot wound, and not the blow, that had killed Sherman.

Chief Constable Spencer was sworn in next. He confirmed Constable Miller's description of the circumstances in which Paul Sherman's body had been discovered and described the investigations that had led him to the Howells.

"And what did you discover when you arrived at the Howell Farm?" Garrett asked.

"We discovered a washtub in the woodshed back of the kitchen, full of soapy water. In the tub was a blue dress. The dress had obviously been set to soak, but it hadn't soaked long enough. When we fished it out, there was still a dark stain on the skirt."

"And in your opinion, what could have made this stain?" the prosecutor asked.

"In my opinion, it's likely a bloodstain."

At this point the clerk held up the dress. The stain was still dark against the blue background, the small flowers blotted out across a section of the skirt.

A murmur ran through the crowd. They had read all about the bloodstained dress in the newspapers, but this was the first time any of them had seen it.

When the constable completed his testimony, it was Ashby's turn to question. He rose, stopped in thought for a moment, took a long look at the jury, then turned to the witness.

"Do you do your own laundry, Mr. Spencer?"

The constable chuckled a little. "No, of course not. My wife does the laundry."

"And do you assist her?"

"No."

"And yet you stated that the dress you discovered at the Howell farm had been … how did you put it? … set to soak."

"Yes." Spencer was alert now. He had enough court experience to understand that Ashby might be headed in a dangerous direction.

"How do you know this?"

"Because I don't know how many times I've come home with my clothes in a state and my wife has sighed and said, 'Give me that, I'll set it to soak.'"

A ripple of laughter swept through the crowd.

"I see," Ashby said with apparent great interest. "And do you often come home covered in blood?"

"I wouldn't say *often*, but it's happened a few times."

"And on those occasions, your wife has, as you said, *set your clothes to soak*?"

"Yes."

"As fascinating as we find the subject of Mr. Spencer's laundry," Justice Stephens interjected, "I'm wondering if there is any particular point you are trying to get to, Mr. Ashby?"

"I beg the court's indulgence. I shall arrive at the point shortly." Ashby turned once again to the witness. "Well, Mr. Spencer, since you have stated that you don't in fact assist your wife with the laundry, is it correct to say that you have never examined your soiled clothes after they have been soaked."

The constable was wary. "I've seen them after they were washed."

"But not *between* the soaking part and the washing part of the process."

"Well, no … I just let the wife get on with it."

"So really, you have no idea what a bloodstain — or any stain really — would look like after it's been soaked in a tub of water for a time."

The constable shifted uncomfortably. "Well, no, I suppose not."

"So, in fact, based on no knowledge whatsoever, you concluded that the stain on the blue dress was made by blood."

"It surely looks like a bloodstain to me."

"But it could just as easily be mud. Or cow manure." There was outright laughter at this. "You really can't say without a shadow of a doubt what caused the stain, can you, Constable Spencer? Because you have no first-hand knowledge of laundry."

"Well, when you put it like that, I suppose not, but …"

"No further questions.

"But …"

"Thank you, Mr. Spencer."

And Chief Constable Spencer was left with no choice but to step down. Thaddeus shot a glance at the prosecutor, but Garrett showed no sign of annoyance.

It was approaching five o'clock by this time, and the judge called a halt to the proceedings until nine o'clock the following morning. Thaddeus waited with Ashby while the courtroom cleared out.

"Are you coming 'round?" he asked.

"Not until later, if you don't mind. I'd like to hear the gossip. Shall we say eight o'clock or so?"

Thaddeus was reasonably sure that Martha would find this a relief, but he was also certain that Ashby's search for scuttlebutt would include a circuit of the taverns and taprooms. He would, no doubt, arrive reeking of smoke, sawdust, and whiskey. It would put a further strain on the evening when all Thaddeus wanted to do was dissect what had happened during the day and what would be likely to happen on the morrow. He supposed if Martha got too snippy with Ashby he could order her away, but she had been too important a part of the investigation for him to shut her out entirely. He'd have to follow Ashby's lead and simply ignore Martha's iciness.

When he arrived home he discovered that he had been correct — Martha had made no particularly special preparations for supper. She had set their places at the kitchen table and, although the pot pie she served up was delicious, it was patently not a company dish.

"Well, how did it go today?" she asked when they had all taken their seats.

"I must admit, I don't really know," Thaddeus said. "There seemed to be a great deal of back and forth, and I think Ashby scored some points with the jury, but whether or not any of it will have a lasting impact on them remains to be seen." He stopped in mid-bite and eyed Martha. "He's coming around later, you know."

"I expected as much," she said. She appeared to be completely unconcerned by this news. Thaddeus noted that Caroline was following their conversation closely, so he launched into a description of the disgusted looks he had been subjected to when he'd claimed a seat in the front row, and actually managed to elicit a small smile from the girl.

It was after nine-thirty when Ashby finally arrived. Martha had long since finished the dishes and shooed Caroline off to bed. Thaddeus was yawning in the parlour chair and thinking of retiring himself when the knock came at the front door.

"I'd nearly given you up," Thaddeus said.

"I was stood a couple of rounds of drinks," Ashby said. "Apparently, everyone feels that I'm affording them a great deal of entertainment. It would have been impolite to refuse."

"I hope you gathered some intelligence along the way."

"I did indeed. But not from my companions. Had I looked at my mail sooner, I'd have been here earlier."

He handed a letter to Thaddeus, then sank down in the opposite chair and closed his eyes. Martha came in and leaned on the back of her grandfather's chair, reading over his shoulder. The letter was from a colleague of Ashby's and concerned a case that had been filed in the Court of Chancery, the judicial body that dealt with contracts.

My dear Towns,

When you first asked me to investigate this title, I assumed that it would be one of those typical messes that accompany early land settlements. However, it turns out to be far more interesting than that. As you indicated, a suit has been filed by a Mr. John Plews, but it is not against a Mr. Howell, as you seemed to think it might be, but rather against two brothers,

Paul and Daniel Sherman. The origins of the dispute
go back to the original survey of the Rice Lake area.

"Is that Plews as in Jack Plews?" Martha asked. "And are those the same Shermans?"

"That's correct," Ashby said without opening his eyes. "Read on. It gets even more interesting."

As was the custom at the time, the surveyor was
expected to provision himself and his assistants, and
was paid, not in cash but with title to a certain number
of the lots that had been laid out. The surveyor in ques-
tion, Benjamin Sherman, had in turn subcontracted the
provisioning to a Mr. Josiah Palmer, who only partially
fulfilled the terms of the contract: the provisions were
substandard or absent, and Sherman was forced to feed
the crew out of his own pocket. When the work was com-
pleted, Sherman's legal counsel advised him to deliver up
the deeds as per the original agreement and then try
to sue for non-performance of contract. Unfortunately,
Sherman did not have a copy of the original agreement.
In order to hedge his bets, so to speak, he gave the deeds to
a third party — a barrister in Kingston — with instruc-
tions that they were to be delivered to Palmer only when
a copy of the agreement was produced. Palmer couldn't
come up with the document either, and the dispute was
further complicated when the barrister's office burned
down, destroying the original deeds. When replacement
deeds were drawn up, they were issued in Sherman's
name, and he must have reasoned that the matter was
closed, because he subsequently disposed of the proper-
ties without any further reference to Palmer.

There has been a cloud over the titles ever since. Heirs and Devisees has by and large allowed possession to pass unmolested, but there have been difficulties with respect to mortgages, as the usual demand for clear title is difficult to meet. And now Mr. Plews, who is a descendant of the negligent provisioner, has, he claims, produced a copy of the original agreement and is asking Chancery to uphold the terms of the contract and award the deeds to his family.

It will be interesting to see what the courts eventually decide, but in any case, it promises to be a long and expensive suit, and in my opinion, probably not worth the effort, even when one factors in the recent increase in value of the lands in question.

Hoping this is helpful in illuminating your current case.

Yours respectfully,

Charles Treverton

"I don't understand," Thaddeus said. "Why didn't the courts settle this at the time?"

"Because at that point there was no court of equity in Canada, and no one was sure whether or not the criminal courts had any jurisdiction over contracts," Ashby explained.

"When I heard that Jack Plews was going to court, I assumed he was suing Howell," Thaddeus said. "That's what everybody else assumed, as well. Palmers and Plews and Dafoes. They'd all benefit from this, wouldn't they?"

"Only if the court ruled in their favour. Charlie thinks it's unlikely. That's what I think, too. The situation has gone on for so long that there's a real case to be made for adverse possession — 'squatter's rights' in popular parlance. The question is, do the Palmer descendants know that?"

"And what about this agreement?" Martha said. "Lost for years and now it's found, just when the value of the land goes up? Convenient, isn't it?"

"Precisely," Ashby said. "Incredibly convenient. Almost like magic, don't you think?"

"Yes, you'd almost think there was divine intervention, wouldn't you?" Thaddeus said. "Except the Lord doesn't normally work that way. But I can think of someone more mortal who is awfully good at making pieces of paper look like they're worth something, can't you?"

"Oh yes, I can see George Howell's counterfeiting fingers all over this," Ashby said. "I don't know if Plews went to him in the first place, or if Howell somehow managed to persuade him that he had a case, but there's no doubt in my mind that Howell provided the missing document. He obviously has a tame printer — probably in Rochester — and there would be little risk to him in producing a bogus document for use in a foreign country."

"So Howell took a cut from the sale of Plews's land when he bought it for Boulton, and now he'll take a further cut if the case is successful at Chancery and the land is returned to Plews?" Thaddeus asked.

"That would be my guess. If Howell was lucky, he could get them coming and going. And even if the case isn't successful, he'd still have the cut from Boulton. He had nothing to lose, really. He must have figured it was worth a shot."

"But how would Paul Sherman know that Howell was behind it all?" Martha asked, her face knotted in thought. "Howell's name wouldn't be on the court papers, would it?" Then her expression cleared. "George Howell went to Burlington. It was in the passenger lists you gave me. But why would he do that?"

"The Palmer clan aren't business people," Thaddeus pointed out. "They wouldn't know anything much about courts of chancery and contracts. They probably left it all to the Major to sort out — after all, he has a reputation as a gentleman and keeps some pretty influential company. But he must have known it was a gamble. You don't suppose he tried to blackmail Sherman?"

"And Sherman wasn't having it," Ashby agreed. "That's why he came to Cobourg — to try to get the agreement away from Howell."

"Even though he'd probably win in court anyway?" Martha asked.

"But only after spending a great deal of money to do it. Either way, it was going to cost him a bundle. He must have tried to get the agreement from Howell some other way."

"That's who left the bruises on Ellen Howell's arm. Sherman must have gone to the Howell farm and threatened her," Thaddeus said. In a way, he was relieved. As nasty as it was, it was a one-time thing and not a continued pattern of abuse from her husband.

"And then he followed Howell to Spook Island," Martha said. "But who murdered him? Howell still has the best motive. Doesn't he?"

"Unless Plews and his family were afraid that Howell was double-crossing them," Thaddeus said. "Considering everything else, it wouldn't be an ill-advised conclusion."

"But if Plews was going to kill someone," Martha persisted, "wouldn't it make more sense to shoot Howell?"

"You'd think so, wouldn't you?" Ashby said, "except for one small detail — Howell still had the agreement, and the important thing from Plews's point of view was to keep it out of Sherman's hands."

"This is a wonderful theory," Thaddeus said. "And it would certainly explain a great deal, but how does any of it help the case?"

Ashby sighed. "That, I don't really know. And I don't know if the prosecution knows any of this. Sherman's brother may have filled Garrett in. He may not have — after all, no one can find either Howell or the agreement, and Sherman is better off if no one knows about it."

"Wouldn't Plews mention it?"

"For starters, I don't think he's even been questioned. And why would he say anything? It would make him a suspect, since he theoretically stands to gain a great deal of money if his lawsuit succeeds." Ashby stopped for a moment while he thought this through, then he looked up at Thaddeus. "You, sir, are brilliant." But he didn't elaborate any further. "I need all three of you to be in court tomorrow. We'll see if Caroline's presence rattles any of the witnesses, and then I'll take it from there."

II

Thaddeus and Martha, with Caroline in tow, arrived at the courthouse early the next morning and discovered that Ashby had spread his coat and his briefcase over the bench just behind his table, effectively reserving their seats. He was vigilant in shooing away anyone who had the temerity to try to move the items, and although many tried, his authority as the defence lawyer and a gruff word or two were enough to stop them.

"Put Caroline down at the end," he said to Martha in a low voice. "I want to be sure the jury can see her."

The first person to notice her was her mother, who glared at Ashby. He shook his head at her. Thaddeus hoped she realized from this that Caroline would not be called to the stand; otherwise, the whole case would fall apart as soon as Ellen stood up and changed her plea.

The second person to notice the girl was Donald Dafoe, the man who had found the body.

Witnesses were not allowed into the courtroom prior to their testimony, but were detained in a side room. Dafoe was led in by the bailiff, but it was only as he placed his hand on the Bible that he happened to glance around the room. His gaze came to rest on Caroline Howell. He was quite visibly disturbed by her presence. He had to ask the clerk to repeat the oath before he gathered his wits enough to focus on the matter at hand.

"Mr. Dafoe, could you please describe for the court the events of September fourteenth as you remember them?" the prosecutor asked.

Dafoe cleared his throat and looked at Caroline again before he began. "I was out fishing in my boat," he said.

"This was on Rice Lake?" Garrett prompted.

"Objection." Thaddeus was startled when Ashby rose from his seat. "My most esteemed counsel for the prosecution is putting words in the witness's mouth."

"Mr. Justice Stephens, the victim was found on an island in the middle of Rice Lake," Garrett returned. "I trust everyone agrees that is the particular lake Mr. Dafoe was fishing in."

"Nevertheless, Mr. Ashby has a point, Mr. Garrett. Please allow the witness to tell the story in his own words."

The crowd murmured approvingly. They hoped that the exchange was the first salvo in a battle to come.

"Please continue, Mr. Dafoe."

"I was out fishing" — here Dafoe hesitated and looked at the judge — "on Rice Lake. I landed a lovely pickerel, and being as I was hungry, I decided to put in to shore at Spook Island with the intention of cooking it up for my supper."

"And could you tell the court, please, what you discovered on Spook Island?"

"I found a dead man. He had a big hole in his chest."

"And what did you do then?"

"I got back in my boat and rowed for home."

"I see." Garrett paused for a moment and pursed his lips. "Did you then report your find to the local constable?"

"No."

"Or to anyone else?"

"Just my father." Dafoe looked a little sheepish as he said this.

"And why was he the only person you spoke to about the matter?"

"I was afraid I'd be blamed for it. I didn't have anybody with me, you see, to act as witness. I was scared. I didn't really know what to do."

The prosecutor looked pleased. He had put one sticking point right out there in the open. The defence would not be able to make a great fuss about it now.

"And what did you do then?"

"My father said I had to report it. So I did."

"Thank you, Mr. Dafoe. No further questions."

Ashby rose and smiled at Dafoe.

"Was it a nice day out there on the lake?" he asked. "Was the weather fine?"

Dafoe looked a little confused, but then he answered. "It was beautiful. You couldn't have asked for nicer on a fall day."

"And were you the only fisherman taking advantage of the fair weather?"

"Well, I don't know." Dafoe shuffled a little in his seat. "I wasn't the only boat out there, but I don't know as to whether or not any of the others were fishing. A lot of people were out to have a look at the railway bridge. And the steamer went by, but it goes back and forth all the time."

Ashby shrugged. "Fair enough. Those all would have been good reasons to be on the lake, wouldn't you say?"

"Is there a point to counsel's questions?" Garrett asked.

"There is indeed," Ashby replied. "I beg the court to allow me to continue."

The justice nodded.

"So there were other boats on the lake that day. What time do you normally eat your dinner, Mr. Dafoe?"

"About five o'clock, I reckon. Like most folks do."

"Don't you think that most folks would have wanted, as the afternoon wore on, to get home for their dinners?"

"Objection. Mr. Dafoe has no way of knowing what anyone else intended." Thaddeus could see that Garrett had spotted the trap.

Justice Stephens agreed.

Ashby changed his approach. "What time did you arrive at the island, Mr. Dafoe?"

"I don't rightly know. I don't own a watch, but I was hungry, so I guess it must have been getting on for dinnertime. That's why I decided to stop and cook my fish instead of rowing home."

"Wouldn't you have noticed that the other boats had left the lake by then and realized that it was suppertime?"

Dafoe shrugged.

"I've never cooked a fish on an open fire," Ashby said. "Tell me, Mr. Dafoe, how long does it take?"

Dafoe shifted uncomfortably in his seat, and again his gaze returned to Caroline. "Not long. If you cover it with mud and put it right down in the coals it cooks pretty fast."

"And you, of course, had firewood in the boat with you."

"Objection!" Garrett glared at Ashby.

"Do I even need to tell you, Mr. Ashby?" Justice Stephens said.

"Let me rephrase. Were you carrying a handy supply of firewood in the boat with you that day?"

"No, there's usually plenty of wood around. Driftwood and such. Or dead branches."

"So you caught your fish and rowed to Spook Island with the intention of gathering some driftwood, letting it burn down to coals, eating your fish, and then rowing home."

Dafoe thought he was clear. "Yes."

"And did you have a lantern in the boat with you?"

"No."

Ashby assumed a look of surprise and consternation. "But wouldn't it have been getting dark by the time you'd gathered driftwood, started a fire, let it burn down to coals, cooked the fish, and eaten it, Mr. Dafoe? If that was your intention, weren't you worried about rowing home in the dark?"

Dafoe finally realized where Ashby was leading him and tried to backtrack.

"Well, maybe it wasn't that late, after all. Maybe I just got hungry a little early. And besides, I didn't cook it after all. I saw the body and rowed home right away."

"But if you had, you would have been rowing home in the dark. Isn't that dangerous?"

"Well, like I said, maybe it was earlier than I thought."

"Just one further question, Mr. Dafoe." Ashby turned to the jury, a slight smile on his lips. "What happened to the fish?"

Dafoe looked a little shamefaced. "I took it home and my father and I ate it later."

"Even though you were distraught over finding a dead body on the island?"

Dafoe shifted uncomfortably. "Well, I can be upset and hungry at the same time."

The crowd tittered. This would be one of the exchanges that would be repeated many times to those not fortunate enough to attend in person.

"No further questions."

The next string of witnesses were those who had testified to seeing the Howells on the afternoon of the murder. Ashby spent a great deal of time questioning each of them. Some of them were quite firm in their answers and definite in their stories, while others grew flustered and backtracked, changing small details and elaborating on others. But with each of them, the crucial question he asked was "Did you see the woman's face clearly?"

And one by one, each witness had to admit that he or she hadn't. The woman's bonnet had been pulled too low. And each time one of them admitted this, everyone's eyes slid over to Caroline, sitting at the end of the front row.

By the time he finished, it was nearly one o'clock, and there was a rustle of approval when Justice Stephens called for a recess. Thaddeus stood and stretched, stiff from the long hours of sitting on the hard bench.

"I brought food," Martha said. She passed it to Thaddeus. "Should I take Caroline home now? I'm worn out with sitting."

"Let's all go outside for a few minutes," Ashby said. "I could use some fresh air. But if you don't mind, I'd like Caroline to stay. I don't like the idea of the two of you alone at the manse just now."

"You don't think there's any danger, do you?" Thaddeus asked. Maybe he should rethink his plan to take the evening meetings that were nearby.

"No, I don't think so," Ashby said, "but I don't want the girls pestered by the newspapers, for one thing. And I'm not sure, but there may be a visit from the chief constable, given the resemblance that the entire courtroom noted this morning. I want to be there if that happens."

When court resumed at two o'clock, Garrett called the deceased's brother Daniel Sherman to the stand. Sherman repeated the story that his brother had travelled to Cobourg on business. "Something to do with a land transaction," he said, but claimed to be ignorant of the details. When his brother failed to return to Burlington at the expected time,

Paul Sherman's wife became alarmed, but it was only when the family read details of the Cobourg murder in the newspapers that they feared the worst. Daniel had travelled to Cobourg and identified the body.

"And was your brother carrying any amount of money?" Garrett asked.

"Yes. I do not know what money he had of his own, but he borrowed one hundred dollars from me before he left. He said he did not want to wait for the bank to open."

"And did you get that money back?"

"No. When I asked about it, Chief Constable Spencer stated that there was nothing in Paul's pockets when his body was found."

Ashby rose to cross-examine.

"Mr. Sherman, you state that your brother borrowed one hundred dollars from you. Is that correct?"

"I've already said so."

"And in what form was this money?"

"Bank of Montreal banknotes."

"Do you always have that much money readily available at a moment's notice?"

"No. I took the money from the bank for another purpose. I just happened to have it when Paul wanted it."

"And what was that other purpose?"

"Objection." Garrett rose. "The purpose is immaterial to this case."

Justice Stephens nodded. "I'm inclined to agree unless you can show otherwise, Mr. Ashby."

Ashby nodded in deference to the ruling and chose another tack. "Are you aware that Mr. Jack Plews has filed a lawsuit against you and your brother?"

The spectators, who had seemed quiet and sleepy after the dinner break, suddenly sat up and paid attention again.

They all knew that Jack Plews was going to court over the loss of his land, but, like everybody else, they thought the suit was against George Howell.

Garrett was on his feet again. "Objection!"

Justice Stephens glared at him. "On what grounds?"

Garrett fumbled for an answer. "Mr. Ashby has produced no evidence of such a suit."

"He doesn't have to. He's merely asking if Mr. Sherman is aware of it. Witness will answer the question please."

Sherman squirmed in his seat a little before he answered. So he hadn't told his barrister after all, Thaddeus realized.

"Yes."

"And is it not true that your brother hoped to dissuade Mr. Plews from the suit?"

"Yes."

"And that was his reason for borrowing money from you and coming to Cobourg?"

"Yes."

"And was he successful?"

"I don't know," Sherman said. "He was murdered before he could tell me."

"But the money is gone?"

"Yes."

Garrett was red-faced. "If it pleases Mr. Justice Stephens, I would like to request a recess in light of this new evidence."

"No, Mr. Garrett. This is your witness. You should have been aware of this testimony before you started. However, you may redirect if you wish, when Mr. Ashby is finished."

"And what, exactly, does the suit allege?" Ashby asked.

"That Plews found some long-lost agreement that would throw a number of land titles into dispute. Including, conveniently enough, the land he recently sold."

"Defence has no further questions."

Garrett rose, but it was clear that he had been caught flat-footed. "Is the suit still pending?" he asked.

"I don't know," Sherman replied. "I haven't been home to find out."

Thaddeus could see that Garrett didn't know where to go from there. He had no idea what the answers to any of his questions might be, and he ran the risk of sinking his own case if he persisted. Any further mention of Jack Plews would only reinforce the notion that someone besides George Howell might have had something to do with the murder, and that there could be some motive besides simple robbery. In the end, the prosecutor did the only thing he could do.

"No further questions."

And the jury was left with a thousand questions they wished someone would ask.

III

"I think you should go straight home," Ashby said as the courtroom cleared. "Don't talk to anybody. Don't stop for anybody. I'll be around in a little while." Which Thaddeus took to mean that Ashby was sorely in need of a drink, but maybe he was being uncharitable.

As they exited the courthouse, their appearance caused a stir among the knots of people lingering on the steps after the day's proceedings. One of the newspaper reporters pushed toward them, notebook in hand.

Thaddeus glared and shook his head to signal that he would answer no questions. The reporter hesitated for only a moment, then pointed at Caroline and shouted, "Is this the daughter of the accused?"

Thaddeus could see Caroline shrinking against Martha's side, her face averted from the crowd of people staring at her.

"What is your interest in this case, Mr. Lewis?" the reporter persisted. "Is the girl staying with you?"

"Will the defence argue that this is a case of mistaken identity?" another man asked.

Thaddeus pushed through them, making a path for Martha, who pulled her cloak up around Caroline to shield her from the gaze of the crowd. Someone tugged at Thaddeus's arm. He whirled to face the man.

"I beg your pardon, sir! I have nothing to say to you and I'd appreciate it if you would unhand me."

Suddenly Ashby was there, on the other side of Martha, one arm around her while the other pushed at the people blocking their way. Thaddeus took Caroline's hand and increased his pace until they were almost running. He slowed down only when they were well down the street and there appeared to be no one giving chase. Caroline's face was tear-streaked.

"I'm so sorry that happened," Thaddeus said to her, "but we're all right now, eh?"

"You should be fine," Ashby said. He still had his arm around Martha, but now she shook it off and moved away from him. "Don't let anybody into the house, and above all, don't talk to anyone. I'll be there shortly."

Digger wagged his tail and wiggled ecstatically when he saw Caroline.

"You should take him outside," Martha said. "He's been in the house all day."

"I'll go, too," Thaddeus said. He wasn't entirely sure what Ashby was so worried about, but he figured it was best if he didn't let the girl out of his sight.

Digger liberally anointed several bushes, then raced up and down the yard after a stick that Caroline threw for him until he became sidetracked by a chipmunk that went to ground under the elm tree in the back corner of the garden. He dug ferociously at the root of it, his tail wagging happily.

"Mr. Lewis." It was James Small hanging over the fence that separated the two yards. Thaddeus walked over to him.

Small's manner was abrupt. "Do you have any suggestion as to what I should do with these?" he asked, holding out a handful of stained paper. "I don't know if they have any value anymore, but they certainly aren't mine."

It was the wad of paper that Thaddeus had jammed into the bleeding wound on Small's head, glued into a lump by congealed blood. Only by looking closely could anyone tell that they were notes issued by the Bank of Montreal.

"I don't want anyone saying I kept money that didn't belong to me," Small said.

Thaddeus knew they were probably counterfeit, part of George Howell's stock in trade. They should go to Ashby. But, he judged, they should probably be put directly into the barrister's hands.

"I'm not sure who they belong to now," he said. "Why don't you hang on to them for the time being and I'll ask what you should do with them."

"Very well."

Small put them in his pocket and moved on to his next point of contention. "Are you planning to lead the men's meeting in Baltimore this evening?" The young minister's lips were pursed in disapproval.

Thaddeus had already decided that he wasn't. He was worried about Martha and Caroline, and even if he hadn't been, he felt extremely disinclined to go. Sitting in court all day had taken more out of him than he'd expected. "I don't think so," he said. "I've only just returned from the court-house, and even if I left right this minute, I would make only the last part of the meeting."

"I see. And I suppose Precious Corners is out of the question tomorrow, as well?"

Thaddeus agreed. "Yes, I expect so. Are you well enough to see to it?"

"I suppose I'll have to be, won't I?"

"No, you don't have to be. If you can't go, the lay ministers can lead the prayers."

"I have to tell you, Mr. Lewis, the congregation is most unhappy at this turn of events. They expect their minister to attend them, not spend all his time at the gaol."

"No, they don't," Thaddeus said. "When I first took this circuit, Bishop Smith suggested that I take as many rest days as I need, and that was made clear to everyone. What they're really upset about is my involvement with the Sherman case."

"Yes, they are. And I think someone should inform the Bishop of the impropriety of your involvement."

"If you feel you really must, James, then by all means, go ahead."

This evidently was not the answer Small had been expecting. He gave Thaddeus a sour look but seemed unable to think of anything to say in response.

"If you decide to go to Precious Corners, you can take my horse." Thaddeus knew that this would only aggravate his young assistant, but truth be told, he was a little nettled by Small's words. Nettled, and not a little guilty. He had made such an auspicious start on this circuit, and now he was letting the advantage slide away.

"And here comes your barrister," Small sneered, as Ashby came down the street with a parcel in hand.

"There you go," Thaddeus said. "That's who you should give the banknotes to."

"Everyone's talking about him as well, you know. I wonder you'll admit him to your house. You should look to your granddaughter, Mr. Lewis. Whatever you choose to do is your business, but you're leading Martha down a perilous path."

Thaddeus had had enough of being lectured by his junior assistant. "That is quite enough, James. In one thing, you're correct. This is my business. Not yours. And neither is Martha." And then he turned and walked back into the house, followed closely by Caroline and Digger, who delivered a parting yap at Small. Just as they stepped inside, Caroline said in a small voice, "Are you in trouble?"

"Yes, probably. But don't worry about it. I've been in trouble before and I dare say I will be again."

"I don't like that man. He shouts. Like the dead man did."

Thaddeus asked, as matter-of-factly as he could, "Did the dead man shout at you?"

"No. Not me. At Mama. And he hurt her. He grabbed her arm."

"I know. I saw the bruises. You must have been frightened."

She nodded, but didn't say anything else. Thaddeus desperately wanted to ask her more, but he knew that it would be all too easy to alarm her. Better to let her tell it when she was ready.

Martha was starving, but as she had been in court all day, supper would be a hasty affair. There was a little side bacon in the cold room and a half-dozen eggs, a sack of potatoes in the woodshed, plenty of pickles, a loaf of bread, and not much else. She'd have to go to the market as soon as she could the next day, especially if her grandfather was going to be home. He expected more substantial fare than she bothered with when she was alone. Potato soup would do for tonight, she decided, with fried bacon and hard-boiled eggs.

As soon as Caroline and Thaddeus came in from the backyard, she put them both to work setting the table. To

Martha's surprise, Caroline had no difficulty with which side of the plates the knives and forks went on, and voluntarily folded the napkins into a triangular shape before she placed them at the head of each setting. She may have grown up in a dilapidated cabin, but her mother had obviously schooled her in the finer points of civilized dining.

Ashby smiled charmingly when she let him in the front door a few minutes later.

"I hope you're recovered from that melee outside the courthouse," he said.

"I'm fine. It wasn't me they wanted to talk to so it was just a question of making my way through it. I did manage to land a couple of good kicks on a shin or two, though."

He laughed and handed her the parcel he was carrying.

"A cake," he said, "for dessert. I've taken so many meals here I thought I should contribute for once."

Martha hadn't really been expecting him to come for supper. He would just have to lump in and make do along with everyone else, she decided. She could scarcely tell him to go away. And, she supposed, the cake was a peace offering of sorts.

"I thought you did well today," Thaddeus remarked as Ashby shrugged off his coat and walked through to the kitchen. "You made an impression with the jury, I think."

"I did indeed. And I hope to make a bigger one tomorrow. Don't forget, all we have to establish is reasonable doubt, and I think we're well on the way to that."

"You're right. I keep losing sight of that fact. You don't have to prove who killed Paul Sherman, just that it probably wasn't George Howell. There's a part of me, though, that wants to bring the culprit to justice."

"The thrill of the chase?" Ashby laughed. "Your son told me that you're a human bloodhound."

No sooner had Martha set the soup on the table than another knock came at the front door, setting Digger off and startling them all. Thaddeus rose to answer it. "If that's James Small I'm going to be really annoyed," he grumbled.

It wasn't. It was someone asking to speak with Caroline Howell.

Thaddeus returned to the kitchen. "I believe you should handle this," he said to Ashby. "It's Constable Spencer. He wants to question the girl."

"Yes, I was expecting this. Stay here, if you would."

Martha glanced at Caroline. The girl's eyes were very wide.

They could hear the conversation clearly from where they sat.

"I would like to ask Miss Caroline Howell a few questions in connection with the Sherman murder," the constable said. "I've been told she's staying here."

"Miss Howell has nothing to say," Ashby returned.

"I believe she may have some information that could shed light on the investigation. All I want to do is ask her a few questions."

"Is she being charged with an offence?"

"No, of course not."

"Then as her barrister, I am advising her to remain silent."

"You're her barrister?" the constable asked.

"Yes. Mr. Lewis has retained me to represent both Ellen and Caroline Howell."

"Oh, come on. It's just a few questions."

"Sorry." And then Ashby firmly closed the door. "I was afraid that might happen," he said when he returned to his seat. "This is a slippery game we're playing." Then he turned to Caroline, as if she had been unable to hear the conversation at the front door. "That was a policeman. He was looking for you."

Her face crumpled. "Am I going to gaol?"

Martha was outraged when Ashby replied, "Maybe. Maybe not. But I can protect you only so far." His voice was harsh.

The silence spun out for several minutes while Caroline sat with her head bowed and everyone else picked at their suppers. Suddenly Martha wasn't so hungry anymore.

She waited until everyone appeared finished with the poor supper she had provided, then brought out the cake. It was a beautiful cake, a bakeshop cake, with fancy rosettes of icing on the top. She served them each a piece and sat down again. Ashby was the only one who attacked it with any enthusiasm. Caroline picked at one of the rosettes, then asked to be excused.

It took Martha a long time to get to sleep that night. It was the first time she had ever seen a trial. She was intimidated by the gravity of Justice Stephens, who held the power of life and death in his hands. She had been a little confused at times by some of the terms used in court, but soon found that she could ignore these and still follow the ins and outs of the evidence presented. And she had been impressed and a little awed by Ashby, who floated through the proceedings with an air of sublime confidence. Brilliant, charming Ashby, who could be counted on to frustrate and annoy just when you thought you might like him.

She didn't know why she let him bother her so. She had no difficulty ignoring James Small, except when he severely provoked her, of course. But James didn't have any charm to temper his shortcomings, she realized. It would never occur to James Small to bow over her hand or buy her a bakery cake.

Oh well, she thought, the trial will be over within a few days and then Ashby will leave Cobourg and that will be that.

She would probably never see him again and she wasn't even sure why that would be a disappointment. And at that, she drifted off to sleep.

Frantic barking woke Martha some time later. She sat upright in bed, disoriented and befuddled. She heard her grandfather groan, and then his feet hitting the floor. Digger seemed only to bark when he thought something was threatening Caroline, but she didn't know this for sure. Maybe a squirrel or a cat had caught his attention and that was what upset him.

She scrambled out of bed and ran to the hallway. Caroline stood wild-eyed at her bedroom door. Digger shot past her and down the stairs to the back door. Martha hurried to catch up with him. He was scratching frantically to be let out.

"I've got it." Thaddeus was right behind her. "Get a lantern." He opened the door. The moon was nearly full, but it cast inky shadows over the yard. The dog disappeared into them and Thaddeus followed. Martha ran back into the kitchen, lit a lamp, and returned to the yard just in time for the arc of her light to silhouette two figures struggling by the fence. She heard Thaddeus grunt, then one of the figures broke away, only to be felled by a flying tackle from the other.

She was about to run forward to see if she could help when she heard someone yell over the hysterical barking of the dog.

"Gotcha!"

"Let me up! Get me away from that beast!"

She kept the light on Thaddeus. He had a man pinned to the ground with a knee in the small of his back. He wrenched the man's arm behind him and pulled him to his feet.

"The dog's got somebody cornered," he said. "Let's go see who it is. Hold the light up so I don't trip."

To Martha's surprise, James Small was at the bottom of the garden, holding a poker.

"Digger, quiet!" Thaddeus said. The dog stopped barking, although he continued to watch his catch intently.

"And who do we have here, I wonder? Hold the light a little closer, Martha." She thrust the lantern close to the man's face. It was Donald Dafoe.

"This man was trying to get into your house," Small said looking at Martha with an earnest expression. "I got him, though. Don't worry, I won't let any harm come to you."

"Thank you, Mr. Small," Martha said, although she was certain that she was not the object of the incursion.

"And who are you?" Thaddeus said. He forced the man he was holding down to his knees beside Dafoe. "What are you doing in my garden the middle of the night?"

The man maintained a sullen silence.

A light appeared in the doorway of the house next door. James's father and two of the brothers hurried across to the manse garden.

"What is it, James?" his father asked.

"Caught this fellow trying to get into the manse. I saw him trying to jimmy open the back window."

Mr. Small turned to the older of the boys standing beside him. "Go get the constable."

"But before you do that," Thaddeus said, "go to the Globe Hotel and tell Towns Ashby he'd better come quickly. Roust him out of bed if necessary."

The boy looked puzzled, but Mr. Small's nod of the head sent him scurrying down the road.

Thaddeus took the lantern from Martha. "Please go and make sure Caroline is all right."

Martha was reasonably sure that Caroline was fine, although she might be frightened by the attempted break-in. Digger was still growling in front of Dafoe, as sure a sign as anything that there was no threat inside the house.

"C'mon boy," Martha said. The dog ignored her.

She shrugged and went back to the house, calling Caroline's name as she climbed the stairs. There was no answer. "Caroline? It's all right. You can come out. They caught the men who were trying to get in."

Nothing. Martha changed her tactic. "Can you call Digger? He won't come in for me."

There was the faint creak of a door opening, so faint that Martha had difficulty deciding where it was coming from. Then, at the end of the hall, she saw the door to the big linen cupboard open slightly.

"It's all right now."

"Are they policemen?"

Martha once again felt a twinge of annoyance at Ashby. He had frightened Caroline badly when he said she might go to gaol.

"No, it's burglars. At least I think so. But Mr. Small and my grandfather caught them."

"I'll come out when they're gone," Caroline said firmly. She shut the door again.

Martha decided that Caroline was as safe in the linen cupboard as anywhere, so she returned to the garden. There was no sign of the constable yet, but she hadn't been standing there very long before Ashby came loping down the street. To her sudden consternation, she realized that she was wearing her nightgown and that her hair was a cascade of tangles down her back. She slowly backed up until she could slip into the shadow of the woodshed.

"You sent for the authorities?" Ashby asked Thaddeus when he reached the group at the back of the garden.

"Yes, but I thought you might like a word first."

Ashby nodded. He hunkered down beside the two men. "Hello, Jack. Donald."

The second intruder must be Jack Plews. Martha hadn't known who he was until then.

"Whatever the girl told you is a lie," Dafoe said.

"Shut up, Donny," Plews said. "I don't know what you're talking about," he said to Ashby.

"I haven't said anything yet," Ashby pointed out. "But while we're on the subject, were you going to kill the girl, too? Or is it just the document you're after?"

Just then the Small brother returned with a constable in tow.

"You're a pair of fools," Ashby said in a low voice. "Was all of this really worth a murder?"

"What's this then?" the constable asked, and Ashby stood up.

"It appears to be a case of attempted burglary or at the very least a break and enter," Ashby said. "Fortunately, Mr. Small here realized someone was in the back garden and he very bravely rushed out to apprehend the culprits."

In spite of the annoyance he had demonstrated at Ashby's arrival, Small basked in the praise.

"Was anything taken?" the constable wanted to know.

"I'm not sure," Thaddeus said. "We were reluctant to search them ourselves. Far better to wait until your arrival, we figured."

"Quite right," the constable agreed.

"I don't think they even got inside," Small said. Martha could see that he was puzzled. "One of them was trying to force a window when I saw him."

"Right, turn out their pockets then."

There wasn't much. A few coins, a key, a handkerchief, and then the constable pulled a clip of banknotes from the breast pocket of Dafoe's coat. As he leafed through them, a piece of paper fell to the ground.

Ashby picked it up and held it to the light of the lantern. "It's a steamer ticket," he said. "Return passage, Burlington to Cobourg. Well, well, well." He handed it to the constable.

"You'd better document this along with the rest of Mr. Dafoe's belongings. Do it carefully, mind."

And then Martha understood why her grandfather claimed not to know if anything was taken, and why he had sent for Ashby. He wanted the constable to search Dafoe and Plews, and he wanted Ashby to be witness to it. There would be no disputing in a court of law the fact of anything found in their possession. By the same token, there could be no carelessness on the part of the constable when it came to writing down the particulars. It would all be in black and white, and in the hands of the police. It may have been a lucky guess that either man would have anything that would tie him to Paul Sherman, but Thaddeus hadn't been taking any chances.

The constable led the men away, with two of the Small boys as escorts. Digger waited until they were around the corner and out of sight before he stopped growling, then ran to the back door and scratched to be let in.

"Move the kettle over onto the stove, would you Martha?" Thaddeus said. "We all need to warm up." Then he turned to Small. "I can't thank you enough, James. It's a good thing you were so vigilant; otherwise the thieves might have been successful."

It was clear to Martha that Small had no idea of the import of his actions, and that as far as he was concerned he had merely interrupted a theft in progress. He drew himself up with a great deal of satisfaction, however. "I'm happy I could be of assistance," he said. "My first thought, of course, was for Martha's safety."

"Good man," Thaddeus said.

Even in the dark, Martha was quite sure she could see a smirk on Ashby's face.

"Well, good night now," Thaddeus said. "Again, thank you." He turned to follow Martha into the house.

"I'll be with you in a moment, Thaddeus," Ashby said. "I'll walk Mr. Small to his door."

Digger ran up the stairs as soon as he was let in. Martha threw a couple of pieces of wood into the belly of the stove and pulled the kettle over to heat before she followed him.

The dog was pawing at the door of the linen cupboard. "You can come out now, Caroline," Martha called. "It's all right." And then she rushed into her room to slip into her dress and give her hair a brush before she had to face Ashby again. The dog had disappeared by the time she was ready, but she heard a couple of muffled thumps from inside the cupboard. She walked over to it.

"It's me," she said, and opened the door. Caroline had jammed herself under one of the shelves and pulled Digger into her lap. "Everything's all right now. The men have gone. If you want, come down to the kitchen and get a cup of tea before you go back to bed."

And then she realized how clearly she could hear her grandfather as he fussed with the teapot and rummaged around for cups. The back door opened and Ashby came in.

"So were they after the agreement or the girl?" she heard Thaddeus ask him.

"My guess is the girl," Ashby said. "Or both."

Every word they said could be heard distinctly. Martha looked down at the floor of the hall. There was a cast iron register covering the hole cut through to let the heat from downstairs rise and warm the bedrooms. She ran into the room where Caroline slept. There was another one under the chair that sat in the corner. The room was directly over the dining room. Caroline had been able to hear them all the time they'd sat there discussing the case.

She went back to the cupboard.

"What girl are they talking about?" Caroline asked.

"You."

"I thought they were robbers."

"They were."

"Were they looking for the piece of paper?"

"Yes."

Caroline thought for a few long moments, and Martha was sure she would remain silent as she had before, but she evidently reached some decision for she turned and reached to the back of the cupboard to pull out the leather satchel she had rescued from the cave-in.

They went down the stairs to the kitchen. The men were sitting at the table waiting for the tea to steep.

Both her grandfather and Ashby looked odd, Martha thought. They had each dressed in a hurry, pulling their trousers on over their nightclothes and stuffing their feet into boots. Their hair was tousled, their necks exposed, their suspenders showing. They both needed a shave. Their appearance made the scene strangely intimate, cozy, as if they all belonged in the kitchen together.

Caroline walked to Thaddeus, not Ashby, and handed him the satchel.

He opened it and pulled out a bundle of banknotes and bonds and one sheet of very yellow paper. He scanned it quickly, then handed it to Ashby.

"It's exactly as we thought," he said. "An agreement between a surveyor named Sherman and a provisioner named Palmer. And just as we suspected, the document is a forgery."

"How can you tell?" Ashby said.

"By what it says there at the top. Cobourg, March 23rd, 1796."

"So?"

"It wasn't called Cobourg in 1796. It wasn't even a town. Back then it was all just little settlements, a few houses here and there, clustered together. And they all had different names — Hardscrabble, Amherst, Hamilton. It wasn't until after the war sometime that it all became Cobourg." He shrugged. "It was one of those cases where somebody royal got married and the town fathers chose the name in honour of the event. Apparently they didn't spell it correctly, but nobody has ever bothered to correct it."

"So whoever cooked up the document didn't know the history?"

"But surely one of the Plews or Palmers or Dafoes would have known that," Martha said.

"I'm guessing they never actually saw it," Ashby said. "Howell just told them he had it and they could go ahead with the lawsuit." He turned to Caroline. "It was you on the island with your father, wasn't it?"

"Yes. Mama is no good in a boat because of her leg."

"The dead man came to your house, didn't he?"

She nodded. "He wanted the piece of paper. He yelled at Mama and hurt her. Then we saw him later on the hill and in the village. Papa said we needed to move everything out of the cave because he was getting too close. He said we should go to one of the islands and see if there was a good hiding place there."

"And then what happened?" Thaddeus said it so softly that Martha could scarcely hear him.

"The man followed us there. He shouted at Papa and tried to take the leather bag. Some papers fell out and Papa shouted back at him. Then he tried to hit Papa, so I threw a rock at him." A tear spilled over her cheek. "It didn't stop him, so I ran at him and tried to push him over, but I couldn't. And then all of sudden he fell over on top of me and I got blood all over my dress and Papa said to run."

She stopped, and then in a confidence so fragile that Martha scarcely dared to breathe, she whispered, "I thought I killed him."

"That's what your mother thought, too, isn't it?" Thaddeus said. "That's why she pretended that the blue dress was still hers."

Caroline nodded. "When Papa came back he said no, the man had been shot, but by then it was too late. Mama was already in gaol."

And it wouldn't have mattered at that point, Martha realized. Ellen Howell had been charged with murder as an accessory to her husband. The charges against her wouldn't be dropped even if her husband came forward. He would be charged with murder, too, and any explanation he offered would only implicate Caroline and lay him open to charges of forgery. And he must have wondered, the whole time he was cowering in the cave, how long he could hide from the Palmer clan.

"One of the men who tried to break in tonight is the man who found the dead body," Ashby said. "Do you remember him from the trial, Caroline?"

"Yes. He kept looking at me."

"Have you ever seen him before?"

She shook her head. "No."

"He thinks you did. That's why he was trying to get into the house tonight."

Caroline picked at her nails with her head downcast.

"Tell me, Caroline," Ashby said. "This is really, really important. Did your Papa have a gun with him?"

She wiped her eyes with the table napkin and blew her nose into it, then shook her head. "No. He was really scared. And after he came back he said that we had to hide in the cave whenever anybody came because Mr. Plews's whole family was mad at him."

"Well," said Ashby. "There you have it. So what do we do now?"

"I think we should have some cake," Thaddeus said. "I wasn't hungry for it before, but I think what we all need now is a big piece of cake to go with our tea. Don't you agree, Mr. Ashby?"

"By all means, Mr. Lewis."

Martha bustled into the pantry and retrieved the cake. She set it in the middle of the table and cut off a large piece for Caroline and smaller pieces for the rest of them.

"Now that's what I call a proper midnight lunch," Thaddeus said. "Nothing but cake," and was rewarded with a small smile from the still-sniffling girl.

By the time they had finished, Caroline was yawning.

"Would you like to go back to bed now?" Martha asked. "You've had enough excitement for one day." The girl nodded and slipped off her chair.

They waited to speak again until they heard her footsteps along the upstairs hall, although, Martha realized, it didn't really make any difference. Caroline would hear them anyway, if she wanted to. She'd been listening all along. It had taken her a long time to trust them, that was all.

"The Palmer clan knew Howell was there," Thaddeus said. "If Leland Gordon could figure it out, so could they. They were watching the whole time. That's why I kept meeting the old man on the road. Howell went back to the farm to get Caroline, and he couldn't get out again."

"But they couldn't turn him in," Ashby said. "They didn't know what he'd done with the agreement."

"And they didn't know if he saw who fired the shot," Thaddeus pointed out. "But all they had to do was keep him bottled up at the farm until the trial was over and Ellen took the blame. Then they'd let him go if he handed over what they wanted."

"The cave-in upset all their plans, didn't it?" Martha said.

"There were too many people around. We'd have noticed them."

"And Howell jumped at the opportunity to get away. A horse all saddled up and ready to go — I expect he just rode into the middle of the construction and blended in with the work crew. Even if someone questioned it, he could pretend he didn't speak English and no one would think twice about it. Even if the Palmers were watching, he could fall in with the wagoners and ride right out of there."

"That explains why he didn't take Caroline with him," Ashby said. "She'd have given the game away."

"Caroline wouldn't have gone anyway," Martha said. "Not until she'd rescued her dog."

"The question is," Thaddeus said, "how do we prove any of this?"

"No," Ashby said, "the question is: how do I introduce any of this in court?"

It was the first time Martha had ever seen him look unsure.

IV

Ashby's first witness the next morning was Mrs. Beecroft, a local dressmaker. He held the stained blue dress aloft for the jury to see once more, and then handed it to Mrs. Beecroft for examination.

"This dress has been altered," she said after she had made a show of looking at it. "It has been taken in and the skirt shortened to fit someone smaller than the last owner."

"Is this a common practice?" Ashby asked.

"Oh my, yes — in, out, up, down. Some dresses, particularly those that are originally of high quality like this one, can be passed around ten or fifteen times before they finally wear out."

"And, in your opinion, would the dress in its current state fit the accused?"

"I would say not, though it's hard to tell unless you hold it up against a person."

"With your permission, Mr. Justice?" And when Stephens nodded, Ashby helped Ellen Howell down from the prisoner's box and over to the witness stand. She must be having a bad day, Thaddeus thought, or the pervasive dampness of the gaol cell was taking its toll, for her limp was quite noticeable. She looked frail and vulnerable, and he could see two or three of the jury members frowning in thought.

Mrs. Beecroft shook out the dress and held it up against her.

"Now, you see, this waist would never go around her," she said. "And the skirt ends just below the knee. No lady would go out in a dress this short."

And again, every head in the room swivelled to the front row bench where Caroline was sitting.

Thaddeus glanced at the prosecutor. He looked furious. Martha was right — it was the sort of detail that would never occur to a man, but one that had the potential to sink Garrett's entire case.

Constable Miller was called next and confirmed that he had arrested two men who had attempted to break into the Methodist Episcopal Manse the night before.

"And could you tell the court the identities of these men?" Ashby asked.

"Donald Dafoe and Jack Plews."

"And could you read for the court, please, the list of their personal effects that you catalogued at the time of arrest?"

Constable Miller took out his notebook and cleared his throat. "Mr. Plews — one key, one handkerchief, one piece of string ..." This caused a small titter in the room. "Three American nickels, four halfpenny Bank of Canada tokens, twenty dollars in Northumberland Bank notes. Mr. Dafoe — one handkerchief, one comb, one English pound, one hundred dollars in Montreal Bank notes, and a return passage steamer ticket from Burlington to Cobourg, Canada West, dated September tenth."

"Objection!" Prosecutor Garrett was on his feet. "This has no relevance."

"I will show relevance with my next witnesses, if it pleases the court."

"Please do, Mr. Ashby, or I'll strike the testimony."

Thaddeus was surprised when Ashby next called James Small, but on reflection he supposed he shouldn't have been. Small had no connection with the case and would make an ideal witness to the events of the night before.

Small kissed the Bible and swore his oath in a firm voice, Adam's apple bobbing up and down at an alarming rate.

"Mr. Small, would you please recount, in your own words, the events of October twenty-first."

"I was riding the eastern portion of Hope Circuit."

"You are a minister, sir?"

"Yes, I am on a probationary appointment for the Methodist Episcopal Church. I had just finished leading a prayer meeting in Sully and was headed south when I met my supervising minister, Mr. Thaddeus Lewis, and his granddaughter."

There was a slight stir in the crowd. Many apparently recognized his name, but whether this was because of his fame as a preacher or the rumours that had spread about him, Thaddeus had no way of knowing.

"Mr. Lewis indicated that he was on his way to George Howell's farm," Small went on, "in order to leave some food on behalf of Howell's neighbours, who were concerned about the welfare of the Howell daughter. While there, a railway crew working at the rear of the farm uncovered a small cave, which had collapsed during the excavation of building materials."

James told the story of the dog rescue in a straightforward manner, but elicited a laugh from the crowd when he related how he had come to with a wad of banknotes plastered to his head.

"And what did you do with these notes after you were taken home?"

"Mr. Lewis instructed me to give them to you, which I did."

Ashby strode to his table and held aloft the handful of blood-stained notes.

"I would like to offer these in evidence," he said. "I should also like to present with them an affidavit I obtained from the auditor of our local Bank of Montreal stating that they are not legal tender. They are, in fact, counterfeit."

A gasp and a ripple of comment went through the crowd. *There's probably not a single one of them that hasn't been stung by a bogus note,* Thaddeus thought. He glanced at Ellen Howell, who had managed to sink even lower in the box as her husband's reputation was blown to tatters.

"I would also like to point out that insofar as the serial numbers on the notes are legible, they appear to be part of the same series as the note discovered on Spook Island." He turned again to Small. "And now would you please tell the court about your experience last night."

"I haven't been sleeping well since my accident, so I was up reading my Bible when I heard a dog barking next door. There was a nearly full moon last night, so I was able to see that a man was attempting to force a ground floor window at the manse next door."

"This is the manse where Mr. Thaddeus Lewis resides?"

"Yes. My first concern, of course, was for the safety of Mr. Lewis's granddaughter."

Martha made a face.

"Stop it," Thaddeus whispered.

"But …"

"Shh."

"By the time I reached the yard," Small went on, "Mr. Lewis had wrestled the man to the ground. At that point I realized that there was a second man at the bottom of the garden, and I was able to hold him until some members of my family arrived to help subdue him. Then we sent my brother for the constable, who searched the men and took them away."

"It was Digger who stopped him," Martha said.

"*Ssh.*"

Had the circumstances not been so serious, Thaddeus would have laughed at the look on the prosecutor's face as he rose for cross-examination. He seemed at a loss as to how to proceed.

"Mr. Small," Garrett said. "You stated that you were struck on the head when the cave collapsed. Could this not have affected your memory?"

"It did for a time, but it was only temporary. I have since regained my full faculties."

"You stated that you first noticed the banknotes when you recovered your senses."

"No, sir. I first noticed them when we were removing debris in an attempt to retrieve the dog. There were a number of loose notes mixed in with the rubble."

"And you didn't remark on this at the time?"

"No sir. At the time we were all engaged in attempting to dig through a wall of dirt without bringing it all down on ourselves."

"I see." It was clear that Garrett was unhappy with Small's answers. He changed course.

"Do you normally keep such a close eye on the Methodist manse?"

"Yes, I do. When Mr. Lewis first agreed to come on the Hope Circuit, he stated that his granddaughter would be keeping house for him, and as she is still quite young, he wondered if our family could assist her should any emergency arise. I have taken this responsibility very seriously." He looked at Martha as he said it.

"Wonderful," Martha whispered. "Now everybody knows that Small is sweet on me."

"I see," the prosecutor said. "Is it fair to say that you would do anything for this young lady?"

And bless James Small, Thaddeus thought, in spite of the fact that the question was a blatant attempt to discredit him, he gave the perfect answer.

"I would do anything within my means and the bounds of my conscience, yes," he said. "But I am a man of God and I therefore hold myself to a high moral standard."

Garrett gave up. "No further questions."

His expression became even gloomier when Ashby recalled Donald Dafoe. Two constables brought Dafoe into the courtroom. He was in handcuffs.

Ashby held in his hand the yellowed document Caroline had given them the night before, although he didn't immediately refer to it. Dafoe seemed to know what it was and he couldn't take his eyes from it.

"Mr. Dafoe," Ashby began, "could you please state your relationship to Mr. John Plews?"

"He's my cousin."

"Are you aware that your cousin, Mr. Plews, has filed a suit in the Court of Chancery against Paul Sherman and his brother Daniel?"

"What Jack does is his business."

"And who, please, is Josiah Palmer?"

"He was our grandfather."

"And is it not true, Mr. Dafoe, that if your cousin's suit against the Shermans is successful, you and your family would gain control of some lands that have become very valuable?"

Dafoe mumbled his answer. "I suppose so."

"Mr. Dafoe, according to the documents filed in Chancery, the case hinges on an agreement between Mr. Sherman's grandfather and your own, which was thought to be lost and has recently been recovered. Can you tell me where and when, exactly, this elusive agreement was found?"

"Objection. Mr. Ashby is referring to documents that have not been presented to the court."

"I apologize, Mr. Justice Stephens. This evidence has come to light so recently that copies of the court documents have not yet arrived. However, as prosecution's own witness has acknowledged the existence of the suit, I fail to understand Mr. Garrett's objection."

Justice Stephens mulled this over, his eyes narrowed. Then finally, he said, "For the time being, Mr. Ashby, you may proceed."

Ashby turned to Dafoe again. "Were you aware of the sudden discovery of this long-lost agreement?"

Dafoe squirmed and hesitated.

"I will remind you that you are under oath, Mr. Dafoe. You have already stated that you would be a beneficiary if the case was successful. I don't see how you would know that unless you were aware of the agreement."

"Yes. Jack told me about it."

"Did he mention how it came to be found?"

"He said it turned up."

"And yet, even though your cousin had discovered a document that would mean a significant improvement in both your fortunes, you didn't think to ask him where he found it or what he had done with it? It wasn't filed with the suit. Didn't you think that was odd?"

"Objection. Counsel is leading the witness."

"Overruled, Mr. Garrett. Mr. Dafoe is a hostile witness and I have already allowed the cross."

Ashby positively beamed. "Well, Mr. Dafoe, did you not think this was odd?"

"Yes, I suppose."

"And what was even odder, and I really don't know why you didn't question this, is that it was in the possession of Mr. George Howell."

"Objection!" The prosecutor was on his feet again, but Dafoe answered before the judge could rule. "Jack said we could trust the Major to look after it."

"Did you personally trust Mr. Howell? Weren't you afraid that he would double-cross you by attempting to blackmail Paul Sherman?"

Silence. "Answer the question, Mr. Dafoe," the judge instructed.

"Jack trusted him."

"Were you aware that Mr. Howell had been passing counterfeit money in the Cobourg area?"

"How would I know that?" Dafoe growled.

"Mr. Ashby!" the justice cautioned.

Ashby forged ahead in spite of the warning. "Did it not occur to you that the agreement might be a forgery?"

"Objection!" Garrett howled.

"I'll withdraw."

At that moment Thaddeus looked at Ellen Howell, whom everyone seemed to have forgotten in the unfolding drama. There were tears streaming down her face.

Ashby paused for a moment, as if in deep thought.

"Constable Miller has testified that he found you with a great deal of money last night. Where did it come from?"

"I just had it."

"And he also found a Burlington steamer ticket."

"Yes. I went there last month to see my cousin."

Ashby walked over to the table and picked up the three heavy ledgers that Martha had searched. "And yet, Mr. Dafoe, your name does not appear on any passenger lists." He handed the ledgers to the clerk.

Then he turned back to Dafoe.

"When did you realize that it was Caroline Howell, and not Ellen Howell, on the island that day?"

"I didn't see either of them."

"Did she see you rifle Sherman's pockets?"

"Objection. Mr. Dafoe has no way of knowing what someone else saw."

"I withdraw. What were you going to do if you found her at the manse?"

"I just wanted to know if she had the piece of paper."

"And one last question, Mr. Dafoe. Do you own a Baker rifle?"

"Yes."

And the courtroom erupted in a commotion that went on for several minutes, until Justice Stephens finally threatened to clear the room.

Thaddeus expected the prosecutor to question Dafoe again after this, but Garrett evidently felt that enough damage had been done, and was reluctant to let his witness dig an even bigger hole in his case. He had formulated one last salvo, though. He stood. "I call reply evidence."

"Fair enough, I'll allow it," Stephens said.

"I call Mr. Thaddeus Lewis."

"Objection!" Ashby was on his feet. "Mr. Lewis has not been sequestered as a witness. He has been present throughout the proceedings."

Stephens fixed Ashby with a glare. "Based on the evidence presented so far, Mr. Lewis appears to have been instrumental in furnishing a great deal of your defence. He could scarcely be categorized as a witness for the prosecution. Objection overruled."

Thaddeus was aware of much craning of heads as he walked to the stand. He knew that his name had been bandied about in connection with the case, but he was less well known here in Cobourg itself than he was in the backcountry, and everyone wanted to get a look at this preacher who seemed to have played such a large part in the story. He stood as straight as he could while he took his oath, and avoided looking at Ellen Howell as he wondered what he was about to be asked.

"Mr. Lewis, your assistant stated that when he met you on the road on October twenty-first, you were on your way to George Howell's farm."

"Yes, that's correct."

"What were your reasons for going there?"

"My granddaughter and I were visiting Mr. Leland Gordon and his mother at their farm near Sully. During the course of this visit, Mr. Gordon expressed some concern as to the well-being of the Howells' daughter. As Mr. Howell's whereabouts were unknown and her mother was here in Cobourg, there was an uneasiness that the daughter had been left alone on an isolated farmstead. She's only twelve."

"And why had Mr. Gordon not attended to this himself if he was so concerned?"

"Because the girl ran away whenever anyone went near the farm. Mr. Gordon thought that, as I am a minister and Caroline had met me previously at a meeting, I might have more success in reaching her."

"Wasn't that an odd thing for you to do?"

"Not really. We were going by on our way home, so it was no inconvenience. I told Mr. Gordon that I would at least try to talk to her."

"And you were successful?"

"Yes."

"Even though Mr. Gordon himself, and no doubt countless other neighbours, couldn't get near her."

"I doubt that I would have either, had the cave not fallen in on her dog."

"Are the Howells members of your church?"

"No."

"And yet you managed to retrieve the girl when no one else could. And not only that, but you took her into your own home."

"Yes."

"Is Mrs. Howell a close friend?"

"No."

"And yet, Mr. Lewis, you went to a great deal of trouble to find a barrister to represent her."

"Yes." Thaddeus felt his face grow stony and tried to will it to relax.

"And the keeper at the gaol tells me you have faithfully attended Mrs. Howell and that you spend your time reading to her."

Thaddeus should have realized that a gaoler named Palmer would repeat everything he saw to his sprawling family, and that any tidbits concerning Ellen Howell would have been repeated many times.

"Yes," he said.

"These were spiritual readings, designed to comfort her in her time of need?"

Thaddeus wanted to say yes, because that's what it was, for her — a reminder of home and happier times.

"No."

"What exactly did you read, Mr. Lewis?"

"A book called *Mansfield Park*. By a Miss Jane Austen."

"And what kind of book is *Mansfield Park*?"

"Well … it's a work of literature. A story."

"Would it be fair to say that it's a romance, Mr. Lewis?"

"I suppose."

"So, for this woman whom you claim you barely know, you retrieve her child, scurry around and find a lawyer, and spend hours reading a romantic novel for her amusement?"

It sounded so ludicrous and silly the way Garrett presented it. In spite of himself, Thaddeus felt his face grow hot.

"Yes."

"You have quite a reputation for solving crimes, do you not?"

Thaddeus could see that Ashby was about to leap up and object, but he knew how to answer this.

"I have no idea what my reputation is," he said. "That's for other people to decide."

"But will you confirm that in the past you were involved in two rather infamous cases?" Garrett consulted his notes. "A peddler who was convicted of killing a number of women, and a case of murder and fraud involving a farmer?"

"I had some small part in finding the truth of those affairs, yes."

"Mr. James Small is your assistant, is he not?"

"Yes."

"And so you hold a supervisory position over him?"

"Yes."

"And has he demonstrated a romantic inclination toward your granddaughter?"

"Yes." Thaddeus hoped Martha would forgive him for this answer.

"Would he be inclined to do anything you ask of him?"

"Objection!" Ashby was on his feet.

"I'll rephrase. Would James Small lie for you?"

"Not in a million years," Thaddeus answered before Ashby had time to object again. And then he steeled himself for the question that must surely come next. The one question he did not want to answer.

To his surprise, Garrett didn't ask it.

Thaddeus was dismissed from the witness stand and took his seat. Martha slipped her hand into his and gave it a squeeze for reassurance.

Ashby rose and began his summation, weaving all of the facts together so that the jury would see a clear picture of what had transpired — an unscrupulous land deal and an old document that magically reappeared when it was wanted most, produced by a man who earned his living as a counterfeiter; an identification made on the basis of a blue dress that was too small for the woman who was supposed to have been wearing it; Donald Dafoe's unconvincing fish story, his possession of the one hundred dollars in banknotes and of the steamer ticket that matched one purchased by the victim, his attempt to gain entry to the manse. Ashby spoke for an hour, laying it all out for the jury to see.

"We have ample evidence that Ellen Howell was not on Spook Island that day," he said. "We have also heard evidence to support the notion that Donald Dafoe had means, opportunity, and motive in the murder of Paul Sherman. The prosecution's case against Ellen Howell rests on the premise that she and her husband formed a common criminal purpose — to wit, the robbery of Mr. Paul Sherman — and that Mr. Sherman was killed in the course of executing that purpose. I submit that the evidence points in another direction, both in terms of robbery and of murder. I must remind the jury that when a case depends exclusively on circumstantial evidence, the circumstances must be not only consistent with the guilt of the accused, but inconsistent with any other rational conclusion. I submit, gentlemen of the jury, that there is an alternate conclusion that is very rational indeed.

"You have one decision to make today — did George Howell shoot Paul Sherman, or could there be some other explanation? It is not up to this court to decide if someone else is guilty of this crime, only that Ellen Howell is not. Nor is her husband. I urge you to acquit Mrs. Howell of the unwarranted charges against her."

If Thaddeus had not been so unsettled by the prosecutor's questions, he would have thought that Ashby was magnificent. Clearly the spectators thought so. Thaddeus could only hope that the jury agreed. It was a shame that the prosecution had the last word.

Garrett did his best to muddy the waters. He avoided any mention of the seamstress's testimony, instead focusing on the number of witnesses who had seen the Howells that day, and the bloodstain on the skirt of the dress. But he saved what he thought was his most damaging argument for the end.

"You have heard testimony from two ministers today. You're probably like me, gentlemen of the jury — you are predisposed to believe that a man of God must be telling the truth. But these men of God are both of the same persuasion. One of them, in fact, holds a superior position over the other, and we may assume, therefore has a great deal of influence over him. James Small has testified that he intercepted Donald Dafoe trying a window at the Methodist manse. His concern, however, appeared to be solely for the safety of the Methodist minister's granddaughter. It was clear to me, gentlemen of the jury, as I'm sure it is clear to you, that James Small holds great expectations with regard to this granddaughter. And so, I ask you, if you were in love with a man's granddaughter — moreover, a man who held your future in his hands — would you not do almost anything to ensure that man's good opinion? Now, I am not saying that James Small is a perjurer — I am sure he told you faithfully what he believes he saw — but I am suggesting that his testimony has been coloured by his emotions and his eagerness to please the man who holds the key to his happiness."

Thaddeus could feel the intensity of Martha's scowl without even looking at her, but he could pay her no attention just then. He knew there was worse to come.

"And now let us consider Mr. Lewis, a senior minister in the Methodist Episcopal Church. A man who has a history of tracking down murderers. A man who visited the accused in her cell, not to grapple with the state of her immortal soul, but to read her romantic nonsense. A man who wished to place himself in a good light in her eyes.

"And what would be most natural for a man who has a history of solving crimes to do? Why, solve another crime, of course, and find a solution that would exonerate the lady in question.

"Mr. Lewis has been remarkably resourceful in providing that solution. He hired a barrister to defend her. He has been in court every day, immediately behind that barrister, directing her defence. He just happened to be present at her farm at the exact moment that so-called *new evidence* was uncovered, and he has no one to corroborate his story but his assistant, Mr. Small. And again, we have only Mr. Small's word for it that someone was attempting to break into the Methodist manse.

I do not mean to say, gentlemen of the jury, that these two men of the cloth are less than sincere. I am merely suggesting that they have been influenced by their emotional states. One of them is in love with the granddaughter; the other is in love with the accused. They have seen what they wanted to see, and said what they most wanted to believe."

Thaddeus couldn't stop himself from looking at Ellen Howell. Her face was a mask of embarrassment. And something else besides, he realized, some emotion that showed itself in a tiny upturn of the lip. Distaste? Repugnance?

And his mortification became almost more than he could bear. He heard little else the prosecutor said, and almost nothing of Justice Stephens's direction. His humiliation was complete. He would not be remembered on the Hope Circuit as the winner of The Great Debate, an orator of the first rank and a saver of countless souls, but as a man who lusted after a married woman and pressed his suit with false words and trashy novels.

And for what? A mirage. A trick of memory.

The jury was out for only half an hour.

Ellen Howell was led back into the prisoner's box to hear her fate. Thaddeus sat with downcast eyes. He would not look at her again.

The clerk of the court stood. "How say you, gentlemen? Is the prisoner guilty or not guilty?"

"Not guilty," the foreman replied. "We find the accused not guilty."

The noise in the room became deafening.

Thaddeus desperately wanted to get out of the courtroom, but spectators and reporters rushed to the front, blocking the aisles in their eagerness to get close to Ellen. It would take the bailiff some time to clear them out.

Ashby was grinning broadly as he accepted congratulatory comments on his victory. He shook hands with several people, then turned to Thaddeus. "This crowd is a menace. They all want to talk to her. I'll see if I can take her back to the gaol for now. Meet me there as soon as you can get out." And then he rushed forward, pushing people out of the way to get to the prisoner's box.

"What happened to Mama?" Caroline asked. "Why is she being taken away again?"

"Your Mama is free," Thaddeus said. "We'll go and get her in a little while."

When they were finally able make their way to the gaol entrance, Ashby met them at the outer door and beckoned them in, shutting it firmly against the reporters crowded around the entrance. Ellen was sitting, not in the narrow cell where Thaddeus had seen her before, but in a comfortable chair in the antechamber. She rose and rushed to Caroline, enveloping her in a tight embrace. They were both crying.

"What happens now? Martha asked. "Do they just put her out on the street?"

"That's more or less it," Ashby said. "It's up to her where she goes now, but the Anglican minister has stepped forward and offered her and the girl a room for the night." He eyed Thaddeus speculatively. "I think that's the best plan, don't you? No one will question it, and he'll keep the newspapers away from her."

Thaddeus nodded. He wasn't sure he was ready to talk to her anyway.

V

Martha and Thaddeus walked back to the manse in complete silence.

Martha was profoundly embarrassed by the remarks the prosecutor had made about James Small and herself. She hoped that the newspapers would not report that part of Garrett's address. She was almost certain that they would. But as she walked along she reflected that she had done nothing to cause any of it, and could protest as much should anyone remark on it. It was different for Thaddeus. He had behaved very oddly with respect to Ellen Howell, but the prosecutor had put the worst possible construction on his actions. He must be appalled.

The day had certainly been a triumph for Towns Ashby, though. Martha couldn't help but feel glad for him, and proud of the role she had played in the case. She wondered if he would come to the manse that night, then decided that he probably wouldn't. He would want to bask in congratulatory attention at the Globe or at one of the less salubrious establishments he frequented. Many people would want to buy him drinks and claim they knew him.

Tomorrow, perhaps. Yes, tomorrow, and probably sometime in the morning. She would slip out to the market and get a chicken. She would use her own money to buy it. And she should make a pie. They could have a celebration. And maybe it would go a little way toward cheering up her grandfather.

Digger barked as soon as they neared the house, but once inside he settled quite readily at Martha's command.

"He's getting used to us," she remarked.

"I suppose I should take him out to the yard," Thaddeus said. "He's been inside all day."

"I'll do it," Martha said, "if you'll put the kettle on."

She slipped the old piece of rope they used as a leash over the dog's head and stepped outside the back door. Digger made a beeline for the yellow rose bush that grew beside the house and relieved himself, then put his nose to the ground and pulled her to the back of the garden. He was following Caroline's scent, she realized, tracing the steps she had made the day before. Martha let him pull her along. He piddled twice more, to make his mark. She turned to pull him back to the house when a voice on the other side of the fence startled her.

"May I speak with you, Miss Renwell?"

It was James Small.

"Yes, I suppose." She was in no mood for James, but she supposed he was owed his say. After all, he had been singled out in court as well.

"In light of today's events, I think it's wise for me to speak frankly. I hope you won't think me presumptuous."

He was at his most pompous, red in the face, Adam's apple bobbing.

"By all means, please be frank."

"I don't think it can have escaped your notice that I may have had certain aspirations regarding yourself."

"It was pretty much announced in open court," she pointed out.

"Yes. Well. I have never been certain what your position is regarding me."

Martha was very certain, but she decided to refrain from baldly stating it.

"I am currently in no position to entertain matrimony, and I know that you are still quite young," he continued.

Oh dear Lord, she thought, *where is he headed with this?*

"I had, however, hoped to reach some sort of understanding with your grandfather so that at some future date I might press my suit."

Martha had a wild mental image of James Small with a sadiron, pressing a crease into his baggy black trousers and managed to stifle a giggle only just before it escaped from her lips.

He drew himself up to his full gangly height, a disapproving look on his face. "Your grandfather's reputation has been severely damaged by this whole Howell affair, as has yours by your association with Mr. Ashby. Given my position in this community, I regret that I must now inform you that I have set aside any intentions that I may have had, and that I will no longer seek any union between us."

"I think that's probably the wisest course, Mr. Small."

"I hope this will not be too painful for you, but you must see that your own actions have influenced my decision."

"Thank you, Mr. Small. I shall endeavour not to feel pain. Good day to you."

"Good day." And with that he strode back into his parents' cottage with an air of great satisfaction at having done his duty.

"C'mon Digger," she said, and tugged him back toward the house. Once inside, she began to laugh. She'd been annoyed with Ashby the night she chased him down on the streets of Cobourg, but if she'd known it would be enough to discourage James Small, she might have done it more than once.

"What are you laughing at?" Thaddeus was at the stove, fiddling around with the tea things.

"Apparently I am no longer the object of James Small's affections."

"What? No. Did he just tell you that in the back garden?"

"Yes. Over the fence. Apparently, we aren't respectable enough for him."

Thaddeus looked at her uncertainly. "Are you upset?"

"Do I look upset? I've never been so relieved in my life."

"Oh. Well. I guess that's all right then, isn't it?" Then he stopped and frowned. "This may be a problem, you know. I expect I'm the talk of the town."

Martha had never seen her grandfather so tentative. "I don't care," she said. "Is there tea yet?"

The dog spent the night in the kitchen, jammed up against the back door, his head drooped over his paws. Occasionally he sighed deeply and whined.

"I'll take him over to the Anglican rectory in the morning," Thaddeus said. "The Howells will no doubt be heading back to the farm and will want him."

But before they'd finished breakfast there was a knock on the front door. Martha rushed to answer it. It would be just like Ashby, she thought, to turn up unannounced first thing in the morning. But when she opened the door she found a boy, who shoved a piece of paper at her and left. She handed it to Thaddeus and read it over his shoulder. It was from Ashby. As usual, he went straight to the point:

Howells leaving Cobourg dock ten o'clock.

Thaddeus seemed hardly to know what to do with the news. He sat staring at the note until Martha finally said, "Maybe you should take the dog to them?"

He looked up at the sound of her voice. "Yes. Yes, that's what I'll do."

Thaddeus was about to leave the house when he remembered the leather satchel that Caroline had clutched so closely. He was sure that the notes and bonds it contained were counterfeit, and in the normal course of events he would have taken them all into the back garden and burned them. Or turned them in at the bank. Or something other than what he was now considering. Ashby's message hadn't indicated where the Howells were going, only that they were leaving. Ellen Howell had no money. The Anglican minister, or maybe even Ashby himself, must have advanced her the funds for steamer passage. She would arrive at her destination penniless. Would Thaddeus be an accomplice to her husband's crimes if he gave her the satchel full of notes to use as she saw fit? Or could he claim that he was simply returning her property and whatever was in the satchel was none of his concern? It didn't matter. He walked upstairs and fetched it from the room Caroline had used.

"Tell Caroline she's welcome to keep the dress," Martha said. "Her old one isn't fit for anything but rags. And if you see Mr. Ashby, tell him he's invited for dinner. At noon."

Thaddeus looped the rope around Digger's neck and set off. As he walked toward the harbour he was acutely aware of the stares coming from the people he passed, at first certain that it was because of the trial and convinced that they whispered to one another after he'd gone by, but after a few minutes he realized that it was more likely because of the dog, who was leaping ahead and pulling him along at a frantic pace. At the foot of the pier, he pulled the rope out of Thaddeus's hand altogether and went racing down the dock to where the Howells were waiting. He leaped at Caroline, nearly knocking her over in his enthusiasm.

Ashby was there to shepherd them aboard the steamer, which was already approaching the dock.

"Thaddeus!" he called. "I thought you might come."

Ellen Howell said nothing at all, but walked a few paces farther down the pier.

"We thought it best to go this morning," Ashby said. "The reporters are still scribbling away at their reports of the trial, but it won't be long before they'll be looking for something more to write about. I didn't want Mrs. Howell pestered."

Thaddeus nodded and walked up to stand beside her.

"I can't begin to thank you for what you did," she said when he reached her side.

"It was only right," he said.

"But not many would have bothered."

Whatever he'd thought he was going to say to her died on his lips at the constraint in her manner. He could never, he realized, tell this woman that the prosecutor had been correct, that he had acted as he did in order to gain her good opinion. Her slip of expression in that one unguarded moment in the courtroom had made Thaddeus see himself as she must — as a wild-eyed country preacher of an unsophisticated creed, dusty from the road in his rusty black coat, an aging fanatic in a backwater colony with nothing to offer but the conviction of his own importance. How foolish he had been. How mad.

The silence stretched out between them.

"Will you ever finish *Mansfield Park*?" she finally asked.

"No. I don't think I will now. I may never know how it ends."

"Happily for some, not so happily for others."

"You'd read it before?"

"Several times," she admitted. "It was still the perfect choice, and there's a paragraph at the end that reminds me of you: *When*

I hear of you next, it may be as a celebrated preacher in some great society of Methodists, or as a missionary into foreign parts.

"No, I think maybe that part of my life is behind me."

She continued to look out across the lake, her eyes narrowed against the glare of the sun on the water, her face in perfect profile. He watched her sidelong, but closely, trying to etch the look of her into his memory.

"Where are you going?"

"For now, to Rochester. My husband has connections there. I expect that's the easiest place to start looking for him."

"You still want to find him? After everything that's happened?"

"What would you have me do, Mr. Lewis?" She turned to fully look at him for the first time. "Whether I like it or not, my fortunes are tied to his. And he's not a bad man. He loves his daughter."

Thaddeus suddenly remembered the satchel he had under his arm. Without a word, he handed it to her.

He could tell that she knew what it contained. Her eyes were full of question as she took it from him.

"It really is over for you, isn't it?"

"Yes."

"I'm sorry."

As the steamer tied up at the dock, Digger barked furiously, running up and down with Caroline in pursuit. Ellen turned to watch them, a frown on her face.

"I don't know what to do about the dog. We can't take him with us."

"I'll keep him. Until you want him."

She nodded. "Goodbye, Mr. Lewis."

She intercepted Caroline, and after a huddled discussion the girl dropped to her knees in front of Digger. He licked her face and wagged his tail furiously. Then she grabbed the rope still dangling from his neck and walked him to where Thaddeus stood.

"Will you take care of him?" she asked, her face streaked with tears.

"Of course I will. And when you're ready to take him back, you have only to ask."

She gave the dog one last lingering pat, then ran up the gangplank without looking back.

Ashby walked up to stand by Thaddeus. Together they watched while the steamer pulled out into the harbour.

"That all turned out rather well, didn't it?" he remarked cheerfully.

Martha said she found Ashby "exasperating," and at that moment Thaddeus knew exactly what she meant. "Will they ever come back, do you think?"

"I doubt it," Ashby said. "Unless Donald Dafoe is indicted, George Howell is still technically wanted for murder. I gave Warren Garrett the agreement, by the way, so that may well happen. But then there would still be fraud and counterfeiting charges for Howell to answer to. No, if she finds him, they'll stay in the States. It's safer. And I don't think there's much of anything here for them now."

"What about the farm? That's worth something, isn't it?"

"I should think so, because of the railway. Mrs. Howell asked me to arrange a sale. She promised to write from time to time to provide instructions."

"And you? Where do you go from here, Mr. Ashby?"

"Back to Toronto. I'm leaving on the one o'clock steamer, actually."

"Oh. Martha was hoping you might come for dinner."

"Please thank her for me. I'll be sorry to miss one of her meals. But business calls." He began to walk back toward shore. Thaddeus fell into step beside him. Had Ashby at that moment suggested that they walk back to the Globe Hotel to settle in leather chairs and order up brandy and whiskey, Thaddeus would have gladly followed him.

Fortunately, Ashby stopped at the foot of the pier and held out his hand. "Until we meet again," he said. "You've been a wonderful partner. I couldn't have hoped for better help with all this."

"So who actually fired the shot, do you figure? Dafoe? Plews? Another one of the Palmer clan?"

Ashby laughed. "I keep telling you, Thaddeus, it doesn't matter."

He could smell roast chicken as soon as he walked in the back door of the manse. Martha was just putting the top crust on a pie, a smear of flour across one cheek. She looked up and smiled at him, then frowned when she saw the dog.

"Couldn't you find them?" she asked.

"I found them. They couldn't take the dog. I said I'd keep him until they could."

"Where have they gone?"

"Rochester. To look for Mr. Howell."

"Oh. I suppose we'll manage, but Digger won't be happy." She crimped the edge of the pastry, then set it in the oven. "When is Mr. Ashby coming?"

"He isn't. He's leaving for Toronto at one."

"Oh … well … we'll have to have our own celebration then, I guess. Just you and me." But Thaddeus could see that she was upset.

It was a glum meal. Neither had much of an appetite, and neither of them seemed able to think of anything to say that wouldn't open a floodgate of difficult conversation.

"Pie?" Martha asked, after they had picked at the chicken.

"Maybe later."

She cleared the dishes away. Then Thaddeus heard her go out the back door. He followed. She'd tied Digger to the fence and was sitting on the back stoop watching him. He sat down beside her.

"Are you all right?" he asked. She was crying a little.

"Yes … No. I'm just being silly." She wiped the tears away with the back of her hand. "I'm not even sure I like him. But I did think that he would at least come and say goodbye."

"He is, as you pointed out to me, a most exasperating man."

"Yes, he is." She pulled out a handkerchief and blew her nose. "There, I'm done."

"No, you're not. But you will be."

He leaned back against the door and closed his eyes. The wind was chilly, a promise of the winter to come, but he could feel the heat of the afternoon sun on his face, and it soothed him.

"What about you? Are you all right?"

"No. But like you, I expect I will be someday." Then a thought struck him. "Did you ever finish the book?"

"*Mansfield Park*? Yes. It's rather silly. Girls with nothing on their minds but finding a husband."

"But what else could they do? It's been pointed out to me that women don't have many choices."

She thought about this for a moment. "I don't know. You're right, of course; there isn't much else for women to do. But I'd never turn anyone down because he doesn't have enough money, like the girl in the book did. She decides she can't marry him because he's going to be a minister, you know." She eyed him closely, watching for his reaction to this.

"Really? That explains something someone said to me today."

He was grateful that she didn't ask him to clarify. She really was very like her grandmother, he thought — she knew when to speak and when to let things lie. They sat in silence for a few moments, and then Thaddeus said, "I'm going to give up preaching. I have no right to do it anymore."

She didn't argue the point with him. "What are you going to do instead?"

"I don't know. I'll finish out my year here, only because the church would find it difficult to fill the position on short notice. But I won't take another appointment."

"But where will you go?"

"I don't know."

"So where will I go?"

He hadn't taken Martha into account in his decision. "Back to Wellington, I suppose. You always have a home with your father."

"But I only just got the manse arranged the way I want it." She jumped to her feet and went to pat Digger's head.

"What's the matter? Do you like it here that much?"

"Yes!" She shouted it at him. Digger looked at her and whined.

"So what is it you want to do?"

"I don't know! Anything but go back home again. I want to see different places. Meet different people. Have an adventure."

"You just had an adventure," he pointed out. "It left you crying on the back doorstep."

"Yes, it did. And it was the most interesting thing that's ever happened to me." She began to pace up and down in front of him. He stayed silent until she was ready to speak.

"If I go back to Wellington, all I'll do is cook and clean and look after until I get married, and then I'll cook and I'll clean and I'll look after until I'm an old lady and so worn out with scrubbing that there's nothing left to do but lie down and die. And all the while I'd be wondering what I missed."

She stopped pacing and stood in front of him. "Do you see? I just want a chance to find out what the rest of the world looks like."

"You'd rather come with me?"

"Yes."

"But I don't know where I'll end up."

"That's the whole point, isn't it? Not knowing where you're going to end up?"

He had to admit that he liked having her around. She was the last of his girls. Over the years he'd lost his daughters, one by one. Then his wife. Martha was oddly like all of them. There were moments when he thought she was the spit and image of her mother. At other times she reminded him so much of Betsy that he would be taken aback. But the ghosts of the little ones — Grace and Ruth and Anna and Mary — they were there, too, and whispered to him in unexpected ways.

He had promised Martha once, when she was very small, that he would never go far from her. He was sure she didn't remember it, but the words came back to him now. Maybe it was time to keep his promise. Maybe he could begin to set himself right again if he did.

He looked at her sternly. "I'd still want you to wash my socks."

"I'll make them soft as a lamb's fleece."

"And you've got to stop moving the furniture around. If I ever stumble home in the dark, I'll break my neck."

"I can do that."

"All right."

She gave a little shriek and threw herself at him in an exuberant hug that nearly knocked him over.

"Careful," he said. "I'm old bones, you know," but he was grateful to her. He had no idea what he was going to do with his life, but apparently he wasn't going to be doing it alone.

VI

It wasn't as bad as Thaddeus feared. The newspapers were full of details of the trial, along with the astounding revelation that George Howell was responsible for the counterfeit money that had circulated throughout the district. There was also a great deal of speculation about who was actually responsible for the Sherman murder, now that it had been decided that George Howell wasn't.

The *Cobourg Star* lauded Ashby as an up-and-coming star in the legal world and published his summation in its entirety. Little about the prosecutor's allegations was printed. He had lost the case, after all, so why would anyone be interested in anything he had to say?

Still, Thaddeus was aware of a new reserve among attendees at meetings. No one said anything, but he could tell that people were disappointed when they discovered that it was he who would be leading their prayers. He was seldom invited for dinner anywhere, other than by the Gordons. He began leaving most of the work to Small, who no longer came to the back door with pie or attempted to sit close to Martha, although Mrs. Small still gossiped over the back fence as fiercely as she ever did.

Donald Dafoe was indicted for murder and brought to trial at the Spring Assizes and once again the Paul Sherman murder made headlines across the province. Thaddeus paid little attention to the case, but he was in no way surprised when he heard that the jury failed to convict. Palmers and Plews and Dafoes. That family always did look after one another. Thick as thieves.

He spent most of his time thinking about the future. He had been a schoolteacher once, but that path seemed blocked now. Even village schools were demanding professional teachers now that the normal school in Toronto was training young people in the art of instruction. He wondered if Martha might like to be a teacher. Tuition was free, but if she were to go there, Thaddeus would need to establish a household, and an income, nearby. The school was close to where his son lived. Perhaps Luke's employer, Dr. Christie, could be prevailed upon to put them up, but Thaddeus rejected this notion almost as soon as he thought of it. It was one thing to welcome a guest who only occasionally stayed the night, but another thing altogether to have two extra people parked at the breakfast table every morning, not to mention the addition of a yapping dog.

The Methodist Episcopal Church was opening a new seminary in Belleville, but he knew better than to apply for a position. They would want highly qualified instructors. And even someone so lowly as a tutor would be expected to demonstrate the highest moral rectitude. There had been too much gossip. He would be dismissed out of hand.

As summer neared, he began to despair. Perhaps he had been hasty in his rejection of another appointment. What if he traded on past favours and asked Bishop Smith for a new posting? A second chance? But the thought depressed him. He had no heart for it anymore.

And then, just as his time on the Hope Circuit was drawing to an end, a letter arrived in the mail. It was typical — no salutation, no greetings, no catching up with personal news, just a bare-bones message and the almost indecipherable signature at the bottom:

> *I have a case I can't make head nor tail of. I need an investigator. Will pay. Can you come?*
>
> *Towns Ashby*

Yes, Thaddeus decided, he could.

The Cobourg–Peterborough Railway, December 29, 1854

The town of Cobourg was in a great state of excitement as the town council, the directors of the railway, and fifty other prominent gentlemen crowded onto the benches that had been hastily installed on twelve flatbed cars. At ten thirty in the morning, pulled by two powerful locomotives, the Cobourg to Peterborough railway left the station at Cobourg Harbour and chugged northward at the unimaginable speed of fifteen miles per hour. A mere sixty minutes later the train successfully crossed the Rice Lake Bridge and reached Peterborough East, where it was greeted by local dignitaries. After three cheers for Cobourg and three for Peterborough, the passengers marched under a welcoming arch to the Town Hall, where a magnificent dinner awaited them. Toasts and congratulatory speeches flowed as freely as the champagne.

The Member of the Legislative Assembly for Cobourg, the Honorable Ebenezer Perry, recalled that he had arrived in Cobourg in 1815, when it was still known as Hardscrabble.

"And hard scrabbling it was," he said, "but since then they have scrabbled up a harbour, plank roads, gravel roads, fine buildings, and now a railway."

But it was stagecoach proprietor William Weller who brought the house down.

"I know why you have called upon me," he said. "It is to hurt my feelings — for you know I get my living from running stages, and you are taking the bit out of my mouth as well as out of my horses' mouths. You are comparing in your minds the present with the past, when you had to carry a rail instead of riding one, in order to help my coaches out of the mud. But after all, I find that I am rejoiced to see old things done away with and new things becoming *Weller*."

More speeches and songs followed, with festivities continuing through the night. The next day the excursionists found their way to the station for the return trip to Cobourg, but not before railway director D'Arcy Boulton toasted their Peterborough friends with a parting glass of champagne. The celebration was but a taste of good times ahead, he said, and as the train chugged its way back home again, everyone's heads were filled with dreams of coming good fortune.

Three days later the Rice Lake Railway Bridge collapsed.

ACKNOWLEDGEMENTS

I am indebted to a number of sources in the writing of this tale, most notably *The Lazier Murder: Prince Edward County, 1884*, by Robert J. Sharpe (Osgoode Society for Canadian Legal History, University of Toronto Press, 2011). Justice Sharpe brilliantly outlines the evolution of the Canadian legal system and clearly explains how different the rules of a criminal trial would have been in 1853. Further insight into the world of Canadian law was provided by *A Class Apart? The Legal Profession in Upper Canada from Creation to Confederation, 1791–1867*, a master's thesis by Sarah Elizabeth Mary Hamill (Graduate Department of the Faculty of Law, University of Toronto).

The rather daunting *Reports of Cases Adjudged in The Court of Chancery of Upper Canada Commencing in December, 1850, Vol. 2, Part 4*, by Alexander Grant (R. Carswell, Toronto, 1877) supplied the delicious details of a late lawsuit based on an early land survey, and further information was provided by *Equitable Jurisdiction and the Court of Chancery in Upper Canada*, by Elizabeth Brown (*Osgoode Hall Law Journal* 21.2 (1983): 275–314).

The articles regarding the Cobourg–Peterborough Railway by Colin Caldwell reproduced on the *Cobourg History* website (www.cobourghistory.ca/histories) proved invaluable, as did *Cobourg 1798–1948*, 2nd edition, by Edwin C. Guillet, MA. (Goodfellow Printing Co. Ltd., Oshawa, Ontario, 1948); *Early Cobourg* by Percy L. Climo, printed in Cobourg in 1985; and the *1851 Cobourg Canada Directory* at ancestry.com.

The happy juxtaposition of *A History of the Canadian Dollar* by James Powell (Bank of Canada, December 2005) and "Counterfeiting: A Rochester Way to Wealth" by Gerard Muhl (*The Crooked Lake Review*, Spring 2002) seemed to naturally present a plot twist.

And once again, the historical Thaddeus Lewis spoke to the fictional Thaddeus Lewis when I returned to the Lewis autobiography of 1865 for details of The Great Baptism Debate.

Thanks go to my agent, Robert Lecker; my editor, Allison Hirst; and, as always, my husband, Rob, for his enormous patience. And a special thank-you to the many dogs who have shared my life over the years and who proved such wonderful models for the faithful Digger.

More Thaddeus Lewis
Mysteries by Janet Kellough

On the Head of a Pin

Thaddeus Lewis, an itinerant "saddlebag" preacher, still mourns the mysterious death of his daughter Sarah as he rides to his new posting in Prince Edward County. When another girl in the area dies in a similar way, he realizes that the circumstances point to murder. But in the turmoil following the 1837 Rebellion, he can't get anyone to listen. Convinced there is a serial killer loose in Upper Canada, Lewis alone must track the culprit across a colony convulsed by dissension, invasion, and fear.

Sowing Poison

After many years, Nathan Elliott returns to Wellington, Ontario, to be at his dying father's side. Within a few days of his return, he is reported missing, and no trace of him can be found. Shortly after, Nathan's wife arrives in the village. Claiming that she can contact the dead, she begins to hold séances for the villagers. Thaddeus Lewis, a Methodist circuit rider, is outraged, and his ethical objections propel him on a journey to uncover the truth about the Elliotts. Religious conflict and political dissension all play a part in this tale set in 1844 Upper Canada.

47 Sorrows

When the bloated corpse of a man dressed in women's clothing washes up on the shore of Lake Ontario, a small scrap of green ribbon is found on the body. The year is 1847, and one hundred thousand Irish emigrants have fled to Canada to escape starvation in their homeland. But the emigrants bring with them the dreaded "ship's fever," and soon the ports are overflowing with the sick and dying. Itinerant preacher Thaddeus Lewis's son Luke, an aspiring doctor, volunteers in the fever sheds in Kingston. When he finds a green ribbon on the lifeless body of a patient, he is intrigued by the strange coincidence. Young Luke enlists his father's help to uncover the mystery, a tale of enmity that began back in Ireland.

The Burying Ground

Someone is digging up the graves at the Strangers' Burying Ground in Toronto — the final resting place of criminals, vagrants, indigents, and alcoholics — and the only person who seems to care is the sexton, Morgan Spicer. The authorities are unconcerned; after all, for years the growing village of Yorkville has been clamouring to have the bodies moved and the Burying Ground closed.

The distraught Spicer enlists the aid of his old friend Thaddeus Lewis, who has unexpectedly returned to preaching on the Yonge Street Circuit. The graveyard's secrets lead Lewis and his son Luke into the hidden heart of 1851 Toronto where they discover a trail of corruption and blackmail tied to an old sexual scandal and a dangerous enemy intent on vengeance.

DEC 1 4 2016